MURDER IN AN
ORCHARD CEMETERY

MURDER IN AN ORCHARD CEMETERY

Cora Harrison

**SEVERN
HOUSE**

First world edition published in Great Britain and the USA in 2021
by Severn House, an imprint of Canongate Books Ltd,
14 High Street, Edinburgh EH1 1TE.

Trade paperback edition first published in Great Britain and the USA in 2022
by Severn House, an imprint of Canongate Books Ltd.

severnhouse.com

British Library Cataloguing-in-Publication Data
A CIP catalogue record for this title is available from the British Library.

ISBN-13: 978-0-7278-9040-5 (cased)
ISBN-13: 978-1-78029-809-2 (trade paper)
ISBN-13: 978-1-4483-0547-6 (e-book)

Typeset by Palimpsest Book Production Ltd.,
Falkirk, Stirlingshire, Scotland.
Printed and bound in Great Britain by
TJ Books, Padstow, Cornwall.

ONE

Reverend Mother Aquinas had finished reading the bishop's letter when a knock on the door interrupted her thoughts.

'It's just Pat Pius; do you want me to tell him that you are busy,' said Sister Bernadette, inserting her head into the room through as small a space as possible. As usual, she correctly read the expression on the Reverend Mother's face and was willing to protect her from intrusion.

'No, you'd better bring him in,' said the Reverend Mother reluctantly. She knew full well why the man had come; would have been able to sum up his request in three words: 'Vote for Me'; knew also that he might take about twenty minutes of her time before she managed to get rid of him. Nevertheless, she was there to serve the community and Pat Pius was part of the parish. Carefully, she put the bishop's letter into a drawer and turned to welcome her guest. Judging by the speed with which he appeared, he had followed Sister Bernadette down the corridor.

'Reverend Mother!' he exclaimed. 'At last!' Theatrically, he sank down upon the nearest chair and placed his hat upon the floor. 'You won't believe this, Reverend Mother,' he said, 'but I've been meaning to drop in to see you for the last six months. You wouldn't credit how busy I am, Reverend Mother. I think of you every time that I pass the convent, but there's always something on my mind, something that needs to be done immediately. But don't think that I've forgotten you. I know the good work that you do in the parish. I know that money doesn't grow on trees. I was brought up hard. Now, before I waste any more of your time, I'll just write you a cheque.'

He did not, though. He had something to say first. He had to tell her in detail about his deep concern for the city, how he was brought up hard, and now wanted to help others in

the city, enterprising people like himself, people who looked
to the newly elected Aldermen to back business and cut the
obstacles to making profit. Rates, he declared, were going to
be his target, didn't want excessive rates to be a burden on
people like himself who were struggling to build up a business, thought people should not have to pay through the nose
for all sorts of things that had been dreamed up by the city
manager: like wages, so much; material, so much; footpaths
and crossings, so much; a new refuse destructor, if you
please; and what was wrong with 'make-do and mend', he
would like to know; and all this nonsense about taking people
out of perfectly good houses and building mansions for them
. . . He ran out of steam, eventually and looked at her with
an expression of a hopeful terrier. It was evident, she thought,
that he wanted a word of encouragement, a hint as to her
intentions.

The Reverend Mother had a short struggle with her
conscience and allowed him to wait while she looked at
him thoughtfully. A true educationist, she thought, would
endeavour to argue with the man; to explain the concept of
social justice to him; that all matters to do with a community
are the concern of that community; perhaps even to quote her
patron saint, Thomas Aquinas on that subject. '*Manifestum est
autem quod omnes communiter pertinet ad omnes partes
communitatis habet.*' She murmured the words below her
breath as she eyed a pile of bills awaiting her attention and
he flicked a rapid and practised sign of the cross in answer
to what weekly attendance at the Latin Mass led him to
guess that the words were probably some holy prayer.

Pat Pius's name was Murphy and he had been christened
Patrick, like another quarter of a million boys at the time.
However, a highly religious mother had pulled her son from
the obscurity of being yet another Paddy Murphy and had
borrowed his middle name from the reigning Pope Pius XI,
so that when he attended the Christian Brothers at the age of
five he had been rechristened Pat Pius and with this distinctive
name had, when still only fifteen years old, set up a business
in Crawford Street, first to repair shoes and then after a few
years, to sell shoes and boots. '*Good as new!' says Pat Pius!*

was his slogan and many a small boy of the neighbourhood got a start in his factory, as he named it, beginning with door-to-door collection of old shoes and graduating to polishing, repairing and rebuilding old shoes into shining and new-looking products. 'Worth a packet, that man!' had stated Sister Bernadette, who got her information from the butcher and baker and various message boys and relayed it all to the Reverend Mother in between cooking meals, organizing cleaning, shopping, answering the door and collecting old shoes for Pat Pius. A clever man, she thought. Had seen a gap in the society of Cork where the rich happily discarded not-so-old shoes and the poor desperately needed footwear for themselves and their children. Had profited from his short years in the Christian Brothers, was reputed to be able to add up simultaneously five columns of figures: pounds, shillings, pence, half-pence and farthings. She watched him as he wrote a cheque fluently, filling in the date with practised ease and writing 'Reverend Mother Aquinas' with a flourish, but then he hesitated, glanced up at her and she pretended to busy herself with her diary. She did not look at him. She was not prepared to give any encouragement or in any way to hint that her vote was for sale.

Even when the scratching of the pen had ceased, she did not look up, but when he came over to her, and deposited the cheque with a flourish under her eyes she could not forbear to thank him enthusiastically and as she rose to her feet to usher him out, she promised that a mass would be offered for his intentions in the convent church.

Five pounds! It was an enormous sum, and in a slightly conscience-stricken way she suspected he had only meant to write five shillings and was nudged towards the larger sum by her silence.

He seemed, thankfully, to be quite satisfied with that promise, perhaps read more into it than she had intended: Cork people were past masters at innuendo, and he took her offer of a mass to be celebrated for his intentions to imply more than she had intended. His face was wreathed in smiles when she left him at the door, and she went back to her desk wishing that she had his simple faith. 'Ask and it shall be given to you,' had said St Matthew, but that didn't happen too often in her experience. Carefully she tucked into an envelope the cheque and a filled-up paying-in slip, addressed it to the manager of the Munster Bank and placed a stamp upon it. Sister Bernadette would post that off as a glorious offset to the many bills that called upon her scanty resources.

Then she turned again to the bishop's letter.

Every year the bishop conducted a retreat for the religious superiors of the Cork schools: the Christian and Presentation Brothers, the Presentation Sisters, Ursuline Sisters, Sisters of Mercy and of Charity all gathered together to spend seven days in prayer and meditation. Absolute silence had been the rule during those seven days of retreat from the normal world. In the past, the Reverend Mother, though slightly irritated by the prospect of seven rather fruitless days taken from her busy life, had welcomed this silence as a time for new ideas to spring into her active brain, but this was now to be changed. The bishop had decided to invite the six candidates for the office of mayor in the city to join them in the annual retreat. And in order that they could profit from the spiritual advice of his brothers and sisters in Christ, he proposed to rescind the usual order of complete silence and wanted his brothers and sisters in Christ to help to guide the five candidates in their search for divine blessing on their work for the city. And, thought the Reverend Mother, in an exasperated moment, probably help his lordship to make up his mind which candidate he would back. She could imagine the surreptitious, little confidential conversations which would take place throughout these seven days.

The bishop, of course, had huge influence in this pious city and whosoever he favoured would probably win the vote of the ratepayers. The Reverend Mother compressed her lips and tried to avoid looking at the stamped envelope addressed to the manager of the Munster Bank, but despite her good intentions, she could not help wondering how many bribes came into his lordship's bank account and then, rather more cheerfully, whether someone else other than Pat Pius might think her influence would be worth a donation. She held the bishop's letter in her hand and stared through the window at the fog and mist that hid almost all the convent vegetable garden from view. But not even the sight of the verdant green of her sprouting potatoes and the frilled leafy clumps of carrots would have been enough to lift her spirits and dissipate the sense of annoyance. Those seven days were going to be wasted and there was something in her which rebelled at the idea that the influence of one man, though he be a bishop, was so considerable in this poverty-stricken city.

'Come in,' she said, in answer to a tentative knock, and then as the door was pushed open very hesitantly and a rather anxious face appeared at the door, she was conscious that her voice had had been curt and unwelcoming and tried to rearrange her features. It was Eileen, and Eileen might be bringing good news, or it might be bad news, but in any case, she had once been a pupil and her sorrows and joys were of the utmost importance to the Reverend Mother. Hastily she put the bishop's letter aside and welcomed her visitor.

Eileen had been one of the cleverest girls whom she had ever taught, but unfortunately at the immature age of fifteen she had been seduced from her studies by the IRA who had recruited her, taught her to shoot as well as any soldier and imbibed her with a passionate desire for the complete freedom of her country and a worship of Michael Collins. That had been over seven years ago. Michael Collins was now dead; his rival, de Valera, was leader of the country and Eileen had gradually been weaned away from a dangerous lifestyle, had got a job and had been induced by the Reverend Mother to go back to her studies. Three years ago, she had won a Honan Scholarship to Cork University.

'The results are out.' Eileen's voice was excited.

'And you failed, of course!' said the Reverend Mother, trying to sound detached, but with a relieved smile. Eileen's face was easy to read and today it glowed with excitement and pleasure.

'Wrong!' said Eileen triumphantly. 'First honours in every subject! Top of the year in English. I thought you might like to know,' she added with an effort to appear indifferent and then, casting pretence aside, she laughed triumphantly. 'I knew you'd be pleased! And, what's more, my Honan Scholarship can be extended for another three years if I care to go on studying.'

The Reverend Mother waited. She could see from the shining eyes that Eileen had an idea in her head. It was no good asking her to sit down; when Eileen was thinking hard, she strode up and down the room, so she sat at her desk and watched the girl.

'I've got it all worked out!' said Eileen, almost breathless with excitement. 'I had a little secret hope, you see, but I didn't want to say anything. And I did need that scholarship. I can't have my mother working in that pub for the rest of her life. I want to pay her back a little, but I don't want a job in an office or a bank or anything. I want to be a lawyer, a solicitor first and then perhaps a barrister, so I'm going to go on studying. I want to do an LLB.'

'You'll need to be apprenticed if you are to be a solicitor,' said the Reverend Mother, her brain busily scanning through the solicitors in Cork from whom she might, perhaps, ask a favour. Eileen, she thought, would have little idea of the cost of such an apprenticeship!

'I know! I've done it! Did it immediately I saw the board up in the *Aula Max* and saw my name up there at the top and saw "Honan Scholarship" opposite to it. Just went straight out, ran all the way down to North Main Street and talked to a solicitor that I know,' said Eileen with a visible effort to reduce her excitement to a businesslike manner, 'and she said "yes", said that she would take me on for nothing and that I could pay her, bit by bit, when I qualified and got a good job. I know her, you see. She's one of the Hogans, Maureen Hogan. Her father is a solicitor and so is her uncle. I knew her brother. He was in the hideout with me a few years ago – he went off to America when he was wanted by the police – so I've heard! Maureen's a member, though she keeps it very quiet, represents the lads in court, though . . .'

She didn't say what Maureen Hogan was a member of, or who 'the lads' were, but the Reverend Mother's lips tightened a little. She had hoped that Eileen would break all connection with the IRA and all those who rebelled so violently against the signing of a compromise treaty which allowed the six counties of the north to remain British. Their aim was for a united and a republican Ireland and all links to be broken with the United Kingdom, a legitimate aim, but their weapons were still the gun and intimidation. However, the treaty provided for the establishment of the Irish Free State within a year as a self-governing dominion within the community of nations known as the British Empire, a status the same as that of the Dominion of Canada. It also provided Northern Ireland, which had been created by the Government of Ireland Act 1920, with an option to opt out of the Irish Free State, which it immediately exercised. The agreement was signed in London on 6 December 1921, by representatives of the British government (which included the English Prime Minister David Lloyd George) and by representatives of the Irish including Michael Collins and Arthur Griffith. And then a bloody civil war broke out and the seeds that it sowed were still appearing above ground from time to time.

Eileen, studying at the university for an LLB and working in a solicitor's office would, hopefully, have little time for illicit action, but an office in the slum precincts of North Main Street rather than in the traditional South Mall did not argue for much of a practice. Eileen would learn little, she suspected from this Maureen Hogan. Nevertheless, now was the moment for congratulations.

'Well done,' she said quietly. 'So, you are all set now for a good career. And a very worthwhile career.'

'There was something else,' said Eileen with a trace of nervousness in her voice. 'You see, when I said to Maureen that I was popping in to tell you about the results, she asked me to . . . well, you see, Maureen, she's very ambitious, you see, and she thinks women should be running the country and I agree with her and . . . well, she's going up for election as an alderman and she asked me to have a word with you, to persuade you, to sort of suggest that you might have a word with the bishop – you know he'll be the one who decides in the end – and when they elect a lord mayor again – when they get tired of that manager – well, she'd have a very good chance of being lord mayor of Cork city – that's if she can get to be an alderman now . . .' Her voice faltered and her expression grew more tentative as she eyed the Reverend Mother's face. 'I shouldn't have promised to ask you that,' she said hastily, and the Reverend Mother smiled at her.

'It's all part of growing up, isn't it,' she said affably. 'Children blurt everything out and all is forgiven but as you get older, you don't make rash promises and you learn to weigh up requests. I'm so glad that you understand that. Now tell me, what would you hope to learn from an apprenticeship?'

Eileen, she was pleased to see, had a rather thoughtful expression on her face when, after stumbling through a few expected outcomes from an apprenticeship to a solicitor, she left to go back to her friends and her celebrations. The Reverend Mother hoped that the girl had not committed herself to this Maureen Hogan and that there still might be time to arrange an apprenticeship with some firm where she would learn the trade and gain useful experience on how to manage the affairs of moneyed clients. She finished her accounts, wrote cheques for the many bills on her desk and then turned to the problem of a family of twelve children whose mother was faced with eviction at the end of the week. Something must be done about them.

'Dear Mr O'Connor,' she wrote, and continued fluently, pointing out to the builder that, although the woman had been newly deserted, there was a possibility that the father of the twelve children might send money from Liverpool and that, in any case, she was sure that a reputable citizen like himself would not want to see a woman and such very young children condemned to sleep on a doorstep. She filled the page with bright optimism and a veiled threat of bad publicity and then, with a sigh, folded her letter, stamped and addressed its envelope, added it to the pile and went off to telephone her cousin Lucy, wife of the foremost solicitor in the city, owner of a large law practice, and employer of four or five solicitors, a practice where surely there might be room for a clever young apprentice.

As she walked down the corridor, she decided on her strategy, announcing Eileen's spectacular results and mentioning her choice of a mentor. She could bet that the name of Maureen Hogan would not meet with approval from

Lucy's husband. Absent-mindedly she gave the number to the switchboard lady, discouraged chat about the lovely weather, thankfully heard the sound of a loud street band in the distance, and then waited in silence for her cousin's voice, knowing that for once privacy would be ensured, and that no bored member of the telephone switchboard could surreptitiously lift another receiver and eavesdrop on the conversation without betraying themselves by a loud burst of ear-splitting music.

'I know,' said Lucy immediately as she picked up the receiver. 'You're ringing up about your retreat, aren't you? Even Ellen knows. When she came to tell me that you were on the line, she said, "The Reverend Mother will be off on her retreat, tomorrow." Of course, it's always around this time of the year, the week before the feast of Corpus Christi, isn't it? And not just nuns, priests, and brothers, this year, either. The *Cork Examiner* ran a front-page piece on it, photos and all. You'll have the five candidates for the alderman vacancy hanging around looking hopeful, listening with immense interest to everything that you have to say and, of course, all of them pretending to be extremely pious. They'll all be very respectful towards you. They know, of course, that, secretly, the bishop is frightened of you.'

The Reverend Mother smiled. She had been about to explain about Eileen, but should have known that Lucy would have all the gossip at her fingertips; would want to talk about the forthcoming election; would know about the undercurrents, also. She might as well milk this source before getting onto young Eileen's future.

'So, who are all those people who are supposed to be joining us?' she queried, endeavouring to make her voice sound indifferent.

'Only one that matters; well, perhaps, two. The bishop is very keen on that builder, Mr O'Connor, quite rich, very keen to be lord mayor. And, of course, it's time we had a properly elected lord mayor before we are all bankrupted by that Philip Monahan with his plans to build millions of houses at the taxpayers' expense! I went to a party last night and everyone was saying that. Of course, the bishop is keen to have some new churches so he'll favour that builder, but that shouldn't be of paramount . . . Not that the churches aren't important, of course . . .' Lucy tailed off in a meaningful way and the Reverend Mother's lips twitched.

'Of course,' she agreed piously. Both of their minds, she was sure, were on that wealthy builder Robert O'Connor and the implications of the bishop's interest in him. He, of course, could probably be relied on to give the bishop a good discount on the building costs of a new church in gratitude for his lordship's support.

'But James Musgrave, another of the candidates, is a really nice man, a neighbour of ours. I'm sure that you will like him immensely when you meet. He's an accountant, a stockbroker, really. His girl was at school with one of our granddaughters. Does a lot for charities. A great speaker. A very religious man in a nice sort of way.' And Lucy, always careful in her attempts to manipulate her cousin, seemed prepared to leave it at that, while the Reverend Mother, who was in a slightly waspish mood, wondered aloud how Mr Musgrave could be deemed religious 'in a nice sort of way'.

'I suppose you are going on about that business of dismissing the cook, but he felt he had to. After all, he had young children who could be contaminated by bad example, especially if she kept the child, as she had wanted to do,' said Lucy. The Reverend Mother thought about James Musgrave. Had met him once, about six or seven years ago at a party he had held to celebrate Lucy's birthday, where he had apologized to Lucy for a badly cooked birthday cake from a new cook and had told the story of the former cook and her lack of morals.

'His daughter is now a novice in the Sisters of Charity order, I seem to remember,' she said.

'That's right. Funny that! She was very wild when she was at school. I wasn't too keen on my granddaughters having too much to do with her. He's had no luck, poor man. He is all alone. His wife is dead, died in a car crash when the children were young – Peter and Paul, the twins, were about eleven and Nellie was just eight, the day before her eighth birthday, poor little thing. Used to be very quiet then, just a little shadow to her mother, always out in the garden helping her with planting and weeding. I can just see the two of them.'

'Very sad,' said the Reverend Mother.

'Dreadful,' said Lucy emphatically. 'Poor man. He was driving, coming back from a party, had a bit too much to drink, I suppose, skidded on a piece of ice on the Straight Road. Spun across the road and crashed into a wall. She was killed, but he was perfectly all right. Poor fellow! He's had a hard life. His daughter in the convent, and his two sons, the twins, instead of following in their father's footsteps and studying accountancy, went off to Australia to try their hands at farming, if you please. A constant drain on the poor man, probably. Does anyone make money with farming? Though perhaps it's different in Australia. Went off when they left school. Not that they are much of a loss to Cork. A wild pair, those twins! Always up to mischief, dressing up, pretending to be Germans or something like that. Could mimic any accent in the world. Do you remember me telling you the damage they did making a dam in that little river at the back of our house? Made an explosive by packing some fertilizer into an iron can and burying it in the mud. Came into the kitchen to borrow a bag of sugar and half an hour later back again. I'll never forget the sight of that boy, Peter, or was it Paul – they were so alike in every way, same blond hair, same enormous pale blue eyes – well, it was one of them and I'll never forget the sight of him, when he rushed into our kitchen, streaming blood! My hands were shaking when I phoned for the doctor. Their cook rushed in with bandages and a terribly sweet raspberry drink for the boys and I drank some myself for the shock.

'An adventurous pair. Probably wouldn't have been suited to accountancy.' The Reverend Mother was automatically on the side of youth and of enterprise.

'Should probably have gone into business. Lots of charm,' said Lucy. 'All the old ladies around loved them for their beautiful blue eyes. A neighbour of ours, you remember Maureen Clay, very frail now, poor thing, though still got all her wits about her – you should hear her about Kitty O'Shea and her two lovers – predicting a dual, she was, the last time

I visited her in the Bons nursing home in Cobh – anyway, she always asks about the Musgrave twins. Loved the pair of them. Said she used to look forward to them coming home from school. Never a dull moment during the holidays. She loved the pair of them! Of course, James had to send all three of them to boarding school after their mother died . . .'

Loved by all, except their father, thought the Reverend Mother. She began to feel a slight prejudice against James Musgrave. A dull, prissy man, she pictured him as, bundling his motherless children off to boarding school, sacking the cook who had loved and cared for the children. Well, he had reaped what he sowed. To have one of your children want nothing to do with you, was, perhaps, not so unusual, but to have all three distance themselves with such finality seemed to show a poor relationship between the widower and his offspring. She began, unfairly she knew, to feel a slight revulsion against Lucy's friend and suspected him of prompting Lucy to get her cousin, the Reverend Mother, to influence the bishop in his favour. At least poor old Pat Pius was open and honest and signed a handsome cheque. And why shouldn't Pat Pius be a better alderman than someone like James Musgrave, born into money and spending his time making more, instead of being more of a companion to his motherless children. Pat Pius had nothing, no expensive schooling, no father to hand down money to him, nothing but his own enterprise and energy to stand between him and destitution.

'I would have thought that your Rupert would be voting for the young solicitor, Maureen Hogan – his own profession,' said the Reverend Mother.

'So, you do know all about the candidates. I thought that you would. You've always got your finger in every pie,' said Lucy, the affection in her voice coming across the crackling phone line. 'Don't be fooled by the brass plate on the door,' she added. 'That's another one that disappointed her father, and mother. Nearly broke her father's heart. Joining up with Sinn Fein and then getting mixed up with the IRA, just like her brothers. But her father daren't let her near his own prac-tice. He'd lose three-quarters of his clients if he did so. She'd be pushing IRA propaganda down their throats, quoting James Connolly at them.'

'Oh dear!' said the Reverend Mother seizing the opportunity. 'Oh, dear! I wish I had known that. I'd have discouraged Eileen from making contact with her. You remember Eileen, don't you, Lucy? Well, she has done brilliantly in her final examination, got first honours in her bachelor's degree and top of the class, her Honan Scholarship extended and now she has plans to study law and to do her apprenticeship with this very same Maureen Hogan. Oh dear!' she repeated and waited expectantly.

'Talk her out of it,' advised Lucy. 'And, yes, I'll have a word with Rupert. That's what you rang up about, I suppose. I know you! Do have a nice time at your annual retreat. And you won't forget to give my best wishes to James Musgrave, will you?' The last sentence was uttered in a careless manner, but the Reverend Mother was not fooled. Life was like that, she thought. A series of bargains. She would gently use her influence with the bishop to bring forth the manifold virtues of this Mr Musgrave and Lucy would persuade Rupert to take Eileen on as an apprentice.

'Why does Mr Musgrave want to be an alderman?' she asked.

'Well, I told you,' said Lucy impatiently, 'there's a vacancy for an alderman and the present lot are all as old as the hills and set in their ways, have been there for years. They just do what that city manager, Mr Philip Monahan, tells them to do. Everyone is hoping that there'll be an election for lord mayor next year and then James, if he gets this vacancy, will have an excellent chance of being elected. The rest of the aldermen are far too old. And, of course, being a stockbroker will give him an advantage as all the other stockbrokers and probably most of the solicitors, all of our crowd, you know – well all these sort of people – they will give him one or more of their votes. And by the way, strictly between ourselves, he's hoping to marry Kitty O'Shea.'

'Kitty O'Shea. The widow of that alderman who died last year. Someone told me she was going to marry the builder.'

'Amazing how you nuns know all the gossip!' said Lucy

tartly. 'All the more reason to encourage the bishop to favour poor James. You don't want all that O'Shea money going to that appalling builder, Robert O'Connor. Rupert is trying to get as many people as possible to vote for James Musgrave. He'll probably succeed in getting him in.'

'I suppose so,' said the Reverend Mother. Rupert's support would be valuable. Like most other solicitors, barristers and stockbrokers, Rupert would have three votes in the election – one for being a householder, one for owning a business premises and one for holding a professional qualification. There were no votes, at all, of course, for people like the unfortunate mother who was faced with eviction from the room which she occupied with her twelve children. 'What does this Mr James Musgrave hope to achieve if he is elected as lord mayor?' she asked.

'Talk to him,' advised Lucy. 'Put ideas in his head. Goodness knows you have enough of them. But don't overdo it. Remember it's the ratepayers who have the votes and they don't want sky-high rates to pay for utopian schemes.'

'Very true,' said the Reverend Mother with a sigh as she put down the phone. In theory, the rich of the city would prefer the poor to live in more sanitary conditions, would prefer not to see rats on the streets or to watch sewage bubble up from drains whenever the River Lee had one of its frequent floods, would like an end to these queues stretching half a mile along St George's Quay of unemployed, tuberculosis-ridden men, patiently waiting their turn to collect some meagre social security payment and spitting onto the pavement, but in practice they were not willing to pay the rates which might have achieved these desirable situations. Normally she enjoyed her conversations with Lucy but this one had not cheered her. And the prospect of this retreat where she would be constantly accosted by ambitious, would-be politicians or worse, the bishop himself, did not cheer her. Even the memory of the delightful apple orchard cemetery at the convent was not enough to soothe her troubled mind. Seven days peace, just seven days, was it too much to ask for, she muttered impatiently as she searched her drawers for an enormous and ostentatious set of silver and jewelled rosary beads that had been gifted to her by the parents of some novice. Surely even an ambitious would-be lord mayor, on seeing this symbol of prayer from a distance, would hesitate to approach her and perhaps she would have some peace if she produced it while sitting among the blossoms in the orchard cemetery.

TWO

The apple orchard cemetery of the Sisters of Charity, the Reverend Mother had always known, had been planted in the last century, during the terrible winter of 1846/47. The 'Black 47' as it was named in folklore, had been the worst winter in a generation with the deadly potato famine followed by a devastating pandemic of typhus fever. The rural poor fleeing from starvation and evictions poured into Cork city; special constables were organized to expel vagrants from the city; the workhouse and the city hospitals were full; starving beggars died on the streets. The cemeteries in the city could not cope with the numbers to be buried. Often, the mass graves contained so many coffins that those interred near the tops of the graves were insufficiently covered with earth allowing the foetid odour of decaying corpses to escape.

Matters were so bad that several convents, though not her own, had consecrated a piece of land for a peaceful resting place for the sisters. But only the Sisters of Charity had come up with this splendid idea of not just consecrating the field beside the convent chapel, but of planting eight rows of apple trees, donated by a farming cousin of the mother superior of the time, and these had been widely spaced so as to leave room for graves. And year by year the spaces had been filled with graves, those from the famine and the fever years headed with modest field stones of limestone and the later graves with more ornate slabs of limestone. The Reverend Mother, who had a practical mind, envied the Sisters of Charity their peaceful and productive graveyard, but had been unable to see any possibility of purchasing land for such a purpose beside her crowded city plot.

There was an air of peace about the place, she thought, as on the fourth day, she opened the gate, closing it gently behind her. The trees were all in bloom, the air faintly scented and the birds singing among the blossoms. The limestone of the

region had been near to the surface and when the trees were
planted and graves dug, great rocks and slabs had been
excavated. And over the years, probably when the site was
occupied by a monastery, the rocks had been turned into a
dozen or so stone pews, carved with great skill. Some were
single seats, while others were long benches, curved into
graceful semi-circles, large enough to fit two people in
comfort. As always seemed to happen during the bishop's
retreat, an unwritten law had arisen where groups of friends
or those who preferred to meditate alone, had established
rights to individual seats or to groups of pews, choosing shade
or full sun according to their preferences.

The Reverend Mother went towards her usual shady seat,
designed for one, but then stopped with a grimace of annoyance. Some large bird, probably a seagull, had perched on
the back and deposited a large and unattractive mess on the
seat. If it were in her own convent, she could have dealt
with the matter quickly and easily, but here she hesitated to
summon the gardener, or to go into the kitchen for a bucket
and a brush. She looked around. A few seats were occupied,
but very few and these were at a distance. Many still chatted
outside the church or had gone to partake of a mid-morning
snack after the morning service, so she was the only one
standing there. After a few seconds she chose the long bench
near to the gate where the stockbroker, James Musgrave,
usually sat, reclining against the sculpted curved end of the
stone and with his long legs stretched out and his shoulders
cushioned by the leather attaché case which seemed to
accompany him wherever he went. A man who seldom
appeared at this time in the morning, but if he did, as he
was a tall man, she would see him instantly he came through
the small gate by the church and could rise to her feet and
either choose another bench or else retire to her room.

She sat down, only noticing as she did so that a new grave
had been dug, last evening, she presumed, just behind the
bench where she now sat. It did not disturb her. An elderly
nun, she guessed, had reached the end of her days and like
the dead leaves and twigs from the apple trees, her remains
would go to enrich the soil. Well over half of the trees, she

reckoned, still flourished, and though now over seventy years old they were, she had heard, still productive so that the living sisters could enjoy their fruits. She sat for a moment, drinking in the atmosphere, and inhaling the scents from the blossom. It was the middle of June, but the cold wet spring had delayed the flowering season and only now were they in full bloom, covered with pale pink, faintly perfumed flowers, and hovered over by numerous bees. She placed a hand upon the warm stone of the bench with a sigh of relief. The almost everlasting fogs and rain through the last nine months had got into her bones and rheumatism and neuralgia had troubled her through the latter part of the winter.

Briskly she reminded herself that this was a retreat, a time for focusing upon matters of the spirit, and she cast her mind over the bishop's sermon this morning. Quite a secular sermon, she thought, and acknowledged a certain degree of surprise that had made her raise an eyebrow when she had listened to his lordship. A rigid, and uncharitable man, she had secretly, in the depths of her mind, classified him, but that sermon which he had just preached had startled her. He had spoken, not emotionally, but soberly and emphatically, and in a worried fashion, of the troubles of the poor in their native city and had urged all who listened to him to bear their troubles in mind; and his eyes had wandered over the row of laity in the front row and then had remained upon them, asking those who proposed a life serving the people of Cork, that if they were elected to high office to remember his words and pray for the strength to serve the poor of that city.

Most unlike the bishop, she thought, as her mind flickered over various meetings chaired by his lordship or services held by him where his sermons related to lofty heights of religious observation and obscure points of doctrine and rarely touched upon any practical work to be done in the city to make the lives of the citizens easier to endure.

She was turning these matters over in her mind when the gate to the orchard cemetery clicked and she realized, to her annoyance, that she would no longer be alone and this bench built for two would invite company since she could not, unlike James Musgrave, stretch her legs along the seat. A nun was coming through the gate. Rapidly the Reverend Mother slid her enormous rosary beads from the capacious pocket at the side of her skirt, but then something about the sweeping movement of veil and habit as the nun turned to close the gate reassured her and with a half-smile she pocketed the rosary and awaited the arrival of Mother Isabelle.

Mother Isabelle, though French born and bred, had spent the last twenty years of her life in the Ursuline Convent in Blackrock, a suburb of Cork. Well-to-do women and men of the city and its surrounds, whose daughters attended her school, spoke of Mother Isabelle with awe and reverence. Her sweeping movements, tendency to lapse into her native language at a moment's notice, when she could stun any parent with a fluent outpouring in the French language and above all, her utter assurance that she always knew best, would quell the most difficult parent.

'*C'est moi,*' she announced unnecessarily and closed the gate carefully behind her, then waited for a few seconds gazing back at the pathway. Pat Pius, distinguished by his multicoloured tweed cap, had followed her, making a few tentative steps in their direction, but to the Reverend Mother's amusement, Mother Isabelle stayed there at the gate, very still, gazing at him with an air of frozen astonishment which would have done credit to any actor on a London stage. Pat Pius removed his cap hastily, looked all around with the air of a man who is seeking to recollect an errand and then hastily turned and retraced his steps. Mother Isabelle remained stationary until they heard his voice greeting someone else coming out from the church and then she crossed the verdant swathe of grass and gathered her skirts carefully before taking her seat beside the Reverend Mother.

'*Ah, ma chère, que c'est ridicule!*' she said with a gesture that encompassed the convent chapel from which they had just emerged, and perhaps also the bishop, whose sonorous voice could be heard and almost certainly the pathetic effort of Pat Pius and his fellow candidates to curry favour with the clergy of the city.

They would, decided the Reverend Mother, continue to speak in French. She had spent a year in France when she was a young girl, and during the last few years had resolutely set herself to read some French every day, if possible. If they were conversing in French then the bishop, who was touchy and ill-at-ease with Mother Isabelle, would not approach, nor would he, though doubtless fluent in Latin, be able to pick up anything from their conversation.

'Rather a surprising sermon. Not like him,' she said in conversational tones. The use of the pronouns '*il*' and '*lui*' for the bishop was a convention that was well understood between herself and Mother Isabelle. She watched with amusement as her sister in Christ flung out her arms and discoursed fluently on the bishop's secret aims and desire to manipulate his audience. Apparently his lordship was worried, feared a great danger from one who was not only a '*terroriste*' but who had the additional failings of being a '*socialiste*', and worst of all in the *opinion* of '*lui*', according to Mother Isabelle, this person had the temerity to be a female looking for high office in the state.

The Reverend Mother nodded. No names would be used between them. That would be dangerous. The description obviously referred to Maureen Hogan. She raised her eyebrows in a query and that was enough for Mother Isabelle to break out again into a fluent speech in rapid French. Times, she said, had changed. There was fear in the city. The *bourgeoisie*, as she designated the merchant princes of Cork city, were intimidated. The 'Jacobites' – by which term the Reverend Mother understood her colleague to be referring to Sinn Fein – were spreading the word, by letters, phone calls, and casual conversations, promising that under the pretext of *Liberté, Unité, Égalité*, to be present at voting halls in order to check on each ratepayer's vote.

Was it possible? Just about, she decided, and in any case enough of a threat to intimidate, and to cause those courageous people who turned up, to think long and hard about where to place their votes.

'*Et lui, que veut-il dire?*' she queried, her mind going through the quite socialist sermon to which they had just listened.

According to Mother Isabelle, *lui* was very *fine*. The initial f of the French word for 'devious' and 'cunning' was hissed by her. 'If you can't beat 'em, join them' thought the Reverend Mother, translating the bishop's intentions from fluent French into good, honest, Corkonian speech. A hint was being passed to all the candidates that they would be wise to preach a socialist doctrine, said Mother Isabelle who always had means of finding out the gossip about the wealthy and powerful in the city. The speeches, no doubt, would be couched in vague terms, she thought cynically. Aspirations rather than firm promises. Probably already the bishop's chosen candidate, Robert O'Connor, 'Bob the Builder', was being coached in how to deliver a very carefully prepared talk to the collected heads of the schools in Cork. The Reverend Mother smiled, nodded and stored, in the back of her mind, Mother Isabelle's information. She was just about to ask a question when footsteps, coming up the gravelled path, made her stop and look in the direction of the gate. Not the bishop, she thought. The sound was of heavy boots, so not the gentlemanly stockbroker, James Musgrave, either. She had made up her mind that it was probably Pat Pius, coming to express a hope that she had not encountered any problems in cashing his cheque, when a broad-shouldered tall figure opened the gate with assurance.

It was Bob the Builder, himself. Sent by the bishop, doubtless, and that would have added an extra layer of self-confidence to his normal air of cool aplomb. A fine figure of a man, she thought, thinking about the well-endowed Kitty O'Shea. Had been brought up in the country, someone had told her. His father had been a small farmer in the rich land of north Cork. It was obvious that he had been well fed. And an eldest son, she seemed to remember. No money spared on him. Had even been sent to secondary school, though had not been much of a scholar. In any case, the custom among farmers in Ireland was to set up the older boys in some trade or business and then, when the father eventually grew too old to manage the farm, it was handed over to the youngest son who had obediently stayed at home and worked on the land. Would the builder win the hand of the wealthy widow, or would she opt for the more well-bred stockbroker from the Musgrave family?

Bob the Builder had the look of a man who was sure of a welcome, but Mother Isabelle was a match for him. Instantly she launched forth a stream of words and the Reverend Mother tightened her lips to make sure that her face remained blank and expressionless as she listened to the fluent French.

At an interesting stage of the narrative, Mother Isabelle decided to notice the invader. '*Oui*, you search *someting* . . .?' she said with a very strong French accent.

'Oh, no, nothing, nothing, lovely day, isn't it?' The builder cast a hasty glance around the blossoming apple trees and the neat graves of long dead nuns, examined the excavation for another grave and then, with an air of a man who has taken all possible notes for a job to be done, he retreated hastily, closing the gate with care and marching down the gravelled path in a determined fashion.

'*Qu'est-ce que je voudrais dire?*' said Mother Isabelle placidly and waited for another few seconds until the sound of the footsteps died away and she had recollected the train of her thoughts and proceeded to explain the bishop's reason for that unusual sermon.

The Reverend Mother listened with dismay. Nothing had changed, she thought, nothing had been learned. This election, like others in the previous years, was going to be stage-managed by violence on one side and corruption upon the other. Was there any chance for Ireland if this went on? And yet there were people around who wanted to steer this newly formed country in a direction where the poor and the powerless could be given the means to lead peaceful lives in decent housing, to have jobs which paid the rent and fed the families, for their children to be educated and medical care given to all. It was, after all, she mused, promised to the people by those visionaries in the 1916 uprising where a guarantee of 'religious and civil liberty, equal rights and equal opportunities to all its citizens; a commitment to universal suffrage', a phenomenon limited at the time to only a handful of countries, not including Britain; and then there was that promise of 'cherishing all the children of the nation equally'. It has not happened, she told herself. And why not? Because of self-interest, because of fear, because of corruption and because of greed. Most of the well-off and the professional classes were trying to ensure the same standard of living for themselves and their families as they had observed in the ruling class of the British, others, like herself, threading a diplomatic path between warring interests.

Had the time come when it was no longer right to be diplomatic? Should she and others like her speak out? She listened in silence to Mother Isabelle discoursing scornfully on the candidates and their inability to express themselves with the fluency which one might expect from those seeking high office and wrestled with her conscience for a few minutes until she decided thankfully that she was probably too old to change. She was about to indulge in a comfortable chat with Mother Isabelle about the bishop's secretary and his inability to understand how much it costs to run a school, when she suddenly realized that they were being listened to, not from the gate which they faced, but from a hedge at the back of the original field where the apple cemetery had been planted. She recognized the man even before he had removed the bowler hat which he wore. His size made him easily recognizable. A small man, almost dwarfish in size, he had been introduced in a rather stony fashion by the bishop on the preceding evening, but he had spoken well, she thought.

'*Il y a quelqu'un qui nous écoute*,' she said quietly and in a warning tone to Mother Isabelle.

'Sorry if I startled you, ladies, but I saw that big hole and just wanted to tell you that I found out from the gardener that there isn't going to be a funeral to disturb us. He just had a few hours on his hands with nothing to do and there are a couple of very old ladies, elderly nuns, I should say, here in the convent and he thought he might as well get the soil loosened and a hole dug, just in case, you know!' He laughed pleasantly and the Reverend Mother looked at him with interest. His name was William Hamilton, but he was known by all, as 'Wee Willie'. He came from Northern Ireland but was of the Roman Catholic faith. A few years ago, he had left Northern Ireland, presumably because he was uncomfortable and possibly found himself discriminated against. And so, he had moved away from Northern Ireland right down to the

county of Cork and had set up a factory for the manufacture
of women's stockings in a small town on the eastern side of
the city of Cork. A genial man, she had thought him to be
and he had been good company the night before when they
had all met over an evening meal. An enterprising one, also.
He had visited her convent quite soon after his arrival and
brought with him a present of a few pairs of stockings, medium
size, jet black in colour and in every way suitable for a convent.
He had adroitly gleaned from her the number of sisters and
lay sisters in the convent, had quickly worked out how long
a pair of stockings would last a nun walking these endlessly
corridors and pacing hard-floored classrooms, discoursed on
the waste of time spent mending old stockings, on the shocking
price of darning wool and had offered her a fair discount and
had immediately secured her as a client.

Wee Willie, she thought, had a healthy air of confidence
about him and showed little deference to the bishop when
the candidates had been forced to introduce themselves to the
gathering of nuns, priests and brothers before dinner on
the first evening. No respecter of dignitaries. She rather admired
his cavalier fashion of ignoring Mother Isabelle's attempts to
freeze him from their company by continuing to speak in
French and with his strong, harsh Northern Ireland accent,
declared his intention of shepherding them back to the flock.

'And ye'll let the gardener finish that job; the poor, wee
fellow had in his mind to cover the hole with a few slabs of
timber and a tarpaulin, but then you ladies arrived. He's
worrying that it's dangerous to have an open hole like that,'
he said with an assured manner, standing sturdily in front of
them with one arm crooked, ready to give them assistance to
rise if needed, but not looking as though he minded one way
or another. Out of politeness she took his arm, though she
prided herself on being able to rise readily from any chair or
seat. Mother Isabelle made use of the back of the bench and
with a quick farewell, still in French, went on her way in stony
silence towards the gate. The Reverend Mother cast a glance
at the depth of the grave that was awaiting the next death
in the convent and then thanked Wee Willie for coming to tell
them about the gardener. He gave her a friendly smile.

'Good idea, this,' he said with a nod towards the neat row of gravestones. 'Great place to put the bodies. I wonder would it work in the city, Reverend Mother? Would the trees take up too much room? High death rate here in Cork – in fact, it may be something the council should be considering. You wouldn't believe it, Reverend Mother, but the death rate in Cork is twice the rate of the Belfast death rate. Now what do you make of that?'

The Reverend Mother considered the matter for a moment. The statistic horrified her, but he was a sober northerner, Scots-Irish and would be unlikely to pluck a figure from the thin air like his more mercurial counterparts here in Cork city.

'The river?' she queried.

He smiled up at her with a congratulatory nod, but then held up one finger. 'Ah, but you see, Reverend Mother, we have a river in Belfast, the Lagan, flows through Belfast, but it's a clean river and the sewage was dealt with over forty years ago, doesn't come near the city. Fifty years ago they built a treatment centre well away from the city and you'd be surprised how few cases of cholera and polio and these sort of things they have in Belfast these days, but down here in Cork we're living in the past, spilling it all into the River Lee. We need to treat the sewage and keep it away from the river. I had polio myself as a wee child and it didn't do me much good,' he said without a scrap of self-pity, but with a determined nod.

'I suppose there is no other solution other than the river and then sea,' said the Reverend Mother.

'There's always a solution if you dig deep enough,' he said briefly. 'They manage better in the country than they do in cities. Everything gets dug back into the soil.'

Cities, she thought, were not good places. And, of course, he was right about the countryside. People were spread out and could dispose of their own sewage – probably like the orchard cemetery – in a useful and productive as well as safe fashion. When she had first embarked upon having hens in her convent garden she had been worried about comments from her deputy, Sister Mary Immaculate, about the pollution from their droppings and the smell they would cause, but her gardener, a country man, reassured her. 'It all goes back into the soil, that's nature's way,' he had told her, and the Reverend Mother, when Sister Mary Immaculate enthused about the fresh taste from their runner beans, had difficulty in restraining herself from mentioning that the flavour came from a liberal amount of hen droppings dug into the soil before planting time.

An interesting man, Wee Willie Hamilton, she thought when they parted at the door to the church and she decided that she would pursue their conversation about sewage, possibly not over dinner, but certainly in the hearing of the bishop, who, after all, had great influence over what happened in Cork. Why should cities have almost every square yard covered by houses and streets? Why not intersperse the streets with city orchards, or woodland copses, where the sewage could be covered with soil and used to grow apple trees and fruit bushes? Too late for the Georgian inner city of Cork, but an idea for the new suburb of Turners Cross where the city manager, Mr Monahan, was striving to build houses for the poor. Yes, she decided, she should do her best to ensure that Willie Hamilton, northerner or not, should have a fair hearing for his ideas on sewage.

Still, it would be unfair of her to concentrate on one candidate and with an inner sigh, she prepared to meet the bishop and the man whom he was obviously determined to introduce to her. So, this was Lucy's friend, James Musgrave. She remembered seeing the house and its beautiful garden. The Musgraves, of course, were an old Cork family, one of the so-called merchant princes and the bishop was obviously most impressed by him.

The bishop, himself, a man of great ability and strength of purpose, had come from a lowly background. His father had been a farm labourer and his son Daniel had attended the village school where his rapid progress had attracted the attention of the local priest who had advised his parents to 'make a priest out of him'. It had been, and still was in country districts, the only sure route whereby a boy of lowly origins could get an education and the young Father Daniel had risen as high as he could, graduating with honours and moving onto post-graduate studies and eventually becoming a bishop. His origins he kept secret; rarely, apparently, visiting his parents when they were still alive and having nothing to do with the rest of the family. Not surprising, perhaps, that he had a weakness for the prominent Roman Catholic families of Cork in whose houses he was now a welcome guest by virtue of his high office. He beamed happily as he introduced James Musgrave to her.

'I feel as though we are old friends, Reverend Mother. Your cousin Lucy and her husband Rupert are my dearest friends, and they speak so often of you.' James Musgrave was a handsome man; in his fifties, she would have thought. Iron grey hair well brushed back from his forehead, clean shaven and well-dressed in a quietly expensive manner. Certainly, highly approved by the bishop, she instantly realized, by his lordship's beaming smile of approval. In fact, she thought, Bob the Builder may have taken a step further down the ladder. A shy novice was beckoned forward and introduced as Sister Mary Magdalen, daughter of Mr James Musgrave. The Reverend Mother greeted her politely but felt that if the girl had entered her convent, she would have disapproved of the choice of such a flamboyant name. Mary Magdalen had been a follower of Christ, had been one who had stood around the cross, but she was remembered by most as a repentant prostitute. An odd name to choose, she thought and looked at the small, pale face with interest. Was Mr James Musgrave, a prosperous stockbroker, with a house in Montenotte, pleased that his young daughter had entered the order of the Sisters of Charity, an order which was devoted to visiting of the poor, especially the sick, in their homes, and also visiting those in prison. There was an unhappy look about the shadows beneath those large pale blue eyes and an unhealthy pallor to the face. The girl, if she had wanted to become a nun, would perhaps have been better placed in the Ursuline Convent of Blackrock where she would have been a teacher of girls like herself. The Reverend Mother smiled an acknowledgement of the introduction, but forbore to ask any questions of the girl as she seemed ill-at-ease and bore the appearance of one who would like to flee the company of the bishop and numerous nuns, priests and brothers who were interrupting the cloistered peace of the hillside convent.

There was no uneasiness about the father, though. In fact, the fond look that he bestowed upon his daughter seemed to show satisfaction rather than concern and he was obviously an affectionate father, holding the girl's hand and patting it from time to time as he chatted pleasantly about all the good work that the Reverend Mother had achieved in a poverty-stricken area of Cork. It was well done, she thought, allowing a smile to encourage him along the lines. It was calculated to please her, but also there were enough mentions of the 'deserving poor' in his conversation to keep the bishop happy. His lordship was all in favour of the 'deserving poor', but like the landlords of the city who made substantial sums of money from the letting of multiple tenancies in the crumbling Georgian houses, he very much disapproved of those who spent money drinking in the public houses of the city.

A fluent speaker and probably a clever stockbroker, thought the Reverend Mother and wondered, with a touch of envy, whether the mother superior of these Sisters of Charity was able to call upon his skills to sort out her accounts before the bishop's secretary could cast a beady eye upon the muddle in which her own accounts frequently ended up. It was, of course, she thought, resignedly, very much her own fault as the muddle was probably a consequence of running two separate sets of accounts side-by-side. The bishop's secretary could never be allowed to see the money spent on sweets, handed out so liberally as rewards, bribes, and sometimes, sadly, as the most positive gesture she could make towards a small child who was struggling to cope with the news of a death or an eviction. Somehow, there never seemed enough time in her busy life to make her accounts look acceptable.

Resolving to have a chat with Mother Isabelle about this matter of fiddling the accounts, she turned her attention to the five candidates: Pat Pius, the shoe manufacturer; Robert O'Connor, nicknamed Bob the Builder; Maureen Hogan, the solicitor with IRA links; James Musgrave, the smoothly-spoken stockbroker; and William Hamilton, known by all as Wee

Willie, the entrepreneur from the north of Ireland who had left Belfast a few years after the six counties in Ulster had taken the decision to separate from the south and remain part of Britain. Of them all, Wee Willie, she thought, was the most interesting. It took a degree of courage and enterprise to leave his family, friends and homeland to start a new life in Cork, the most fiercely republican of all cities in Ireland.

Which one of them would be elected to the position of alderman?

THREE

The Reverend Mother rose later than usual on the fifth morning and realized that she was feeling more refreshed than she had felt for a long time. There was, she thought guiltily, something to be said for these religious retreats. They refreshed the body and the mind as well as the soul. She washed and dressed, luxuriating in the realization that no one was going to bring her a problem during that day which stretched ahead of her. The convent was set at a little distance from the small church and the walk for early morning mass and communion was a pleasurable one in this unusually good summer weather for Cork city. But, whereas in her own convent on the flat of the city the increased warmth seemed to bring out a rash of fungal spores even on the well-polished furniture and corridor floors, up here, on this hill, the air was fresh; the sun, for once, was strong and its heat had begun to burn off the mist that still clothed the city below them.

There was no one outside the church, although the doors stood open, and a quick glance inside showed her that she was one of the earliest to arrive. And so, she indulged herself by prolonging her walk for another few minutes, climbing the hill and then pausing for a moment beside the orchard cemetery and drinking in the scented air from the fruit trees. The gardener, it seemed, had taken immediate advantage of their dispersal yesterday. The ugly pit had been roofed in with planks and covered over with a dark-green tarpaulin, tastefully decorated by an assortment of potted plants, and the gnarled ancient apple tree nearby cast a gentle shade over the arrangement. The Reverend Mother smiled a little. The presence of the grave had not bothered her, nor did the realization that the body of a nun would soon go to feeding next year's fruit on the nearby tree. Judging by the amount of blossom upon the knobbly and contorted branches, this was still, despite its age, a high-yielding tree and she considered fleetingly whether she could persuade the bishop to permit her body to be buried in this fruitful place. In life, she thought, as she went back down the path towards the church, she owed the bishop absolute obedience, but surely, once dead, she could have her own way. In her mind, she began to draft a letter that was to be given to his lordship after her death. Her cousin Lucy's solicitor husband would surely be the one to do that service for her, she thought. An unsealed envelope, she decided. The bishop would thereby be subtly reminded that the prominent citizen, Rupert Murphy of South Mall, would probably be fully aware of the contents of the letter. Yes, an unsealed envelope with its flap neatly tucked in. That would be the way to handle the matter.

And with that resolution she entered the church and took her place beside Mother Isabelle. They had been separated at dinner and throughout the previous boring evening spent listening to the bishop, supposedly interviewing the candidates, but in fact, telling each what he believed was their role and inviting their acquiescence – 'and, of course, I'm sure that you agree' – was the bishop's style of interviewing. Once this morning's mass was over, she and Mother Isabelle could stroll back together to sample the excellent breakfast which would be spread out for them and perhaps then they could have a little private conversation. Like herself, she guessed, Mother Isabelle would have a clear memory of a past pupil.

The small convent chapel was cool and dark, so the sun when they came out, hit everyone with a sense of shock. The mist had completely dissipated, and Cork lay before their eyes in unusual beauty, the two channels of the River Lee, curving through the streets of the city and the sunlight bringing a sparkle to the old limestone buildings.

'Would'ya look at the place; all *balmed* out in the sunshine,' said Pat Pius with a friendly smile in the direction of the Reverend Mother and she smiled back. A good, old Cork expression, she thought and hastily, before she had to explain its meaning to Mother Isabelle, she asked her question in low, rapid French, noting, though, how Pat Pius' smiling face changed to a scowl as he gave an angry look

at James Musgrave who was chatting with the bishop at
the doorway to the church. There was bad blood among the
candidates; that was obvious. The builder, Robert O'Connor;
solicitor, Maureen Hogan; and Pat Pius all looked back with
an annoyed expression at the bishop and his advisor. Willie
Hamilton, also, had a slightly unpleasant smile on his lips
when he surveyed the stockbroker.

However, the Reverend Mother averted her mind from
political matters and nodded at the answer to her gossipy
question of Mother Isabelle. It was as she had thought. The
Musgrave girl – now, and for ever more, to be known as
Sister Mary Magdalene – had been a pupil at the expensive
Ursuline school in the exclusive district of Blackrock. No,
said Mother Isabelle shaking her head vigorously, no, not at
all pious, not at all subdued, *au contraire* – headstrong,
opinionated, and a worry to her unfortunate widowed father,
some scandalous behaviour, even . . .

'*Un coup de foudre!*' was Mother Isabelle's opinion of her
erstwhile pupil's vocation to the cloistered life. Shocked and
astonished the whole convent. *Incroyable!* Not just the choice
of entering the convent, but the choice of an order. Mother
Isabelle echoed her own thoughts on the matter. The life was
hard and the work – these Sisters of Charity were expected
to scrub out the rooms where the sick lay in terrible squalor.
The French word *dure* seemed to sum up the life that the
daughter of James Musgrave had swapped for a life of luxury
and ease, living in Montenotte and going to school in
Blackrock. The poor of the city would have been, previously,
something glimpsed only from the safety of her father's car
with the windows firmly fastened and permitting no stench to
be inhaled.

Still, none of my business, thought the Reverend Mother,
listening to another piece of gossip about how the builder,
Monsieur O'Connor, had built a new house, *toute près* to the
Ursuline Convent, just between them and Blackrock Castle,
not only spoiling the community's view of the castle itself but
completely obscuring the restful vision of the River Lee as it
entered the upper regions of Cork Harbour. With a thinly
disguised satisfaction Mother Isabelle strongly feared that he

may have overspent on his magnificent mansion. He had been expecting to marry a wealthy widow, named Kitty O'Shea, but now this Kitty had apparently plumped for his rival, James Musgrave, the stockbroker and had left him in the lurch.

And, related Mother Isabelle, the bank manager had been observed by two of her sisters taking a *petite promenade,* to have called out to the house recently. The sisters, apparently, had noticed that the builder looked very pale as he escorted the bank manager to his car after their conversation.

The Reverend Mother enjoyed the story, especially as Mr Robert O'Connor had been recently involved in trying to render homeless some parents of children in her school. She hoped to receive further enlightenment and that she and Mother Isabelle could lay claim to that bench in the orchard cemetery after they had done justice to the excellent breakfast. She was interested to hear some more gossip and to listen to the shrewd verdict of the Frenchwoman on those candidates for the lofty position of alderman. The parents of children in her own school would have no interest and no information, but it would have been a different matter with the rate-paying parents of the Ursuline Convent pupils.

They were to be disappointed, though, once they strolled up to the beguiling scent of apple blossom. The bench where they had previously sat was already occupied by James Musgrave and the mother superior of the Sisters of Charity. The bishop himself stood in front of them, smiling benignly. James Musgrave, she thought, looked very relaxed and pleased.

'The chosen one, what do you think?' she murmured, wondering whether *choisi* or *élu* was the correct word, but plumping for the latter as sounding less like its English equivalent.

Mother Isabelle was inclined to think that if that were true, then the bishop was showing good sense. Mr Musgrave was a very pleasant man, most helpful – so he did do the convent's accounts, surmised the Reverend Mother with a moment's envy – moreover, said Mother Isabelle, with emphasis, he would command the respect of the *bourgeoisie* and protect the city from the horrors of such candidates as the little man from the north of Ireland, who spoke so strangely and who had tried once to sell her stockings for her affluent convent at a bargain price. Or that revolutionary young lady solicitor or even worse the low-bred man who sent barefoot children from house to house collecting old shoes. In the meantime, they would go for a *petite promenade*, which the doctor had recommended for her health.

They both enjoyed the walk. Over the years they had learned to trust each other's discretion and so were able to exchange information and even discreetly to share their opinion of the bishop wasting their valuable time in what should be a purely secular matter. As for the candidates, Mother Isabelle, personally, had made up her mind quite some time ago and she was happy to endorse the bishop's choice, if he chose the right man, and to place such little influence as she possessed in encouraging fathers of her pupils to vote in the same way. Mother Isabelle lowered her voice as they came around a corner and found four of the candidates standing in a cluster, looking across the cemetery at the sight of the bishop sitting upon the bench in the orchard in animated conversation with that gentleman candidate for the office of alderman, Mr James Musgrave.

He had a very pleasant voice, one of those quite high baritone voices which carry for long distances. A great public speaker, Lucy had said. In demand for all occasions. Charities loved him! That's what Lucy had said, and the Reverend Mother could see why. Though sitting close to the bishop on the bench and a good hundred yards from them, every word could be heard by those on the path.

'These Sunday collections, though all very well in their own way, are too irregular,' he was stating in a pleasantly authoritative manner. 'What you need, my lord, is a guaranteed sum which could be paid into an investment. I'd advise asking for a yearly sum from as many as you think would accept this way of paying their debt to God and to the church and you would be able to invest this. If your lordship wishes I could advise a few safe and lucrative shares. I'll draft a few details for you this afternoon once lunch is finished. If I could have the use of this bench and perhaps the gardener would bring me a small table, or even a box to put my papers on.'

Bother! thought the Reverend Mother. Once again, he's going to claim the best seat in the grounds for himself. She had already planned to take herself off there for the interval between the end of lunch and the beginning of the afternoon's sermon – a time when most took themselves off for an after meal snooze. James Musgrave, she thought crossly, was one of these men who used charm to get him privileges that those less adroit might snatch. He took it for granted that the bishop would ensure that he had this prime seat in the convent grounds reserved for him during the afternoon break on this warm June day and that all would keep their distance lest they disturb his thoughts.

His daughter was now sitting beside him, having been released from her duties while her fellow novices doubtless were now occupied in scrubbing and dusting like other novices all over the city. A man who found charm got him everything, assumed all would be done as he asked. The girl had now got to her feet looking awkward and ill-at-ease.

'Off you go, now, my dear,' he said benignly. 'Prayers, I suppose.'

A shy girl, perhaps. Muttered something. And then, without any farewell, she strode off through the gate and passed the cluster of visitors to her convent without a greeting or a look of recognition. The Reverend Mother frowned, but said nothing while the bishop went off to command a table for Mr Musgrave.

Only when all the fuss had died down and she and Mother Isabelle were making their way to the church, she said cautiously, 'I was surprised that Sister Mary Magdalen did not greet you.'

Mother Isabelle shrugged. 'Ah, *ma chérie, ces jeune filles gâtées!*' from which the Reverend Mother inferred that the daughter of James Musgrave had been a difficult pupil – spoiled, perhaps, and that the relationship between pupil and headmistress was still somewhat soured and past rebukes had neither been forgiven, nor forgotten.

Her attention just then was taken by the builder, Robert O'Connor, who rapped out an oath and then apologized with a guilty look towards the two nuns. He had, she guessed, heard the offer and correctly assumed from the animated conversation going on that the stockbroker might be more lucrative to the bishop than his own small discounts on a building scheme. Wee Willie was more forthcoming.

'Ye may's well pack y'r bags, laddies,' he said. 'Gentleman Jim'll get the prize so far as his lordship is *consarned*,' he said, and the Reverend Mother speculated in a detached way on how strong an influence the Scottish language still had upon the people of Northern Ireland – especially when one remembered that it was more than three hundred years since, during the reign of James I, the warlike Roman Catholics of Northern Ireland had been evicted from most of Ulster and the land filled with Protestant Scots, who had never truly amalgamated with the natives and had preserved their customs, accents and religion.

Why had Wee Willie left his native city of Belfast and come down to this most Catholic and most revolutionary city in the whole of Ireland? Was there something in his background that had made it impossible for him to stay in the north, something that would have made British rule and British justice a danger to him. It was, she thought, an interesting speculation. There must have been some pressing reason. After all, Cork was not in any way a prosperous place, not a place which would have appeared ripe for new business. There was huge unemployment and huge poverty in the place and even the well-off, such as doctors, solicitors, stockbrokers and successful businessmen, were certainly far less wealthy than they had been before the wars of independence and the civil wars. Her cousin's husband, the foremost solicitor in Cork, incessantly mourned the downturn in the economy, according to his wife.

Still, none of my business, she told herself as she smiled mildly at poor Pat Pius who wore the resigned look of one for whom fortune seldom smiled. Perhaps someone with his drive and his energy might have been better off taking the boat to America and devoting his gifts of innovation, perseverance, and courage to becoming an entrepreneur in that land of enterprise. Maureen Hogan, she thought, wore a thoughtful look, rather as though she were planning something as her eyes swept over the neat array of ancient apple trees and lines of graves. A clever young lady: she certainly had that appearance. A most determined chin and an air of indomitable courage about her. The Reverend Mother sighed a little when she thought of her star pupil, Eileen, who was also clever and self-willed and had the knack of getting herself into dangerous situations because of her devotion to the cause of a united Ireland. It would be the worst possible thing for Eileen to work in such close proximity to Maureen Hogan. These four men: James Musgrave, Robert O'Connor, Willie Hamilton and Pat Pius wanted the office of alderman because of the monetary success that it would help to bring them, especially if it led to the status of lord mayor, but Maureen wanted it in order to bring revolution into the city of Cork, to rake up the fires of nationalism which had recently died down to smouldering levels. There was a cold look in the girl's eye, a look that the Reverend Mother had seen in many of the heroines of the rising; such as Mary and Annie MacSweeney and also the Countess Markievicz, a look that seemed to say that, having pushed themselves, in the past, to do deeds that would be considered alien to their sex, that from then onwards they had kept a wary eye on their impulses and geared themselves to be ready for further action.

Perhaps, she thought, Lucy is right. James Musgrave might be the best candidate, after all. Brought up to money, sent to university, made a success of his original accountancy degree, risen to the heights of stockbroker; now very well-off, one of the Montenotte crowd and he would probably be above taking bribes unless they were very subtly offered in the form of a directorship or something of the sort. Whereas Robert O'Connor, the builder, was probably still hungry, doing well, but needed to do even better, especially now if he were to be disappointed in his courtship of the affluent widow, Kitty O'Shea. Pat Pius certainly would need more money if he were not to lead a 'hand to mouth' existence for the rest of his days. As he said himself, he was brought up hard, and that, in her experience, often meant that the hardness was transferred to his dealings with others. And Willie Hamilton, the Northern Ireland man. What about him? She didn't think that a northerner would have too good a chance in the strongly partisan

Cork city, though he might have concealed resources. He was, she decided, as she went into church, the mystery man and her mind went to a tale that she had heard once from her friend and physician, Dr Scher. It had been a complicated story involving a boat, an island, some Germans and a man from Ulster. She resolved to ask him about it when next they met.

FOUR

There had been, thought the Reverend Mother, a rather poor atmosphere over lunch. The lay members of the gathering were tense and uncommunicative. Even the charming James Musgrave ate his fish with the air of one whose mind is on other things. He had worn a dinner jacket the evening before, and though he now appeared in a lounge suit, he had embellished it with the silver and blue stripes of a Clongowes Wood College tie, pinned to his shirt with a small, neat pioneer badge, thereby signalling to the bishop that he had attended the most expensive and most exclusive school in Ireland, and was, moreover, a teetotaller after the example of Father Matthew, a saint much venerated in his native Cork city and whose memory was preserved by an enormous statue next to the Patrick Street bridge.

The other candidates for high office were ill-at-ease with James Musgrave, thought the Reverend Mother, and she sensed that there was going to be some bad feelings among them as the day progressed. It was unwise of the bishop to display his preference so openly.

It was, she thought, probably the fine weather that made everyone rather discontented. In the past when only the members of the religious orders had been invited, they seemed to have had bad weather with either rain or fog, encouraging all to either keep to their bedrooms or sit quietly in the library reading, or praying in the chapel. But now everyone wanted to be out of doors. The grounds, for those wearing their best shoes, were limited in scope, enough room for a short brisk walk, but no more and now the orchard had been barred to all except James Musgrave.

There was a feeling of unrest, a tense atmosphere. None of the candidates, she suspected, felt like ever repeating these tedious few days. Even she, herself, had begun to tire of the worldly company of Mother Isabelle and was filled with an

impatient desire to get back to her own convent where she
was sure that some real-life problems were waiting to be solved.
Seven days were long enough, she thought, as she made her
way to the chapel where she would not have to talk to everyone. She noted with amusement that, despite the sun, most
were going upstairs towards their bedrooms and would
probably spend the afternoon with a book or sleeping on their
bed until the hour for dinner approached. This day was going
to drag its endless length and by now everyone was sick of
this enforced companionship. Even the sun, she thought, as she
entered the darkness of the chapel, had begun to pall and
she found herself worrying over various vulnerable pupils and
hoping that Sister Mary Immaculate was following her instructions to make sure that no suspicious men were hanging
around the gate when the pupils went home after school. Some
of these barely adolescent girls were easily seduced with
the offer of a meal and would then be plied with some strong
Guinness or Murphy's Stout. She tried to pray but realized
despairingly that lists of instructions which she had written for
members of her staff kept intruding upon her mind. More of
a Martha than a Mary, she thought, and Jesus had reproved
Martha for her solicitousness about worldly matters rather
than prayer. Kneeling in the empty church she murmured,
'*Dixit illi Dominus, Martha, Martha, sollicita es . . .*'

And then, her low voice was drowned by an explosion, a
terrible thunderous burst of sound, near, raw, ear-splitting!

The Reverend Mother jumped to her feet and went to the
door. Not for a moment had she thought that it was thunder.
Anyone who had lived through the wars in the streets of Cork
city during the last years recognized instantly the raw, shocking
explosive sound of a bomb and would not ever mistake it for
the throbbing clap of a thunderstorm. A bomb meant danger,
but she did not hesitate. Lives were lost, but not always. Bodies,
even of the most severely wounded, could be reclaimed,
rebuilt. As she went through the door, she loosened her veil,
made from the strongest material it had seen a lifetime of
service, but was still strong enough to form a tourniquet for
a desperately bleeding wound.

The bomb, as she had thought, had exploded quite close to

the chapel. As she came through the door she could see where it had been situated. Clouds of smoke rose up; dust and dirt darkened the sunlight; the sun was hidden, and the air was filled with an acrid smell. The first thing that she noticed was that an enormous gnarled apple tree was lying across the pathway with its roots in the air. The cemetery itself was gone from view, just a bomb site veiled in dust.

'Get someone to phone the Mercy Hospital, quick, phone for an ambulance, doctors, nurses!' She snapped the words at a terrified novice and saw her run down the path towards the convent before she turned in the direction of the gate to the orchard cemetery.

The dust was beginning to clear from the air, to subside in layers on the trees, the tombstones, and the verdant grass. The Reverend Mother hesitated for a second. One bomb, she knew from experience, was often followed by a second, but she guessed that, in this place, at this hour, and for a particular reason which had inserted itself into her mind, there would have been just the single bomb. And so, she took the risk. There would be only a chance in a million that anyone could have lived through that explosion, but strange things happen. She knew of a house that had been blown up, but a baby strapped securely into a pram, had landed safely on the soft grass of a well-kept lawn outside the porch where he had been sleeping.

The fragile wooden gate was lying in splinters, but the heavy limestone blocks that formed the wall had been scattered and blocked the entrance. It took her a few minutes to scale them. Not a large bomb, she thought. Now that the air was clearing, the damage was minimal, apart from the gate and the one tree . . .

And, of course, the beautifully curved limestone bench.

The Reverend Mother said a quick prayer for courage and looked for a way to get further in.

And then she saw something which caused her to stop for a moment. Lying across one of the more ancient gravestones, not far from the gate, oddly stripped of clothing . . .

It was a human leg.

The Reverend Mother looked at it for a moment and then

turned and went back towards the shelter of the church. Her life, she knew without any false self-esteem, was a valuable one, and there would be no justification for risking it just to reclaim a dead body. Let the authorities come. The fire brigade, the army, ambulances and the police themselves all had plenty of experience in dealing with an atrocity such as this. She should, perhaps, go and check that the novice had obeyed her instructions, but she thought that the girl had looked alert and intelligent.

And yes, there was Mother Isabelle, accompanied by Mother Teresa, the superior of the Sisters of Charity, coming rapidly up the path. Was it religion or experience which gave her fellow mother superiors an ability to respond to all crises with calmness and a prayer? A quick glance at the scene from both; both glances pausing at the spectacle of the blood-covered leg, a murmur of a prayer from Mother Teresa – *Requiem aeternam dona eis, Domine* – and all three made the sign of the cross and then turned to each other.

'The ambulance and doctors are on the way,' said Mother Teresa and the other two nodded. It was interesting that Mother Teresa, in her prayer, had used the Latin word '*eis*' meaning 'they'. As far as the Reverend Mother knew, the only occupant of the orchard cemetery had been the stockbroker, James Musgrave. But of course, Mother Teresa, as manager of the convent and its grounds might have known otherwise. For the first time, the Reverend Mother thought of the obliging young gardener and breathed a quick prayer hoping that he had not been present.

But then the sound of a siren came to their ears. The streets leading from the city were narrow; the hill was steep, and narrow, too. A siren, if the ambulance and perhaps fire engine were to make progress, was essential for safety, but the Reverend Mother wished that it had not been necessary. It immediately attracted attention. A cluster of novices, faces as white as their wimples, emerged timidly, but stood their ground in front of the convent waiting for instructions. And then some other nuns, a priest, the bishop, and then last of all, the candidates for high office in the city, mostly fresh from their beds, judging by a slightly dishevelled look, but coming bravely up the path towards the three nuns: William Hamilton from the north of Ireland; Pat Pius Murphy, the shoe seller; Maureen Hogan the solicitor; and Robert O'Connor, the builder.

But not, of course, James Musgrave the stockbroker – stockbroker and father.

The Reverend Mother's eyes went to that cluster of novices at the bottom of the path. Instantly she took the decision to interfere. The superior of the convent was present, but the stunned expression on the woman's face, a face blanched with fear, eyes wide with horror, made her reluctant to pile more troubles upon Mother Teresa, who was waiting, with as much dignity as she could muster, for the arrival of the ambulance, the fire brigade and the police. The novices would be the last matter on her mind at this moment and so the Reverend Mother made the decision to use her own initiative.

A quick '*Excusez moi*,' to Mother Isabelle, then back down the path towards the cluster of girls outside the front door of the convent. 'Come with me, my children,' said the Reverend Mother quietly and with outstretched arms she ushered them in through the front door.

The convent of the Sisters of Charity had once, about eighty years ago, been the home of some wealthy and titled family and when their daughter had converted to Catholicism and had entered the order, her heartbroken father, a widower, and without any other children, had endowed the order with the house and had returned to his native town in southern England. The place still looked more like a country house than a convent and the Reverend Mother had no idea of the whereabouts of the novices' quarters. In this emergency, though, protocol did not matter so she immediately ushered them into a ground-floor parlour, carpeted with a thick Axminster rug and furnished with overstuffed couches and armchairs. As the girls stood around, shocked and indecisive, the Reverend Mother delved in her capacious pocket and produced her enormous and ornate rosary beads and handed them to the most sensible looking of the novices.

'Call out the rosary, my dear,' she said quietly. 'The sorrowful mysteries.' No need to say any more.

She had made a good choice, she thought as she left the

room. The girl's voice was quite steady as she announced, 'The First Sorrowful Mystery: "The Agony in the Garden" . . .' and then embarked upon the Lord's prayer and then the first of the ten 'Hail Mary' recitations. By the time the girls finished the sixty prayers that made up the rosary, their nerves would be steadied, and their minds would be calmed so that they could absorb the bad news without hysteria.

For one of them, there would perhaps be a greater shock, but that would have to be dealt with by the girl's own community, and so the Reverend Mother made her way down towards the convent kitchen, still housed in the basement of the stately Georgian home.

The lay sisters, having fed lunch to the visitors and the choir sisters of the convent were now, she guessed by the animated voices, having their own meal. She knocked politely but did not wait to be invited in, and so entered as a man's voice was in the middle of a story. 'If it hadn't been for the fact that I was missing a bag of fertilizer I'd have been in there myself. I'd be in a thousand pieces by now.'

He stopped abruptly as the Reverend Mother appeared.

'Sit down, everyone,' she said immediately, and then addressed the gardener. 'I'm pleased to see you. I was afraid that you might have been killed.'

He fumbled awkwardly with his cap and remained standing until she hastily took a spare chair and sat at the table. Then he sat down, also. 'I was just telling everyone, Reverend Mother, that I would have been in the orchard cemetery myself except that I couldn't find my bag of fertilizer, so I was busy in my shed, turning the place upside down, looking for it,' he said. 'Lucky for me! You see, I had planned to give the apple trees a bit of feed before the blossoms fell and the new season's apples began to form,' he explained.

'God spared you,' said one of the lay sisters, making the sign of the cross, which was quickly copied by the other sisters. She was probably the cook, possibly the unofficial superior of the other lay sisters, a woman past middle age, judging by her lined face, but still vigorous and active, thought the Reverend Mother. Rather like her own Sister Bernadette who ruled the convent and knew everything that was going on.

'I fear that someone has been killed,' said the Reverend Mother, and saw by the faces that they knew the news already. She asked no questions. There was, however, one matter on which she could get information.

'Was your shed very near to the explosion?' She directed the question at the young gardener but noted that there was a slight stiffening in the figure of the lay sister who had made the sign of the cross.

'Just around the corner,' he said cheerfully. And then with a look at the lay sister, he said confidentially, 'Sister Mary Agnes is afraid that I'll be blamed for it.'

'How on earth could you be blamed for it?' asked the Reverend Mother and caught a warning glance sent from Sister Mary Agnes to the young gardener, almost a maternal glance. He was probably young enough to be a son of the middle-aged lay sister, she thought and knew a moment of regret that these lay sisters were pushed into the convent at the age of fourteen when they were really far too young to make a decision about their future. Many of them later, she had learned, regretted that they had not been wives and mothers. Families, in her experience, could be quite cruel about getting rid of a few of the extra mouths to feed and the older ones were often sacrificed for the sake of the younger ones, the parents salving their consciences with platitudes about the will of God.

'Time you were getting back to work. They might be looking for you,' said Sister Mary Agnes. Her words were roughly spoken, but her glance at the young man was certainly quite maternal. The Reverend Mother, however, had been intrigued by the question of blame and she got to her feet.

'Will you walk back with me?' she asked. The gardener immediately seized his cap and escorted her, walking ahead and opening a door that led into the yard.

'Why on earth should anyone blame you if a bag of fertilizer is missing?' she asked again, once they were out in the open.

'It's the Shinners,' he explained. 'The Sinn Fein, you know, Reverend Mother. They steal fertilizer. I should have kept the shed locked, but, you know, I didn't think that they'd steal from a convent.'

'What on earth would they want fertilizer for?' The Reverend

Mother was genuinely puzzled. An image of the banned members of Sinn Fein hiding out in the hills and growing potatoes with the aid of stolen bags of fertilizer came to her, but she rejected it. Ever since she had had the inspiration of rooting up the useless shrubs of Portuguese Laurel, hydrangea and rhododendron in the convent garden, she had taken a keen interest in growing potatoes to feed hungry children at lunch time. Potatoes, she knew, should be planted as near to St Patrick's Day on the seventeenth of March as possible, not in June and in any case, these warlike young men were more likely to steal potatoes than go through the long drawn-out process of growing them.

His eyes widened at her ignorance. 'They makes bombs out of it,' he said.

'Bombs!'

'That's right, Reverend Mother. They use fertilizer and diesel sometimes.' He was enjoying her ignorance. 'You can even make a bomb out of fertilizer and sugar, you know.'

'Never!' she exclaimed, and enjoyed the expression of pleasure on his young face. She scanned her mind for information. Had she ever seen a bomb? She couldn't remember. 'What does a bomb look like? Is it like a big metal ball?' she asked cautiously as they made their way around the house.

He laughed heartily. A child of the troubled times, she told herself. His growing-up years would have been marked by explosions, gunfire, raids and executions.

'You get yourself a bag of fertilizer and a can of diesel and a match, Reverend Mother, and you have a bomb,' he said with an air of huge enjoyment at instructing her. And then, as they rounded the corner and confronted the paraphernalia of violent death – the ambulance, the fire brigade, and the police car – his assurance fell away from him and he came to a full stop.

'You wouldn't tell them about the bag of fertilizer, would you, would you do that for me, Reverend Mother?' he pleaded. 'You could explain that I didn't think that the Shinners would raid a convent. You see, I'm awful busy just now. No time to be talking to the guards – have to see to earthing up the potatoes. Can't waste any more time, today.'

She nodded. Wrong of her, perhaps, but she doubted that he could have had anything to do with the theft. There had been very little Republican activity in recent months, and she could not see why the convent would have been a target. The whole matter was very strange, and she was relieved to see the familiar figure of Inspector Patrick Cashman beside the throng of vehicles at the entrance to the convent.

It was only then that she suddenly thought of Maureen Hogan – a very respectable professed solicitor, but also a prominent figure among the *'Cumann na mBan'*, the women's branch of Sinn Fein.

And now Maureen Hogan was a candidate for the position of alderman in the city of Cork.

FIVE

Inspector Patrick Cashman was leaning on the roof of the Garda car with a pair of binoculars held to his eyes. Beside him was his assistant and at a little distance some ambulance men, shrouded in protective clothing and wearing large gloves. An ominous stretcher and a large body bag were on the ground beside them and they stood very still, looking at the scene of ruin ahead of them.

For the moment, only a couple of members of the fire brigade were within the orchard cemetery enclosure, and these were heavily protected with helmets, masks, leather coats and thigh-high boots. Wouldn't do them much good if another bomb exploded, thought the Reverend Mother, but she was too accustomed to the casual bravery of the city services to comment on the matter, as she silently came and stood beside Patrick.

'Like to have a look, Reverend Mother?' Patrick handed over the binoculars and went to have a word with his assistant, Sergeant Joe Dugan. The Reverend Mother put the binoculars to her eyes and instantly the whole scene sprang to life in magnified detail. The bench was gone; one piece of jagged stone protruded from the trunk of a distant apple tree but otherwise there was no sign of it. And the neatly disguised grave, with its tarpaulin covering and its decorative pots of plants, was now an enormous and gaping hole in the ground. As the Reverend Mother watched, holding the binoculars as steadily as she could, one of the firemen bent down and picked something up, turning back towards the laneway and shouting something. In a second Patrick was back beside her and immediately she returned the binoculars to him. His eyes were fifty years younger than hers and this was police business. He gazed for a moment, lifted an arm in acknowledgement and then lowered the binoculars and turned to his assistant.

'Piece of metal, an alarm clock, perhaps,' he said, and Joe

nodded in casual acceptance, while the Reverend Mother suppressed her instinct to exclaim or to question. What was an alarm clock doing in the neatly cared-for rows of apple trees and of graves? She asked herself that question and was puzzled about the relevance of this find. She, herself, had spent much time there in the orchard cemetery during the last two days and had not seen anything other than well-mown grass and an immaculately raked gravel path. Certainly, no rubbish. It definitely had significance, though. Already Joe was noting the discovery in his notebook, looking up from the position of the afternoon sun to the church behind them and with a pointed pencil estimating a position for the find, still held up in the air by the fireman's arm. How useful it was that every church had its altar on the eastern side of the building! Wherever there was a church within sight, no one needed a compass to check a location, even on a foggy or cloudy day, but today the sun helped to ensure an accurate location and Joe nodded with satisfaction and, in his turn, held up an arm. The fireman came forward now to the gate. Joe delved in his bag and advanced to meet him with a small cardboard box in his hand.

'Doesn't look like anything,' he said. And from what the Reverend Mother could see, it certainly did not. Just a lump of twisted metal.

'Bet you that it will turn out to be a nice little alarm clock. Handy to get you up in the morning, Joe. No more excuses from him if he is late to work, isn't that right, Inspector,' said the fireman with a wink at Patrick, and he and Joe laughed with no appearance of strain. These young men would have attended many scenes like this and would have watched as firemen and ambulance men risked their lives. The Reverend Mother stood at one side and hoped that the pale and rather impassive face, which she saw in the mirror every morning as she straightened her veil and wimple, would not betray her feelings of horror and, she had to admit, a slight frisson of fear. What if there were another bomb? Or if, for some reason, part of it had not exploded. She had known of such happenings in the streets of Cork, the most violent and heavily bombed city in the country of Ireland.

And then came the moment which she awaited. One fireman beckoned the two ambulancemen and they came forward with the stretcher and the body bag. The Reverend Mother forced herself to stand her ground and, for once, was glad of her fading eyesight. She had seen plenty of death during her time as superior of a convent of aging nuns, but solemn careful routine had no place here. The men first picked up the leg which she had seen originally and then moved here and there, bending from time to time, picking up something and placing it in the bag. They wore large white gloves and as she watched the gleam of this immaculate colour faded and the gloves became stained and dark. She remained there, as impassively as she could and, in her mind, she said, *If they can bear it, so can I.* Death for the elderly should be a matter of custom; for the young it was an abomination.

When they came back with their burden, she raised her hand to her forehead and made the sign of the cross and murmured a prayer. One of the men said, 'Thank you, Reverend Mother.' But the other looked embarrassed. The first, she had an impression, may have been a pupil of hers. The boys she knew less well than the girls. They left at the age of seven and moved onto the Christian Brothers. As had Patrick Cashman, now Inspector Patrick Cashman, and to him she turned with more practical aid.

'It was a bomb, was it not?' she queried, and then, not waiting for the obvious reply, she said, 'The gardener has missed a bag of fertilizer from his shed.'

That startled him. 'Fertilizer!' he exclaimed. Then: 'So, it was a Sinn Fein operation. They make them sometimes from fertilizer and diesel.'

She waited. He was experienced and astute. It was for him to ask the questions, to weigh up the evidence and to guess what might lie behind this terrible slaughter. She would help him with any piece of information that he required, but for now she would be silent and allow him to consider what lay behind this strange event.

'Who was the victim?' he asked after a moment, looking at her very directly.

'I'm not sure,' she said. That was the truth, but, of course, there was more to it than that and she forced herself to go on. 'The principal teacher from each school in Cork city was invited to come to this convent for our annual retreat, Patrick,' she said and saw him nod. He had known that.

And he probably knew also of the bishop's strange decision for this one year.

Nevertheless, she went on with her explanation. 'For once, this year, we were joined by the five candidates for the post of alderman on the city council. You know who they are, Patrick. Mr William Hamilton, who has a stocking factory; Mr Pat Pius Murphy, seller of shoes; Miss Maureen Hogan, the solicitor; Mr Robert O'Connor, the builder and . . .' She stopped for a moment and then forced herself to go on while silently uttering *God have mercy on his soul*. 'And Mr James Musgrave.'

His eyes went to the stretcher, which had been cautiously edged into the ambulance, inserted with such care that no individual part of the body would roll from beneath the cover which had been placed on top of it.

'And the victim,' he repeated. 'Could you hazard a guess, Reverend Mother?' His eyes, like hers, were fixed upon that stretcher. The door had not yet been closed. The ambulance men had done their part and now they awaited instructions.

'I think that it may have been Mr James Musgrave,' she said after a moment and tried to ensure that her voice remained as steady as did his.

'The stockbroker,' he said. There was a note of astonishment in his voice and once again she was conscious of a feeling of surprise that he knew so much of the ins and the outs of Cork society. It was, she herself had thought, most unlikely that someone of James Musgrave's breed and lineage had anything to do with Sinn Fein or the remnants of Protestant resistance. He belonged, from what she knew of him, to one of those old Roman Catholic families in Cork city. People who kept their Catholic religion, obeyed the law that, until almost a hundred years previously, forbade Catholics to engage in the professions, but who used their brains and their ingenuity and their family influence to engage in commerce and when the time of Catholic Emancipation arrived, those accumulated fortunes

served to educate their sons, and recently their daughters, to
take their rightful places in the professions of the country –
doctors, lawyers, accountants and university lecturers. No, she
agreed with Patrick's unspoken comment; no, there was little
chance that James Musgrave could have been a member of
either faction, of those who followed Michael Collins and his
pragmatic moderate compromise which involved losing control
of the six counties of Northern Ireland, nor of the de Valera
revolutionaries, who had never accepted the divided country
and the remaining link with Britain. Many violent deaths in
the city these days resulted from this enmity. But it was, she
felt, most unlikely that James Musgrave had taken part in any
of the sporadic fighting and military conspiracies that were
behind most sudden and violent deaths in the city.

However, if that were the case, how had it happened that,
when sitting peacefully in a convent garden, he had been blown
up by an amateur bomb made from garden fertilizer and
diesel? Perhaps, she thought suddenly, I might be wrong. Why
should it be James Musgrave? Perhaps the man had finished
his trawl through his documents, had put everything back into
his case and then had gone for a walk. Judging by the time
that it had taken the ambulance men to search through the
bomb-strewn lumps of flesh, the body might be indistinguish-
able. Identification would have to be made. The man was a
widower; his twin sons had emigrated to Australia. The only
near relative was the young novice here in the convent and
she might have to give a formal identification, but in the
meantime, something needed to be done and the Reverend
Mother nerved herself to make the offer.

'Is there any possibility of identification now, at this
moment?' she asked in a steady tone of voice and then added,
'the daughter, a young novice here in the convent, is the only
near relative and I would like to spare her if possible. It may
not be James Musgrave,' she added, but was conscious that
her words lacked conviction.

'Just a minute.' Patrick left her and went towards the ambulance. She waited, watching the conversation. They spoke in
low tones, too low for her to make out what they were saying,
although they were quite near to her. But she could read their

faces, read their body language. They were uneasy, unwilling. She guessed at what they were saying, but stayed there, very still. The responsibility was theirs, but she suspected that they would leave it up to Patrick now to make the decision.

And Patrick had known her since he was a four-year-old boy. She hoped that he would feel able to trust her.

The men had turned back to the stretcher. Fresh gloves on their hands, she noticed. They had thought their grisly task was at an end and that others in the morgue at the hospital would take over. She waited calmly, breathing a quick prayer to her patron saint to give her courage and when, after a couple of minutes, Patrick turned and came back, she asked no questions but moved towards him, following him with a steady step and doing her best to make this as easy as possible for the unfortunate ambulance men who were being forced by her to revisit the corpse which they had covered so neatly.

It was, however, impossible to distinguish any features from the hollowed out and blood-clotted head. She gazed at it long enough to make sure that there was no possibility of any identification. She was just about to make the gesture which they awaited, her permission to cover the pieces of what once had been a body, when her eye was caught by a pile of what seemed like raw meat but had on top of it a strip of material. It was heavily stained with blood, but some portion had escaped. A strip of blue and silver, with a bloodstained circle – a badge, she thought and pointed at it.

'Is it possible to wipe the blood from this – I think it might be a badge, don't you?' she asked, looking back at Patrick. His had to be the authority for doing this.

He nodded, but it was left to one of the ambulance men to take a soaked swab from a bucket and delicately wipe the object. It was as she had thought.

'It's a pioneer badge,' she said aloud. 'I noticed that the man I mentioned to you had a pioneer badge, inspector, I noticed him wearing it during our lunch.'

Everyone received that remark respectfully and in silence, although she noticed that two of the ambulance men exchanged glances. It was left to Sergeant Joe Duggan, Patrick's assistant, to venture a doubt.

'Very popular, in Cork, these pioneer badges,' he remarked.

'Knew a man who wore one, day in and day out, and only took it off when he went to the pub of an evening,' said one of the ambulance men, emboldened by that remark from the police.

'Yes, of course,' said the Reverend Mother. 'You're quite right. Yes, many men would have been wearing a pioneer badge. It's just that the tie is the same, also. Luckily, there is a fragment that hasn't been soaked in blood.' She leaned over the body, beginning to feel more at home with the situation and concentrating hard upon saving poor young Sister Mary Magdalen from having to identify her father from these awful remains. 'You see, inspector,' she said addressing Patrick, 'I recognize that tie. It would only be worn by someone who had been to a particular school near Dublin, a school called Clongowes Wood College, a boarding school, a most expensive school, indeed,' she added. 'Mr James Musgrave, the stockbroker, wore this tie at lunch and I noticed that it was pinned to his shirt by a pioneer badge.'

'Not likely anyone walked in off the road wearing a posh tie with a pioneer badge stuck into the middle of it, Jim,' said one ambulanceman to the other.

'Ruin a good silk tie,' said the other. 'Funny he didn't pin it to his lapel.'

The Reverend Mother gave him an approving nod. Cork people, she thought, with a moment's pride, had sharp wits. She had thought the same thing herself at lunch time and had come to the uncharitable conclusion that it had been placed in the centre of the tie in order to attract the attention of his lordship the bishop.

'That seems good enough for identification,' said Patrick briskly. 'Off with you now. Take him to the morgue. The sergeant will be along later.'

The Reverend Mother felt vaguely comforted by the way in which the body was now referred to by the pronouns 'he' and 'him'. She had thought only to save the young novice from the ordeal of trying to identify a body which was nearer in appearance to a tray of meat than a human being on a hospital stretcher. Now her evidence and her deduction had resulted in the use of the word 'he' and prayers for the dead could use the word. She made the sign of the cross and murmured, '*Requiescat in pace*,' and slightly awkwardly the ambulance men also made the sign of the cross and murmured, 'Amen' as she stepped back and went to stand beside Joe, leaving Patrick to give a few last instructions or commands.

This was murder, she thought. An appalling and brutal murder. But was this apparently innocuous stockbroker the intended victim or was he just the wrong man, in the wrong place, at the wrong time. She waited until the ambulance had turned and then was driven slowly and cautiously down the path. It stopped outside the convent and in the distance the Reverend Mother heard a familiar high-pitched sound from the horn of Dr Scher's Humber Super Snipe car

'You've met Mother Teresa, haven't you?' she said to Patrick, guiltily aware that she was nothing but a guest in this convent.

'Spoke to her on the phone,' he said briefly, and then with more animation, he exclaimed, 'That's Dr Scher, I'd know the sound of that horn anywhere. I should have phoned him. Excuse me, Reverend Mother, I'll just go down and explain to him. There's nothing for him to do here, but we should have waited for him.'

And then he was off. The Reverend Mother did not follow him. He would make his peace with Dr Scher without her help; there was no man who minded about protocol less than Dr Scher. She, however, had a more important task ahead of her. In her own mind, she was certain that the body of the man blown up by the bomb, placed near to the bench in the orchard cemetery, was that of the stockbroker, James Musgrave.

And James Musgrave, whose wife had been dead for over ten years and whose sons had emigrated to Australia, had only one member of his immediate family left here in the city of Cork. And that was Sister Mary Magdalene, novice in the convent of the Sisters of Charity.

I must see the superior, immediately, thought the Reverend Mother. She nodded at Patrick but did not offer to accompany him to greet Dr Scher. In the distance, she could see Mother Teresa in conversation with the bishop and she made her way towards them. Not a very competent woman, she thought as she approached. It was, perhaps, an uncharitable conclusion, but the Reverend Mother had long since learned to accept herself and to accept the razor-sharp accuracy of her appraisal of her fellow members of the religious community in Cork. As long as the judgements were lodged securely within her own soul and were betrayed to none, she had decided, no harm was done and she wasted no time in confessing the sin of uncharitable judgement, in uttering platitudes, or on expecting more from people than they had the capacity to give. There was, she had often thought, a clarity of vision, an understanding of human frailty in the portrait painted of the humanized Christ by the gospels written by his apostles and she consoled herself with the memory of his sharply accurate verdicts upon Peter and his other followers.

But now, Mother Teresa had to be made to understand that her support would be needed for one very vulnerable member of her community and the Reverend Mother walked steadily towards her and the bishop.

'The body is being removed, my lord,' she said, addressing both, but by convention using the bishop's title only. 'And a preliminary identification has been made. The person who was blown up was wearing a blue and silver tie from Clongowes Wood College in County Kildare and there was a pioneer badge pinned to the tie. I observed earlier today, as perhaps you did also, my lord, that Mr James Musgrave was wearing both at lunch time.

The bishop bowed his head sadly. 'I had thought that it must be he. I was just about to say this to Mother Teresa when you arrived. Poor man! His last minutes were spent in working for our holy mother, the church. God be with him!'

The Reverend Mother, as all three solemnly made the sign of the cross, wondered fleetingly whether going through a set of possible investments was as much God's work as feeding the hungry and housing the destitute, but she had more important matters upon her mind and so she turned to Mother Teresa.

'Mr Musgrave's wife is dead, and his two sons are in Australia, so my cousin, Mrs Rupert Murphy, told me recently.

His only close relative is his daughter, Sister Mary Magdalene, here under your care.'

'The novice I spoke of, my lord,' said Mother Teresa to the bishop. There was an undertone to her voice which the Reverend Mother interpreted as meaning that Sister Mary Magdalene was a problem novice.

'Will she have to identify the body?' asked the bishop and there was, to the Reverend Mother's slight astonishment, a note of pity in his voice. She hastened to reassure him and to inform him of the realities of bombs.

'The body was blown into many pieces, my lord,' she said bluntly. 'Smithereens' was the word that the ambulance men had used to the police sergeant, but she thought it might be an inappropriate word for his lordship. 'There is no chance of his daughter identifying anything – it was pure chance that I noticed the Clongowes Wood College tie and the pioneer pin which the late Mr Musgrave wore at lunch. I don't honestly think that there is any point in confronting his young daughter with the carnage.' She did not wait for an answer but instantly turned to Mother Teresa. 'May I offer my services to you when you break the news to the girl,' she said and added quickly before her offer could be declined, 'I think it might be consoling to the girl to know that I have identified the body of her late father. Do you not think so, my lord?'

The bishop, of course, was immediately in agreement. To give him his due he had a shocked and slightly sick look and had obviously taken in the implication of her words.

'I'm sure that Mother Teresa will be most grateful for your help, Reverend Mother. Now I must leave you both because I see that the police inspector is waiting to see me and to make his report to me.'

The bishop went swiftly in the direction of Patrick and Dr Scher and left the two women together. There was still an undecided look on Mother Teresa's face, but she said nothing as the Reverend Mother walked by her side towards the front door.

A cluster of nuns broke up swiftly as they approached and only one was left when they reached the steps leading up to the building.

'Mother Carmel, will you send Sister Mary Magdalene to me in the back parlour.' The words were curt, but a glance of understanding passed between the two women. Not much pity in either face, thought the Reverend Mother. More an expression of exasperation. She remembered the conference between the bishop, Mother Teresa and James Musgrave and she wondered whether the conversation had been about the young novice. She said nothing, though. It was not her place and there had been little rapport between herself and Mother Teresa during the years when she had come to spend the annual retreat at the convent of the Sisters of Charity. In silence she followed the mother superior into the back parlour – she surmised that the front parlour, a more comfortable room, would be left vacant in case the bishop needed to make use of it in his conference with Inspector Patrick Cashman or the police surgeon, Dr Scher.

They had not long to wait. The click of Mother Carmel's shoes and the shuffle of the pair of slippers worn indoors by the novices came closer. The door was opened and Mother Carmel was standing there with her hand on the knob, ushering in the girl with the demeanour of a prison officer. She did not follow in, but with a glance at her mother superior, she closed the door with a careful click.

Sister Mary Magdalene knew the truth. The Reverend Mother could see that by the terribly white face and the swollen eyes. She advanced and stood obediently in front of the two nuns, but it was with an effort and the place where she had stopped was still at some distance from her mother superior. The child would faint in a second! The Reverend Mother ignored protocol and the ordinary politeness of a guest in someone else's home and dragged a chair from under the heavy table and placed it behind the novice.

'Sit down, sister,' she said, and pressed upon the girl's shoulder.

She sat. One thing the convent did for these girls was to train them into immediate obedience.

The Reverend Mother went back to Mother Teresa who so far had said nothing, but who was looking appraisingly at the girl, now slumped in a chair a good ten feet away. She had made no effort to approach nearer to the novice but stood very still and appeared as though she were turning matters over in her head.

The Reverend Mother took advantage of the distance between them and the girl and said in a very low voice, 'Would you like me to tell her, tell her what I saw?'

There was a moment's silence. A look of annoyance upon Mother Teresa's face, but the offer was a plausible one. After a moment she said stiffly, 'That would be most kind of you, Reverend Mother Aquinas.'

The Reverend Mother did not hesitate. She dragged out another of the heavy chairs and placed it to one side of the girl's chair. She reached out and took the two cold hands within her own. 'I'm afraid that I may have bad news for you, my dear,' she said gently. She pressed the fingers – how very thin this girl is, she thought – before saying, 'A bomb has exploded in the orchard cemetery and I fear that your father may have been there and that he may have been killed.'

And then she waited. She wasn't quite sure what she expected, even after almost thirty years of being the principal in a convent and having had, over the years, to be the one who had to break bad news about a family death; even after all of those events, it was, in her experience, impossible to foresee the reaction. Hysteria, exclamations, pious words, dead silence, all were to be expected, but silence from this reserved girl fitted with what she had already observed of James Musgrave's daughter. Her instinct was to send for a close friend from among the novices, but this was not her community; she had broken the news as carefully as she could, but now it was for the mother superior to deal with the child and so she looked across at Mother Teresa and waited.

'I think that you may be excused your duties for the rest of the day, sister,' the woman said coldly. 'Go to your bed now. Someone will bring you something to eat, later. Please thank Reverend Mother Aquinas for her kindness and go straight up to the dormitory.' She did not attempt to approach the girl or offer even the consolation of a hot water bottle in the bed or the companionship of a friend.

The Reverend Mother stood her ground. She could not leave

someone not too far past childhood in this manner. 'Do you
have an aunt or a cousin, Sister Magdalene?' she asked and
was surprised when the girl shook her head. Most unusual in
a city full of large families. 'What about Mrs Murphy, your
neighbour, you were friendly with one of her daughters, weren't
you? Shall I phone her?' Lucy, she knew, was kind-hearted to
the young. She did not wait for an answer but swept on. 'Go
to bed now, my child, try to sleep.'

She waited until the door had closed behind the novice
before turning to Mother Teresa. 'I fear I have to impose upon
your kindness and use your telephone, once more, Mother,'
she said quietly and barely waited for a nod before leaving
the room. There would be a queue for the telephone once
every school principal and visitor realized the anxiety
caused in the city when news of the explosion in the hillside
convent had been broadcast. She would not hesitate to invoke
the authority of the mother superior as she apologized for
jumping the queue.

SIX

The only person to be seen where the telephone, like her own, was installed in a dark back hallway, was someone who had no responsibility for a school. The tall thin figure of Miss Maureen Hogan, the solicitor, with face to the wall and her free hand forming a funnel between the mouthpiece of the telephone and her mouth, was speaking in a low voice. Excellent hearing like all the young! When the Reverend Mother came near, she immediately stopped talking. She did not, however, finish her conversation and hand over the telephone to someone so much older and of so much more of importance than herself, but held it firmly with her left hand now clasped over the earpiece as she swivelled around and glared at the intruder. This tactic might have worked with the other members of the ill-fated 'retreat' but it didn't worry the Reverend Mother in the least and so she waited, deliberately not moving away or even pretending not to listen. She waited with her expressionless face which she hoped conveyed to the young lady that she should finish up her conversation as quickly as possible. It would certainly have worked with every other member of the laity, or even of the clergy. Maureen Hogan, however, was made of sterner stuff.

'Just a minute. Someone is here,' she said into the mouthpiece and then transferring the phone to her left hand, with earpiece once again firmly blocked, she said in an imperative and rather high-pitched tone, 'Yes?'

'I wish to use the phone,' said the Reverend Mother sternly. 'So, if you have finished . . .?'

'I haven't finished,' said the young solicitor.

'Then may I suggest that you postpone private conversations until no one else needs the telephone urgently,' replied the Reverend Mother promptly.

The young woman had spoken with an arrogant rudeness

that surprised the Reverend Mother. Many members of Sinn
Fein were, she understood, very anti-religion, partly because
of the bishop's threat that members could be denied the last
sacraments in their dying moments and partly because of the
stance he had taken against the hunger strikers, heroes in
the eyes of their comrades, but guilty of mortal sin according
to the bishop. Nevertheless, she, personally, had never encountered any hostility. Most Sinn Fein members recognized the
good that she had done among the poor of the south side of
the city and saluted her with respect whenever she came across
them. Now, faced with rudeness from this young lady, she
waited with an impassive face, but deliberately did not take a
step backwards.

There was a short silence, but then Miss Hogan capitulated.
With an abrupt 'I'll ring back', she slammed down the phone
and stalked off to a perch on a draughty windowsill without
a word to the Reverend Mother, who immediately gave Lucy's
number to the telephone exchange, quashed any desire of the
telephonist to gossip by commiserating on how busy they must
be, and then when her cousin came to the phone, said briefly,
'I need your help, Lucy, and your car. You remember the matter
of which we spoke.' And then she rang off and returned the
phone to Miss Hogan. Lucy, she guessed, would by now have
heard all – Cork was a city where gossip flew rapidly from
the flat of the city to the lofty heights of Montenotte.

'Thank you,' she said to the young solicitor. She was inclined
to add *'but please do remember that many here will have
important phone calls to make'*. However, she resisted the
impulse. There was, she felt, little profit in annoying the girl
and it was, she always felt, better to lead by example rather
than by precept. In any case, this girl might be a source of
valuable information. Both Patrick, Inspector Patrick Cashman,
and the humble young gardener had viewed the theft of the
bag of fertilizer as a significant link to Sinn Fein. She looked
thoughtfully at the girl before she went away. It was a good
face, she thought. An intelligent face. There was character in
the set of the chin and in the determined expression of the
dark brown eyes. One girl with two older brothers. She
would have had a struggle on her hands to win her father's

acceptance that she should study law rather than something innocuous like English literature and now, instead of doing the easy thing, and joining her father's practice, she had set up on her own in the not too salubrious surroundings of North Main Street.

It would be a good half hour before Lucy arrived, thought the Reverend Mother as she hesitated in the main hallway of the convent. She decided not to return to the company of Mother Teresa, and it would be impolite to wander upstairs towards the novices' dormitory without the mother superior's permission. The sunrays slanting through the stained glass of the hall door decided her and she turned the knob and went outside. There was no sign of Patrick which slightly disappointed her but, on the other hand, the bishop had disappeared so she could regard herself free to walk around and perhaps pick up a few pieces of information. Her mind felt puzzled. The police had cordoned off the path leading to the orchard cemetery, presumably in case there was still some buried explosive material, though she would have thought that the fire brigade had searched the area completely. But the barrier meant that the church was also barred off and that meant, she told herself with a slightly guilty feeling of pleasure, that they could no longer have any of those church services that seemed to be degenerating into political polemics. She preferred, she thought, a more private connect with the Almighty, though she was sometimes guiltily aware that her prayers seemed these days to be more like begging letters.

'Reverend Mother!' Dr Scher was coming towards her, hands outstretched. Normally his manner towards her was rather ironic, and matter of fact, but now he seemed to be quite moved at the sight of her. She guessed that he might have been alarmed by the news of a bomb at the convent where she was making her annual retreat and so she returned the slight pressure of his hands. 'You're safe and well,' he said, rather unnecessarily, but she welcomed his concern.

'This is a strange affair,' she said briskly.

'And you're in the thick of it, like everything else that happens in the city of Cork,' he said, and she was warmed by the affection in his voice.

'The man was blown into pieces,' she said and hoped that he would not notice the slight tremble in her voice. He, she thought, would have the unpleasant duty of examining what was left of the body.

'An IRA business, according to Patrick. They must be running out of funds from American republicans – back to the good old fertilizer, apparently. Patrick has been on to the *Cork Examiner* to put a warning to gardeners to lock up their bags. The farmers know that already, but the gardeners think that no one will bother about the odd bag here or there. And the dead man. A stockbroker, according to Patrick. You know all about him, I suppose.'

'Barely enough to find it all very puzzling,' said the Reverend Mother. Her spirits were beginning to revive. An abstract puzzle, a question of 'why?' and of 'who?' was better than the memory of the scattered body parts and the devastated daughter. 'He was a widower with twin sons, both out in Australia, and a daughter who is a novice here in the convent.'

'Poor girl,' he said with such compassion that she bore in mind that, if necessary, she would ask Mother Teresa to allow Dr Scher to prescribe a soothing drink to allow the girl to have a few hours of sleep. That matter would have to be approached tactfully, though, so for the moment she shelved it and returned to the mystery.

'Why?' she said aloud and then when he looked puzzled, she went on. 'Was he killed by accident, I wonder? I cannot see him being involved with either side. People of his kind keep out of these matters and mostly, in my experience, they are permitted to keep out of them. *Musgrave* – I remember his father, I think. There was a Mr Musgrave who had a house by the sea in Ballycotton where we used to go when I was young, and he had some sort of clothing factory. Made a lot of money, I believe.'

'Nothing to do with the Sinn Fein crowd, then.'

'Nothing,' she said emphatically. 'These sort of families, even when they wanted an independent country, never wanted it to be achieved by violence but, on the other hand, he was not from a family that might have had anything to do with the law, with a judge that might have jailed some IRA volunteer. The Musgraves, I'd say, were a purely commercial family. Well-off, but James Musgrave is probably the first of his family to enter politics.'

'But do you think that the Sinn Feiners didn't want him. I understand that they have their own candidate. By the name of Maureen Hogan, someone told me.' Dr Scher, as usual, had picked up the gossip of the city.

'She's a solicitor,' said the Reverend Mother. 'I can't see that she would have played any very active part in IRA activity. She would merely have been a follower of Eamonn de Valera, like a lot of quite respectable people.'

Dr Scher gave a cautious glance around and then lowered his voice. 'Patrick is wondering whether it was a case of mistaken victim. Happens very often, you know, when it's a question of a bomb. And, in this case, if it really was a bag of fertilizer and diesel or whatever was needed – I'm not an expert on bomb-making, but even I know that this would have to be set up in advance.'

'I must say that Mr James Musgrave did occupy that seat during the first few days of our retreat. The gardener, the young man over there talking with Patrick, he had dug a grave and then covered it over with some planks, a tarpaulin and even put some potted plants on top,' said the Reverend Mother. She strove to make her words sound neutral but heard a note of doubt in her voice.

'There's been a death, then, in the convent.' Dr Scher echoed that note of doubt. He sounded puzzled.

'No,' said the Reverend Mother. 'The gardener explained that one of the very old sisters is not expected to live too long and as he had some time on his hands, he decided to dig the grave and have it ready.' Though very conscious that her voice held a decided note of doubt in it, she did not endeavour to suppress it. And she thought it was justified. It was, she had thought at the time, a very odd proceeding and certainly not one that she would have permitted within her own convent precinct if she had been so fortunate as to possess an orchard cemetery like this.

'A bit strange that!' said Dr Scher, echoing her thoughts. 'How on earth could he know that there might be a death within days, apart from a piece of gossip? Mostly I don't know myself and I certainly would never be sure enough to give instructions for a grave to be dug. You know yourself, Reverend Mother. Think of Sister Assumpta! She, according to herself, was on the point of death for over twenty years, and even I was surprised at how long she lasted. If that young man dug the grave on his own initiative just because someone told him that an elderly nun was on her way out, then it does seem odd. What if it rains, or, I suppose, since we are talking about Cork, I should say, what about *when* it rains? Well, Patrick is letting him go now. Coming over to have a word with you, I'd imagine.'

They waited in silence, with the Reverend Mother endeavouring to banish from her mind the grisly task that awaited Dr Scher. Patrick, however, looked unmoved as he approached, removing his cap. The sun caught the silver bullion wire of his inspector's badge and she noticed how his glance went to it before he tucked it beneath his elbow. It had been, she knew, a tremendous struggle and nights spent studying for Patrick to attain the rank of inspector and she felt proud of her erstwhile pupil.

'Anything you want me to look for, Patrick?' asked Dr Scher. 'Not that I'll be able to find much with the body in that state,' he added, and the Reverend Mother tightened her lips and repressed a shudder.

'See if you can find the teeth,' advised Patrick. 'Easy enough to find James Musgrave's dentist, and I'd like to have a firm identification in place before we set other matters in motion. The bishop thinks that the man was about fifty so he may have had false teeth, but you never know. Don't worry too much about it,' he said as Dr Scher began to move away. 'We are virtually certain. If it wasn't he, well, where is he now? And if it wasn't he, well, who was it? Everyone else has been accounted for.' He waited until Dr Scher had begun to back out his car and then said, 'I've been wondering, Reverend Mother, whether Mr Musgrave was the intended victim.'

The Reverend Mother looked at him with interest. 'He does seem an unlikely target for the IRA, doesn't he?' she said cautiously. 'My own knowledge of him is minimal; I probably know more about his father and grandfather than I do of him, but my cousin, Mrs Murphy, who will be here shortly, knows him well. He is a neighbour and a friend. But to answer the point you made, do you think that someone else was targeted?'

Patrick hesitated visibly. 'What do you think about the bishop, himself? It would have been feasible that he would have been sitting on the bench that afternoon, wouldn't it? Alone or with someone.'

The Reverend Mother thought about this and acknowledged the possibility. Anyone who wished to kill the bishop would not have worried too much about collateral damage in the form of other members of the clergy or of those on retreat in the convent. 'You are thinking that this might be a political assassination?' she queried. She glanced around. They were both speaking in low tones, as there was a certain amount of people coming and going. The lay sister from the kitchen, Sister Mary Agnes, was superintending the delivery of a sack of flour and a couple of sacks of sugar, giving a long explanation as to why the order for more sugar had to be added at the last moment. Another lay sister was polishing spotless windows and keeping an eye on the ruined orchard, while the gardener was snipping rose heads and gazing anxiously back at the police around the small shed nearby which, she presumed, was where he kept his tools, his pots, and his supplies of fertilizer.

'I think it is a possibility,' he said.

She turned the matter over in her mind, but then shook her head.

'I don't think it likely, Patrick,' she said. 'That hole, which was dug for a grave, was only open and exposed for a short time, so I doubt whether news of its presence could be known to those in the city. In fact, I, and the superior from the Ursuline Convent in Blackrock, were sitting there when Mr Hamilton told us that the gardener was worried about leaving that gaping hole. If I remember correctly what he said was: "The poor, wee fellow had in his mind to cover the hole with a few slabs of timber, but then you ladies arrived and he's worrying that it's dangerous to have an open hole like that."' She did not attempt to mimic the northern accent, but saw Patrick give one of his infrequent smiles at her words – a slightly gap-toothed smile. Suddenly she saw the small boy in him, the ragged, underfed boy, whose teeth had suffered from inadequate feeding in his youth, now almost completely subsumed in the competent, well-dressed police inspector.

But then the rare smile vanished in a second as Patrick bent his mind to the problem.

'So the chances of someone from the city knowing that there was a huge hole in the ground, an ideal place to conceal a bomb in order to blow up whoever sat on that bench at a given time – the chances of that happening are very slight,' he said and the Reverend Mother did not contradict him.

It was he himself who after a minute, said, 'Unless, of course, the IRA had someone within the walls, someone who knew exactly what was going on and who was able to quickly seize an opportunity.'

The Reverend Mother thought about the matter and then she shook her head. 'I don't see the IRA wishing to blow up the bishop,' she said. 'Cork is a very religious city and the IRA are not too popular just now. To be implicated in the murder of a bishop would finish any support that is remaining to them.' Her mind went again to the girl with the phone in her hand and the other hand covering her mouth as she whispered into the phone. Maureen Hogan had links with the IRA; even Eileen had not denied that. Maureen Hogan wanted to be an alderman and then, perhaps, lord mayor of Cork, following in the footsteps of the tragic pair of former lord mayors: Thomas McCurtain who was murdered by English soldiers and Terence MacSwiney who died of hunger strike in an English jail.

'You will be seeing everyone here before they leave, I presume, Patrick,' she said.

He looked at her sharply and bowed his head in acknowledgement. He had picked up on the hint. She mused upon him with interest. Patrick as a boy had, of course, only stayed with the nuns until the age of seven, when after making his first confession and his first holy communion, he had been moved onto the Christian Brothers. During these few years, he had never stood out as being clever in any way. She remembered him for his tenacity, for his stubborn pursuit of an idea, but for little else. He had, she thought, grown with the job and that tenacity had served him better than a quick brain had served many of his contemporaries. From being just hard-working and reliable he had advanced to being also sharp-witted, adroit, and alert.

'I've spoken with the bishop,' he said. 'His lordship suggested that he would arrange for a parlour to be available to me. He's been most helpful and has given me a list of those in attendance.'

The Reverend Mother bowed her head in gracious acknowledgement of the bishop's helpfulness, but she did not offer to move away and to leave him to his work. He gave her one sharp look and then went back to his notebook where she could make out a neat list of names, headed by her own. Then he took a typewritten list from his case and scanned it. He murmured the names of priests, brothers and nuns, all headmasters and headmistresses of the numerous schools in the city of Cork. From time to time he looked at her with a quick sharp glance, but she said nothing and made no move. He replaced the list in his attaché case and went back to his notebook.

'Miss Maureen Hogan,' he said in a low voice. He gave a swift look around, so rapid that it was hardly noticeable, but the Reverend Mother guessed that he estimated the distance of all, even the man delivering the grocery supplies to Sister Mary Agnes.

'You know the name,' she said and her tone, like his, was subdued, and would, she knew from experience, not carry beyond his ear.

'She has come to our attention a few times,' he said briefly.

'She was most anxious to keep her telephone conversation secret, and was not particularly polite when I, also, wanted to use the telephone, but that could be her age, her dislike of Reverend Mothers, of those in authority, a hundred and one reasons. But, obviously, anyone in contact with those who make bombs, must be of interest to you, Patrick. But then she is only one among many who knew that the bishop had more or less told all to keep away from the benches in the orchard cemetery as Mr Musgrave would be doing some valuable work for him – something to do with stocks and shares, I understand. And he asked Mother Teresa to arrange for a table to be taken out for him.'

'So, if I were present at that lunch I would know from the bishop's announcement, that Mr Musgrave would be sitting on that bench during the afternoon.'

'Would be sitting on the bench during the later part of the afternoon,' agreed the Reverend Mother. 'But then he has been sitting on that bench every day since the beginning of the retreat. The custom is that all retire to their bedrooms for private prayer after lunch and then there is a church service at two o'clock where we pray for guidance in our lives and for help in doing the Lord's work. And then we walk, pray, talk with each other, ask questions, sit on benches in the orchard or generally fill the time until supper at six and then another church service. So,' she summed up, 'even if the decision to kill the man was made after the bishop's announcement, then there would still be a couple of hours for preparations, hours during which very few would be around. The nuns here, young and old, rise at half past five in the morning. Many do hard physical labour, scrubbing out disease-ridden tenements and ministering to the sick and the dying. The afternoon bedrest is taken by order and the visitors fall in with this routine. The grounds would have been empty for these couple of hours.'

'That's useful information,' said Patrick, making a few notes and outlining a neat timetable on a fresh page.

A laconic man, thought the Reverend Mother, but she guessed at his meaning. It would be easier for the police and for the investigation into the murder of the stockbroker if it turned out that it was a routine assassination by the IRA. There was, although she was sure that he was aware of this, a danger of thinking too readily of the IRA when any crime occurred; even the theft of a suit of clothes from a shop window in a north Cork town was recently laid at their door in the *Cork Examiner* news section.

'And if they knew that there was a deep hole, already dug, then it might occur to them that this would be an excellent place in which to conceal a bomb.' Patrick frowned a little. 'The time was short, very short to plan and execute something like this. But from experience I know that the boys in the IRA can work fast and expertly. And, of course, there is a strong possibility that the gardener was in their pay, or one of them.'

'Or terrorized,' put in the Reverend Mother. 'What would be their motive though, Patrick? Why should the IRA assassinate James Musgrave? I can't see that he would have too much to do with politics.'

'I don't bother my head too much about politics, Reverend Mother. To me a crime is a crime no matter who commits it.' He hesitated a little and then said, 'Joe told me that Eileen was thinking of being apprenticed to Maureen Hogan. Do you think that you could have a word with Eileen, Reverend Mother? She would only laugh at me, thinks I'm a stuffy old stick, but I don't think it's a good idea, do you? Maureen Hogan . . .' Patrick stopped and made a few more notes and the Reverend Mother could understand how his mind worked. There was, after all, a connection between the victim and the IRA and Maureen Hogan was the link. And Eileen was linked to Maureen Hogan.

SEVEN

Eileen had heard the news two minutes after she walked into the offices of the *Cork Examiner* newspaper the following morning. She had been looking forward to holding the floor for a few minutes at least. The reporters there knew all about her exams and most of them were a party to her ambitions and to her bouts of optimism and of despair. She opened the door with the words: 'Guess what!' on her lips and then stopped. The place was a hive of activity. Reporters speaking on the phone, one hand holding a receiver and the other scribbling words onto a notebook. others were already bashing out stories on the elderly typewriters and did not lift their heads. Few of those on calls even looked in her direction.

'What's up?' For the past three years, Eileen had been supplementing her meagre university grant with writing up stories for the *Cork Examiner*. She had even earned her own seat in the reporter's room and now she slid onto the bench beside a young reporter. 'What's up?' she asked.

'IRA bomb. In the orchard cemetery of the Sisters of Charity. The boss is looking for you.'

For a moment she thought he was joking, but the chief reporter at the desk by the window had seen her. He continued typing with one hand, but the other one crooked a finger and she went forward and stood patiently until he had finished writing his paragraph at top speed. He unrolled the sheet from the typewriter, read it through carefully and then once again crooked a finger, this time at one of the messenger boys. Normally they waited downstairs but when there was a big news coup, they acted as runners, rushing between the reporters' room and the compositors, carrying messages between them. The compositors were highly skilled. As well as laying out the letters with rapid flicks of their fingers and arranging them at top speed, they were also responsible for checking spelling and punctuation and returning work which might be too long or too short. Even the head reporter would have to wait now until the word came back that the piece was acceptable. He would, Eileen knew from experience, have less than five minutes before his attention would be focused on a rewrite or a new piece, so she strained every nerve to hear him above the din of voices and the clacking of typewriter keys. There would be no time to get out her notebook, no possibility while he spoke, for even the fastest shorthand. She would have to do that afterwards, now she had to listen and memorize and only ask the most essential of questions.

'Been an explosion in the orchard cemetery of the Sisters of Charity. Get up there quickly and find out everything. Be back as soon as possible.'

And then the messenger was back, waving the sheet of paper. 'Forty-five words too long,' he gasped breathlessly and with a curse, the boss grabbed it from him. Eileen flew from the room and clattered down the stairs.

That would be it. She had her instructions. Her motorbike was outside. She had forgotten to attach the padlock in her eagerness to get inside the newsroom and tell everyone about her triumph and the scholarship, but there were plenty of messenger boys hanging around to keep an eye on it for her. The excitement of the news of the bomb had spread to them and each knew that the *Cork Evening Echo* would be a sell-out and that their 'farthing a newspaper' wage would mount up rapidly, especially as tips were more frequent when the news looked exciting.

'How do I get to the Sisters of Charity convent?' she shouted as she kicked her engine into life and hardly waiting for their shouted instructions as she roared off down Academy Street and daringly shot across the traffic into the busy St Patrick's Street.

'Sisters of Charity,' she repeated to herself as she sped down the busy street and then slowed to a halt beside a *Cork Examiner* billboard. A lorry beeped angrily behind her, but she was able to dart ahead quickly enough so that the driver did not squeeze past her on the narrow street. The words: BISHOP and RELIGIOUS RETREAT had been in large letters

and that had been enough. The Reverend Mother had said that
she was going on the retreat when Eileen had popped in to
tell about her triumph. With a feeling of apprehension Eileen
wove her way in and out of the traffic and changed into a
lower gear to tackle the steep hill ahead of her. She had just
reached the top of the hill when a figure, dressed in a gabardine
raincoat, with a slouch hat pulled down over his brows, stepped
out into the road and almost blocked her path. An arm was
raised, gloved finger pointing to a side road and Eileen swung
the wheel and pulled into safety.

'You nearly got me killed, Padraig,' she said, but she had
not thought of refusing the summons. She was no longer a
member of the IRA, but Padraig MacDonnell had been leader
of the Barrack Street branch for long enough to have obtained
her instant obedience to any command. A very quiet man, who
used one word where another would use ten sentences. It was
said of him that he never uttered a threat; he dealt in action,
not in words. But the young recruits to the organization had
a deadly fear of him. The less he was heard to say or seen to
have done, the more the apprehension grew and there was a
feeling that his reserve and steely politeness were the bars
behind which a murderous and ruthless assassin sheltered.

'You're off to the convent,' he said and jerked his head
towards the top of the hill.

'Yes,' she said. No point in denying it or in trying to elude
him. He was reputed to know everything that was going on
in Cork, to have spies in every organization and business in
the city.

'Musgrave, the stockbroker, has been killed. Maureen Hogan
feels she's under suspicion. Do your best for her. Pin it on
someone else. Let the blame fall on the right shoulders.'

A feeling of resentment rose in Eileen. 'Who did it, then?'
she asked and tried to inject a little sarcasm into the query.
She was pleased to hear that her voice sounded steady, and a
little indifferent. She already knew a little about James
Musgrave. Stockbrokers, she thought, would not have much
to do with the IRA. She was sorry for Maureen Hogan. She
knew from her own experience that any membership of the
IRA or even of Sinn Fein, was enough to bring an innocent

person under suspicion by the police. Nevertheless, she resented being ordered to do something by this man who now should have no power of authority over her.

He looked at her for a long minute, for the space of time for the tram to trundle past them and then he decided to answer her question.

'Bob the Builder,' he said.

She knew who he meant. Robert O'Connor. The man's name was plastered all over hoardings. He specialized in cheap, small houses in places like Turners Cross and St Luke's Cross. Houses for bank clerks, reasonably well-paid workers in Fords and Dunlop factories, prosperous shop owners and schoolteachers. The houses were reputed to be badly built, made from the cheapest materials, but that did not stop them being snapped up by people desperate to get their families, their children, out from the disease-ridden flat of the city with its continual flood of sewage-choked drains and miasma of fog for most seasons of the year.

'Why should Bob O'Connor murder the stockbroker?' she queried. He was going to tell her, anyway, in his autocratic way, so she might as well ask and get away from him as quickly as possible.

'You don't keep up with the city gossip, do you? The stockbroker was doing his best to walk off with the woman that the builder was going to marry. A pretty wealthy lady, name of Kitty O'Shea. Widow of the alderman who dropped dead with a heart attack.'

Eileen shrugged her shoulders. 'Nothing to do with me,' she said. 'And come to think of it, Maureen O'Hogan is nothing to do with me, either.' That was not strictly true, but she had thought over the Reverend Mother's words, and had decided that it would be best to cut the ties with the past, and to find someone who would give her an apprenticeship and an opportunity to experience different aspects of the law without involving her in any more dubious connections.

'Don't betray your old comrades, Eileen!' The words were an order, not a suggestion, and held a sharp note of criticism. She stiffened, clenching the handlebar, and making the engine roar a little. He gave her a long look and she looked back with

as much courage as she could muster, but then her nerve failed
her, and she slowed the engine while he hissed in her ear.
'O'Connor has overspent on that flashy new house of his,
builder or no builder, fancy materials cost money. Needs the
job of alderman, needs the widow's wealth. Bribed the bishop,
promised him a good price on that new church, but the word
on the town is that the bishop, once he had signed the deal,
taken the bribe, decided that the stockbroker was the more
useful of the two and O'Connor knew he had wasted his money
if he didn't get rid of the stockbroker. He could be a prime
suspect if you play your cards right. And there's a story going
around that he's asked for time from a debtor.'

'So?' She made her voice as indifferent as she could but
felt a quick beat from her heart.

He narrowed his eyes at her. 'No good looking at me as
though butter won't melt in your mouth and as if you don't
know what I am talking about. You've got that *garda*, Inspector
Patrick Cashman, eating out of your hand, so they tell me.
You just get up there now and convince him of the truth: that
the builder murdered the stockbroker. This wasn't an IRA job,
Eileen! Someone is using a trademark and trying to shift the
blame and I'm not having it. None of us put that bomb in a
convent. You're in with some of these people so you can find
out what is going on. And don't forget your own. Patriotism
is not a bit of an old shawl that you can throw away whenever
you think you've got too grand for it! I'll be keeping an eye
on you, so make sure that you do a good job. And that's a
warning, Eileen, not a bit of begging.'

She stared back at him as defiantly as she could manage.
He did not move, nor did he say anything for a few minutes.
A man walking a bulldog came past and she saw Padraig step
aside hastily and inwardly sneered. Not so brave. Could
threaten a girl but was afraid of a dog. She knew these men,
though, and knew that the more nervous were often the most
vicious. For a moment she wished that she owned the bulldog
and could set him on Padraig MacDonnell. It would give her
a great sense of power, but then she changed her mind. He
had thrust his left hand into his trouser pocket and the movement disclosed an ominous bulge in the pocket of the gabardine

which, despite the warmth of the morning, he wore like the uniform it was. He had a gun in that pocket, and she knew that he could use it and disappear so fast that he could not be arrested. They were well trained, these IRA men and, of course, it was the survival of the fittest and the most adroit. Any threat from that friendly looking bulldog and he would shoot the poor animal and then melt into the back streets.

He was watching her now, waiting until the man and dog were away and there was an unpleasant smile upon his lips.

'You're a city girl, Eileen, aren't you?' he said softly. 'Never seen a pig killed, have you? I used to think it great fun when I was a youngster. Very friendly animals, pigs, they never learned the meaning of the knife. Be so pleased to see you. They'd be nudging up to us, trying to lick us and then the knife would slice their throats. Used to make me laugh. They'd make a sound like this.'

It was an unearthly and appalling squeal, that shuddered right through her.

'They say that people are like pigs when you cut their throats,' he said in a soft voice. 'They make the same sort of squeal. Someone told me that once. Not true of men, though. I know that much. Cut plenty of men's throats in my time. Not sure about young girls. Perhaps they do sound like that. I suppose I'll find out.'

And with that, he removed his hand and stalked off. She deliberately raced her engine and swung the motorbike around, missing him by a few narrow inches, and then, her cheeks burning with fury, she went back onto the main road, wove her way in and out of the traffic and kept a good speed until she reached the gates to the convent.

There was no sign of the Reverend Mother though the day was fine and sunny, and many other nuns, brothers and priests strolled around, chattering in groups. Not much praying going on, said Eileen to herself, noting that the bishop in his epis-copal robes was talking animatedly with a group of elderly, white-haired priests while a Franciscan monk chatted with a couple of nuns. Patrick was there, not interviewing anyone, but standing out in the middle of the apple trees. So that was the famous orchard cemetery, she thought. The crater was enormous. Definitely a bomb, though most bombs that she had seen the results of, had been planted in buildings and on bridges.

Reluctantly her mind went over the words from Padraig MacDonnell. She did not like the man, but she trusted his word in his denial of responsibility. He would be the first to take credit for a bomb if he or the party had arranged it. In any case, it did not make sense. Why kill a man, a solitary man, with a bomb that could kill dozens? Why waste a bomb? Why not a marksman behind the wall, or even concealed behind an apple tree? One shot and James Musgrave would be dead. And there was a good chance that no one would have heard or taken notice of the shot if the man was sitting there, alone. That would mean that the assassin could quietly escape, and no one would ever be sure of who had fired the shot.

After all, the aim, surely, was just to kill this one man. Why on earth plant a bomb in a convent? According to Maureen Hogan, the bishop had made sure that not one of those influential heads of schools, private schools as well as state schools, would want to vote for anyone with socialist ideas. Maureen had been very bitter about his sermon on the opening evening which seemed to make a comparison between the Sinn Fein Party and the terrible events in Russia where the communists took control of the country, murdered the tsar and his wife and all of his children, including one sick little boy. It was not as if the nuns were taking any part in the struggle between the rival parties, Sinn Fein or Cumann na Gael. And these nuns, in particular, did very good work among the poor of the city, sending out the sisters to nurse sick children and adults in the teeming tenements of the disease-ridden city. No, she decided, this was not an IRA matter. Someone, to quote Padraig MacDonnell, had stolen the trademark.

'Eileen!' A quiet voice from behind her, made her swing around.

'Oh, Reverend Mother, I'm glad to see you alive and well,' she said impulsively.

The Reverend Mother smiled, but then she cast a glance over to where Patrick was standing. 'Should you be here, Eileen?' she asked.

'This wasn't a Republican bomb, Reverend Mother,' said Eileen earnestly. 'It's just someone trying to shift the blame. What happened? A bag of fertilizer and some diesel – that's what I heard. Put under the bench where the man was sitting. That's the story, anyway,' she finished as the Reverend Mother shook her head.

'Not under the bench, Eileen, near to it. The gardener had dug a grave – rather ahead of time, but there was an elderly sister on the point of death for several weeks, so as he had no other job to do, he busied himself with digging a hole.'

'So, anyone who passed, or who was looking down from that road up there, would see the hole and decide that it was a good place to shove the fertilizer and the diesel.' Eileen looked up at the road and narrowed her eyes. She had excellent sight, but it was, from where she stood, impossible to see anything, but a winding white line. She doubted whether someone standing up there would notice a hole beneath the large and flowering apple trees.

'The outer fence is also at a considerable distance.' The Reverend Mother had read her thoughts and then, when Eileen turned to look at her, she added, 'As a matter of fact, the hole was only visible for a day or so. I understand that the gardener had been about to cover it, went off to his shed in order to get some planks and a green tarpaulin but unfortunately I and Mother Isabelle from the Ursuline Convent in Blackrock, interrupted his work by coming and sitting on the bench.'

'Saying your prayers,' said Eileen with a slightly mischievous look. She would not have dared to say that a few years ago, but now she was a university graduate, a grown woman with a good future ahead of her.

The Reverend Mother smiled a little. 'I fear we were indulging in gossip, though in French so as not to give scandal.' She half-smiled at her own words, but then added, 'Mr William Hamilton, one of the candidates for the position of alderman, came along after a while and told us that the gardener was waiting to cover over the grave. We got up instantly and moved away. The next time that I saw it, the following morning, I think, it was well covered with planks and a tarpaulin and even had some potted plants upon it, so that it would be quite unlikely that anyone would know that there was a six-foot hole between the bench and the nearest apple tree. I suppose,' she said thoughtfully, 'that those few people, the gardener, Mr Hamilton, Mother Isabelle and myself, could be deemed to be suspects, since the makeshift bomb was probably placed beneath the covering of that tarpaulin.'

Eileen felt protective. The Reverend Mother sounded quite worried, rather as if she needed comforting. In some ways, now that she was a grown-up university graduate, the Reverend Mother treated her more like a friend than a schoolgirl. The thought sent a rush of pride through her and she was determined to do her best to help in the solving of this mystery. Of course, a murder of a man who had been sitting on the same bench where the two nuns had sat the previous morning must be a very upsetting thing for a very elderly person.

'And speaking for myself, I really haven't the slightest idea of how you could make a bomb from fertilizer and why you need diesel as well,' went on the Reverend Mother thoughtfully.

'Jesus! Reverend Mother! Nobody thinks you did it!' exclaimed Eileen, shock allowing the forbidden use of the holy name to be jerked from her.

The Reverend Mother gave her a reproving look but didn't comment.

'It's the nitrate,' Eileen said hastily. 'There's nitrogen in fertilizer – it's good to make things grow, a bit like sunlight someone told me. Something to do with sugars, I think, and then they soak the fertilizer in diesel, and I suppose that gives the extra boost of sugar. I'm really not too sure, Reverend Mother, but I know a fellow in UCC – top of the class in chemistry – explained it to me once. Something to do with a sudden release – can't remember anything else. I can find out from him and let you know.'

'Perhaps it might be best to wait for a while before you make these enquiries. We don't want too much talk about bombs and fertilizers,' said the Reverend Mother. She sounded to Eileen as though she were slightly abstracted from the subject of the conversation and then she said, 'Eileen, do you see that young man, boy, really, talking to Patrick's assistant,

Sergeant Duggan. Do you know who it is? Do you recognize him?'

'I don't think so,' said Eileen. The young man was dressed in a grass-stained pair of breeches, tucked into sturdy boots. He looked out of place in this convent full of nuns, brothers and priests and she was certain that he was not anything to do with the election of an alderman – their faces had been on posters all over the city for the last fortnight – nor was he a reporter. No, she thought, that's the gardener. Who would be more likely to have possession of a sack of fertilizer and even a few pints of diesel than a gardener? And who, apart from the nuns, brothers and priests staying at the convent would be sure to know of the six-foot hole conveniently dug quite close to the bench where the dead man had been sitting at the very moment of the explosion. And, of course, Maureen Hogan, Bob the Builder, Wee Willie Hamilton, and Pat Pius, all of them wanting the position of city council alderman.

'I've never seen that young fellow before, not that I can remember. And he's not a member of the IRA, unless he joined after I left,' she said, reading the Reverend Mother's mind. 'I bet he is under suspicion, though,' she added as her mind ran through the opening lines of the story that she would write for the *Cork Examiner* and its sister paper, the *Evening Echo*. Short and eye-catching for the *Evening Echo* – if she managed to get back in time – but longer and more atmospheric for the *Cork Examiner* which would be printed in the middle of the night.

'You don't mind if I use your name, Reverend Mother?' she asked anxiously. 'The chief reporter is very keen on having the human interest of the story and, sure, all Cork know you. It'll put the heart across to them all. And they'll all be praying and making novenas to thank God for sparing you,' she added.

'Well, in that case, I suppose that you may use my name if it's in such a good cause as getting people to pray,' said the Reverend Mother. 'I suppose that the Holy Father himself would approve.'

A wonderful woman! thought Eileen. A narrow escape from death and there she was able to chat and even, just now, seeing the joke about getting people to pray by giving them a juicy piece of news. She looked across at the gardener again. The sergeant had finished taking notes. A nod, and Joe was back reporting to Patrick and the young fellow was left on his own. He saw her looking at him, but he didn't move away. He seemed hesitant and she gave him a sympathetic smile. She wouldn't move; that might be enough to get Patrick or Joe to come up and ask her what she was doing – and if they did that, the chances were they would say that they had already given all possible news to the *Cork Examiner* reporters. And so, she stayed where she was. She had, she told herself, a perfect right to come and enquire after someone who had been her teacher and had coached her for the Honan Scholarship.

'Would you like me to drop in at your convent and tell everyone that you are well, Reverend Mother. I could say that I had been talking to you and that you were as well as could be expected?' she enquired, hardly hearing the answer while she kept an eye on the young gardener. He was on the grass lawn between them now, plucking up a weed and self-consciously fidgeting with the soil in the hole left behind. In a moment, he was beside them.

'Well, looks as though I might have to water the grass,' he said cheerfully. 'Never did that in a month of Sundays! How are you, Reverend Mother?' He spoke to the elderly lady, but Eileen knew that his attention was on her while the Reverend Mother thanked him for his enquiry and said that she was very well.

'Most have been a terrible shock to you, too!' Eileen said. It would be a wonder if he were not under suspicion, she told herself. His hole, his bag of fertilizer, and perhaps a can of diesel from his shed also.

'At least I had no diesel,' he said, as though reading her thoughts. 'Whoever stole the fertilizer had to bring his own diesel. I never use the stuff, just a few sticks and a few twists of the *Cork Examiner* – very good paper for lighting a fire. Sister Mary Agnes in the kitchen saves them for me. I keep a pile of them in the shed on the top shelf to keep them dry.'

'You weren't too near, were you?' Eileen did her best to put a note of concern into her voice. Young fellows like that liked a girl to take an interest in them.

'Naw, I was in my shed, on a ladder, searching the top shelves for the missing bag of fertilizer. Heard the bang and turned around, saw it. Like a sheet of flame. Gave me the shock of my life! I can tell you; my hands were trembling like I had a fever.'

I can do some good stuff from that, thought Eileen. She surveyed the convent grounds carefully, looking from the crater to the small wooden shed. She would start with a description of the desecrated ground, and then move back in time and relate all through the eyes of the gardener. It could make a good dramatic story told like that from the point of view of a boy on a ladder in a shed. Eagerly she questioned him, forcing him to pull small impressions from his muddled brain. What did he hear? What did he see first when he looked through the window? Where were the other people? Who spoke? Who did he go to? Where had he kept the bag of fertilizer? She poured out the questions but left her notebook in her pocket. Any minute now Patrick would arrive and tell her politely that she had no business here. She would have to rely on her memory and strong visual impression of the scene.

Maureen Hogan was hovering at a distance, but Eileen ignored the young solicitor. Who was Padraig MacDonnell to give her instructions? In any case, he was wrong, completely wrong. Patrick, she told herself, would be more likely to be suspicious of the young solicitor if she were to endeavour to persuade him that Maureen Hogan had nothing to do with this murder. I'm keeping out of it, thought Eileen. The very idea that the Reverend Mother and other teachers had been so close to losing their life in an explosion filled her with horror. If the IRA or Maureen Hogan had anything to do with that matter – and it did seem to her that the IRA were more likely suspects than Bob the Builder – well, in that case, she told herself firmly, she, Eileen, wanted nothing whatsoever to do with the matter.

'I'd better be off, before I get thrown out,' she said eventually while the gardener was endeavouring to hold her attention by describing, once again, how he shook, and how he was soaked in sweat. 'Very relieved to see you safe and well, Reverend Mother, I'll be sure to drop in at the school and let them know,' she called out in a clear and carrying voice, meant for Patrick's ear, and then without greeting either him or Joe, and totally ignoring Maureen Hogan, she grabbed her motorbike and wheeled it towards the gate. It was only after she was through the gate and had mounted the saddle that she looked back and saw the furious expression on the young solicitor's face.

'Well, there goes my chance of an apprenticeship,' she muttered to herself. But she didn't care. Something would turn up and the worst thing of all for her now was to return to being entangled in the affairs of the IRA. If that was the price that Maureen Hogan demanded, then she, Eileen, was not willing to pay that price. She wanted to make a success of her life, to pay back her mother for all the years of drudgery, long hours every day spent cleaning out pubs and scrubbing floors and making do with very little food when her daughter had given up her schoolwork in order to go off and join the IRA. She was years older now and hopefully, she said to herself, I have a bit more sense. She then banished the thought of Maureen Hogan from her mind and concentrated on putting words together to form an exciting and attention-grabbing article for that night's *Evening Echo*.

EIGHT

Patrick felt a little awkward with the young soldier. He had saluted and called Patrick 'sir' – but Patrick felt that the soldier was the knowledgeable one and he was the inexperienced recruit. He said nothing, though and listened in silence.

'I see,' he said at the end. The man was English which gave him a strange feeling. Among Cork people, the English soldiers – both the regular soldiers and the Black and Tans, who were known as the 'auxiliaries' but who were reputed to be mainly jailbirds, remnants from the Great War who had for some reason or other ended up in prison – did not have a good reputation in Ireland, but oddly some of them had decided to stay behind and to join the new army and the new police force. This man was about his own age, had joined the English army when he was only fourteen years old, lied about his age and had been trained as a bomb expert; he had told Joe all of that. He had been busy and terse with his team, but now seemed to be waiting with a touch of impatience for questions.

'How do you like Cork, Sergeant?' Patrick asked the question tentatively, thinking that if they were to work together on this puzzling case, then friendly relations should be established.

'Like it well enough. Especially the beer, Murphy's Stout and the *craic*!' said the soldier briefly. 'Feel at home here, inspector. Mam was from Cork and Dad from Liverpool. Got a few cousins here in the city. My second name is Patrick. First name Christopher, known as Chris.'

Patrick nodded. This was different. If his own father had bothered to get in touch with the wife and baby he had left behind and, of course, to send money from wherever he went to after disembarking from the Cork to Liverpool ferry, then he himself might have been brought up in Liverpool. It was an odd thought.

'Call me Patrick,' he said. 'Joe and I drop all this inspector/

sergeant stuff when we're on a job. Now tell me how this bomb worked.'

'Well, I've found out how they did it,' said Chris. 'Kept finding bits of metal and trying to put them together, but the gardener here recognized one bit and he cleared up the problem for us. Said that there were rust holes in a downpipe from his shed and when he replaced it, he kept the old pipe in case it came in handy. One of the bits that we picked up had the curve on it – swan neck, he called it. So, myself and the constable, we worked out how it was done. Took a bit of a risk, igniting it, I'd say, but if the man was busy reading, well then they might have taken the chance on not being seen. Apparently, he always sat on that bench.'

'Petrol, or diesel, what do you think?'

'Well, we don't know, really,' said Chris. 'The fertilizer was stolen from the shed, but the gardener said he didn't use petrol or diesel. Cuts his grass with a scythe.'

Patrick thought about it for a while. He hated to confess to ignorance. Not even to Joe would he say, 'I don't understand', but would sit up for hours at night, going over and over matters in his head. But bombs were not something that he thought he could read up about. He didn't suppose that he could take a book about bomb-making out of the library. Even if he could find one, he would be the talk of the town if he did.

'Of course, the IRA use fertilizer to make bombs, don't they?' he said tentatively after a few moments.

'That's right. Easy to steal, especially in the spring when the farmers have a ton of the stuff stacked up in sheds ready to put on the fields once the soil warms up a bit. Good stuff, fertilizer. Course they need a bit of sugar with it to make the explosion, so they tip the diesel into it. Diesel is full of sugar, you know. A man I know, had a dog that died from licking diesel from his garage floor, liked the taste of it, poor dog.'

'I see,' said Patrick. He still did not know why fertilizer was used for bombs, or why sugar was needed, but perhaps Joe might know, or might even ask the question. Joe, he thought, didn't mind too much if he did not know something. He just immediately went to find someone to explain it to him. Patrick hated revealing ignorance. He turned back to Chris.

'Looks like an IRA job, then, do you think? More the army business than mine, in that case.'

Chris shook his head. 'Don't see the IRA wasting time like that, stuffing the fertilizer into a rusty drainpipe, and blowing up a single man in a convent cemetery. If they wanted to get rid of him for some reason, they'd shoot him one day, shoot him in the street, or in his house – he lived alone, so Joe told me – easy enough to take a potshot at him when he walked around the garden on a fine sunny evening. Bombs would only be used for crowds, normally.'

Patrick nodded. He wouldn't ask the man to do any more speculating. He had been sent down to identify a bomb and he had come up with an explanation. He probably wanted to be off, back to his mates in the barracks at the top of Wellington Road.

'How long would it have taken to make this bomb?' he said, looking at the piece of broken metal.

'I'll take you through the process and then you can make your mind up.' Chris's voice was brisk. He was keen to finish up his task and get back to barracks. This was not going to be army business; that was obvious to both, thought Patrick. This could be a clumsy effort to make a private killing look as though it had something to do with the IRA. He would, he decided, leave all speculations until he was alone with his own sergeant.

'Go ahead,' he said, and took out his notebook and indelible pencil.

'As far as I can guess, the fertilizer was stuffed into the pipe, diesel, probably, poured over it, and then a fuse, rope, candle, taper, whatever, was lit and as soon as the flame reached the fertilizer soaked in diesel, it exploded. I'd say that from the fact that the body was in bits, and from looking at the hole, that the pipe was very near to the bench where the man was sitting. Risky, but it worked. That's about all I can tell you, as a bomb expert.' He gave a bit of a grin and added, 'But if I was Sherlock Holmes, then I'd not have the gardener on my list of suspects, because, to be honest, we

mightn't have tumbled to the drainpipe business if he hadn't
recognized the twisted bit from the bottom of the pipe, the
swan neck, he called it. The fellow from the fire brigade
thought it was a bit of an alarm clock, but it wasn't. No alarm
clock! Nothing like that! This was detonated with a piece of
rope soaked in diesel or something like that.'

'So not a very professional job.' Patrick mused about that.

The bomb expert shook his head. 'Amateur,' he said. 'This
guy picked up a few ideas, perhaps studied chemistry, something like that. Heard about bombs that had been made from
fertilizer. Might even have put his own life at risk. Depends
on the length of the fuse – probably a length of rope, I'd
say. Could be an IRA fella, not experienced and a bit of a
maverick, acting on his own, but most unlikely, I'd say. Much
more likely that it's someone with a grudge against this Mr
Musgrave and who wanted the IRA to take the blame.'

'I see,' said Patrick. He was conscious of a feeling of
regret. So much easier if it were the IRA. Sooner or later
someone would talk. They were all at daggers drawn, Sinn
Fein, Cumann na Gael, all bloodthirsty and alike in wanting
to kill each other. He was fairly sure that the dead man,
the stockbroker, was not a member of either party, not the
right type, not the right age. Some of these lawyers and
accountants and doctors might do a bit of messing around
with the IRA when they were young students, but that usually
finished once they qualified. And this man was in his fifties
– so Joe had found out.

'Well, many thanks,' he said, holding out his hand. 'Safe
journey home!'

He was conscious of a feeling of relief when the bomb
expert climbed back into the truck and roared off. Joe and he
would ask questions and listen to the answers today and then
they would go back to their barracks and put their heads
together. And if he didn't feel like talking today, well Joe
would ask no questions, but would be available whenever he
wanted to open his mind. However, he was always punctilious
about letting Joe know all the evidence which he had picked
up, so now he went in search of him.

Joe was busy with his notebook, sketching the scene when

he found him, sitting on the convent wall. He had quite a gift for sketching, and Patrick knew that when they were both back at the barracks, that this sketch might prove invaluable as a check to their memory of the position of the buildings and the paths. Nevertheless, Joe had looked up with an expectant look when he heard him approach and Patrick immediately answered the question in his sergeant's eyes by a quick shake of his own head.

'No,' he said, 'no, they don't think it was the IRA. Too amateur for them, according to the bomb expert. Would never waste setting up an elaborate bomb, which might or might not work just to kill one man. Much easier to aim a shot at him. In any case, they've searched and searched and found no sign of an alarm clock, or any other timing device.'

'What about that piece of metal?' Joe had, thought Patrick, grasped the difficulties that were ahead if this turned out to be a murder committed by one of the convent occupants. He looked hopefully at Patrick who shook his head.

'It turned out to be part of a rusty drainpipe which was taken from the gardener's shed. That and the bag full of fertilizer. They either put some bags of sugar in with it, or else they added diesel. Either way it exploded. But since it had no timer, as far as they can make out, the murderer must have been present to detonate it, probably with a rope soaked in diesel, but it could even have been some newspaper and a match.'

'Seems a most complicated way of killing a man,' said Joe, dubiously.

Patrick shook his head. 'Not if you are a very respectable citizen and want to direct the police's attention in the direction of the IRA,' he said.

'And the hole?' asked Joe.

'The hole,' said Patrick, 'was dug by the gardener because he had time on his hands and knew that one of the elderly nuns was reputed to be on her last legs and it was nice, fine weather and the soil was easier to dig than it would be after a week of rain. So he told the bomb experts. Sounds a bit odd to me.'

Joe shrugged. 'Why should he want to blow up a respectable gentleman. Doubt he ever even spoke to him in his life.'

'Still, we'd better interview him, just out here, nothing too formal.'

'I'll fetch him,' said Joe. 'He's been bobbing in and out of the shed for the last half hour. Doesn't know what to do with himself. Sorry for him, really. He's just a young fellow.'

Seen close up, and without his cap, the gardener was quite a young fellow. Not much more than seventeen or even sixteen, thought Patrick and so he tried to put him at ease.

'You're the man who has the place looking so good,' he said and then thought it was not too sensible an observation as the lad's glance went immediately to the terrible wreckage within the orchard cemetery. Patrick moved on quickly to getting the details.

The gardener's name was Martin Maloney. He was sixteen years old. He lived in a small cottage at the gates of the convent and paid almost half of his wages in rent for it. That surprised Patrick. He would have thought that it would have made sense for someone as young as that to live at home and save the rent.

'Your previous address?' he asked, his eyes still on his notebook. There was a pause, long enough to make him raise his eyes and look at the boy.

'Greenmount.' The answer came slowly and reluctantly and then in a rush of words: 'They taught me gardening. I used to do the lawns and the paths and look after the shrubs.'

'Taught you very well, too,' said Patrick, and hoped that he did not sound falsely enthusiastic. Poor fellow. There was always a mark on those children from orphanages. No wonder he was willing to pay out half of his wages in order to have a place of his own.

'I hear you have been a great help to the army fellas,' he said. 'Solved the problem of the piece of twisted metal for them. Now, tell me why you dug the hole.'

'It was Sister Mary Agnes in the kitchen said to me that old Mother Brigid didn't have long to go and it might be just as well to have a word with one of the nuns and ask them where they would want her buried, just so that I was all ready for the funeral,' he said.

'And who did you ask?' Patrick continued to write as he waited for the answer to the question.

'I chose it myself,' said the boy. He shot an uneasy look at Patrick and added, 'The nuns don't mind. Some of that ground is terrible to dig because of the limestone being near the surface in some places, but I've picked out the good bits during the time that I've been here.'

'So no one but you decided on that spot,' said Patrick.

'That's right. Can I go now? I want to select some vegetables for the dinner tomorrow. Sister Mary Agnes will be after me if I don't have good ones, and plenty of them with the crowd that is here for the retreat.'

'You can go,' said Patrick. He had a vague feeling of unease, but he was sorry for the boy.

'They gave them a hard time in some of those orphanages, so I've heard,' he said to Joe after the gardener had disappeared. 'Not surprising that he's a bit jumpy. Can't see why he should have reason to murder a stockbroker,' he added and shut his notebook with a snap and looked away from Joe's surprised face.

A few of the young nuns were coming through the gate, novices, he thought, noting the difference in their habits and veils and he remembered that one of them was the daughter of the dead man. A terrible thing for the poor girl. He hoped someone was looking after her. He had no intention of bothering her today, but he would have to see her at some stage. Preferably in the company of someone sympathetic to the girl.

And so, with that in his mind, he changed his plans and went in search of the Reverend Mother. He had known her since he was four years old and he trusted her more than he trusted any other living being. She was walking on the terrace, talking with one of the other nuns and he hesitated to disturb her, but when she saw him approach, she instantly left her companion and came towards him. The terrace was filled with nuns and priests and brothers – he thought that he recognized a Christian Brother who had taught him mathematics – and so he did not move near but stood and waited for her, taking off his cap and feeling the sun on his head.

'Beautiful day, Reverend Mother,' he said. Very few conversations in Cork started without a preliminary reference to the weather. She would, he knew, be quick to know what had brought him towards her and would already be sorting out matters in her clear and decisive mind.

'This is a terrible thing, Patrick,' she said gravely, refusing to comment on the weather.

'Indeed,' he said. 'May God have mercy on his soul.' This customary Cork phrase came easily to his lips and allowed him to wait for more information from her without showing impatience. 'You would have known him,' he added.

'He was a widower, you know,' she went on with a nod. 'He has two sons out in Australia and a daughter who is a novice here in this convent, Sister Mary Magdalene. Poor girl! I'm hoping that my cousin, Mrs Rupert Murphy, who was a neighbour and friend to the family, will be here shortly and she may have addresses for the two sons, but of course, it will take about a month before they could return – if they do. So, the poor girl may have to bear this terrible sorrow on her own.'

'I shall have to see her, as briefly as possible, of course, but I hope that you and Mrs Murphy might be present.'

She bowed her head. 'Certainly,' she said, 'that is, of course, if the mother superior of this convent will permit it.'

So, the mother superior was obviously a difficult character. That was about all that was needed. In the meantime, since she didn't appear to be on the scene, he would make the most of his chat with the Reverend Mother. She was always one to know Cork people, especially the wealthy and the well-connected.

So, if the Reverend Mother's cousin was a friend and neighbour of Mr Musgrave, then he was one of the Montenotte crowd. Rich and with rich friends. Money and class, he thought. Not the type to be mixed up with the IRA or their rivals.

He voiced his thoughts aloud. 'Not a gentleman to be mixed up with the IRA, as far as I know,' he remarked in a judicial fashion.

The Reverend Mother bowed her head. 'I think that you are probably right, Patrick,' she said quietly.

He nodded in a satisfied way. He knew that tone of voice. The IRA were to be ruled out of the investigation. Yes, he would do a few perfunctory enquires, just to keep the superintendent happy, but he wouldn't waste too much valuable time. He turned his mind from political to private motives.

'Mr Rupert Murphy, being a close friend and neighbour, probably has the will,' he commented. He knew enough not to ask a direct question and he received no answer, but the Reverend Mother bowed her head again and he knew that meant that she considered him to be probably correct.

However, if the IRA and Sinn Fein were ruled out, it wasn't immediately obvious who the suspects were. Two sons out in Australia and a daughter in the convent. Not murdered for his money, he thought. Politics, money, two of the most frequent reasons for these secret murders.

'Would have been a rich man,' he stated aloud, not wishing to question her about her cousin's friend and his money but hoping for a lead to the solving of what appeared to be a senseless atrocity.

'You are probably right, Patrick,' said the Reverend Mother, once again giving him the seal of approval, but this time she said it in a fashion of one brushing the matter aside. Her eyes, beneath the snowy white of her wimple, were thoughtful, not looking at him but fixed upon a small group of the laity, clustered protectively together. Patrick ignored the men – knew them all – their faces had been on every hoarding in the city for the last month, but he was interested in the young solicitor, Maureen Hogan. She had been a member of the IRA at some stage, a few years ago certainly, but possibly still a member in a more discreet way, so he made a mental note to have a chat with her as soon as possible. The others, the three men, he did not know anything against them. Never been in trouble with the police, any of them, he was sure about that and his memory for names and faces was a good one. He took little interest in politics – just a lot of talking, he thought.

Best thing ever that the people of the city had done w to take the law to their city council, to bring them to t court, to disband the councillors, replacing them with

efficient and hard-working city manager, like Philip Monahan. Wouldn't do it nowadays, he thought. Too many fat cats, ruling the roost. Yet, back then, in 1924, a nine-day inquiry, held in Cork's courthouse, was thronged. The public galleries were full, the inquiry held in the courthouse – and quite right, too. It was a trial of inefficiency and corruption, with the corporation charging huge rates and doing nothing with them, just making themselves and their relatives and friends as rich as could be. Whole families working for the corporation, drawing big wages, just because a distant cousin was a councillor. *It's not who you are, what you can do, but who you are related to that counts*: that was a saying on everyone's lips.

All sorts of excuses for this state of affairs, of course. There had been the war of independence and the civil war. City Hall burned to the ground and the library. Patrick Street burned in 1920. Yes, they had a hard time during the early years, but then, when things settled down and the English army had left, well then, they could have done something for the city, but they didn't. It was only when they were thrown out and Philip Monahan was appointed that a few efforts began to be made to improve the roads and to build council houses for the poor unfortunates stuck in these crumbling old Georgian houses, in lanes so narrow that two people could not pass each other without standing sideways – no lavatories, no water, rats everywhere. These county councillors didn't care about these unfortunate people as long as there were enough prisons to lock them up when they broke the law. And now, thought Patrick, they were trying to bring back another batch of county councillors. A bunch of people who wanted to be powerful in order to make money, he had thought and dismissed them all with indifference, resolving not to waste his time in voting for any of them. Nothing to do with him. He was not a politician; he kept well away from politicians of all kinds, didn't belong to a single society or a single coterie in Cork – no friends, either. Friends were trouble; he had decided some time ago. They always wanted you to do them a favour, had other friends for whom they wanted their policeman friend to go easy on, or to swear

false evidence. Joe was the nearest thing he had to a friend and even with him he was wary in case he could be accused of favouritism.

Now he looked at this bunch of people with sharp interest. As the Reverend Mother had explained to him the previous day, the presence of the bishop, priests, brothers and nuns was to attend an annual 'retreat' and everybody knew about these retreats. He hadn't been on one himself since he had left school, but his mother, he knew, enjoyed them immensely and always declared that she felt a new woman after one of them. Odd, though, that these candidates for the office of alderman had joined these members of the holy orders. And certainly, since one of their number had been murdered, he was most interested in the others.

'It seems strange that the bishop arranged for these candidates for the position of alderman to come on the retreat,' he said in a low voice to the Reverend Mother.

'The bishop,' she said and then paused while she, he guessed, considered how to put the matter. 'I imagine that the bishop felt they would benefit from divine guidance,' she said in guarded tones.

'I see,' said Patrick. He didn't really, but the bishop was a law, not just to himself, but to all officialdom in the city. No doubt he had his reasons and it wasn't for a police inspector to question him. 'I just wondered,' he said.

She guessed his meaning. A very sharp brain, the Reverend Mother. Must be as old as the hills – had been a century old when he was a small child, or so they used to say. She looked little different now as she glanced at him sharply. He knew that look.

'You'll let me know when Mrs Murphy arrives and when you . . .' He stopped and rearranged his sentence. The Reverend Mother was always very punctilious and here she was a guest, not a ruler. 'Just a message when it would be possible to see the daughter of the dead man,' he finished, and she bowed her head in a stately manner, but reverted to their previous topic.

'Yes, indeed,' she said. 'The candidates, the four gentlemen and the lady are here for a seven-day retreat. You have, of course, all details about them, but you may wish to make a few additional notes or ask me some questions.' She waited until he had produced the notebook and indelible pencil and managed, he noticed, to stop herself warning of the danger to his health as he automatically licked the tip. He remembered that she had always tried to stop children using these as she was worried about the danger to their health from the dye used in the pencil lead, but of course everyone did it. When used wet, its tip moistened repeatedly by water or saliva, it produced a bright purple ink and was a permanent record, accepted as evidence in the courts.

He scanned the facts about each of the candidates and then stopped at the name MISS MAUREEN HOGAN.

I've heard a few details about this young lady,' he said with a slight frown. 'Miss Hogan may have been keeping her republican connections secret from the bishop, but the use of an IRA type of bomb makes her presence rather significant to the police,' he added in a low voice. He beckoned to Joe who had approached. 'The army expert said that he didn't think it was a professional bomb, but it was a fertilizer and diesel job,' he continued, explaining the matter to Joe, but with an eye on the Reverend Mother.

'It's true, then, is it, that bombs can be made from fertilizer by the IRA? How very extraordinary!' said the Reverend Mother. 'And they work like real bombs,' she said with a note of interest in her voice.

'True enough and yes, they do work,' said Patrick quietly, thinking of all the mutilated bodies that he had seen during his time as a policeman.

'Easy enough to do,' said Joe. 'I remember a couple of lads experimenting with fertilizer after we had a chemistry lesson. I didn't go myself, didn't want to get into trouble, but one fellow burned his eyebrows and a patch of hair from the top of his head and got caned by the teacher for saying that the moths ate them. I remember there was a workman in the classroom fixing the gas light – could have been Bob the Builder, now that I come to think of it – and he said to us after the lesson, when we were going home: "Ye have a life of Reilly in these 'Proddy' schools!"'

'How extraordinary to learn these dangerous things in a chemistry lesson,' said the Reverend Mother. 'But what fun,' she added. 'And I'm sure that everyone in the class remembered that piece of chemistry,' she added.

Patrick smiled a little at that story. He could just imagine a purple-faced teacher's reaction to the joke about the moths. Funny how some lads didn't care. Thought it was worth a caning to get a laugh out of the rest of the class. He had not been like that, had been terrified of being caned. Perhaps that was why he had ended up being a policeman while some of his classmates were over in America busy becoming millionaires. Patrick looked across at the tall figure of the young lady. Might have ended up in gaol if her father had not been a well-known and highly respected solicitor, he thought.

'I'd say that if she wanted a bomb, she'd know a few people who could manage to make a better one for her,' he said. 'But why would she want to get rid of Mr Musgrave? He was a stockbroker, I understand. Not in the same line of business.'

'Not in the least,' agreed the Reverend Mother. 'Did you study Shakespeare's play, *Macbeth*, when you were in school, Patrick? A great play and a great portrait of a flawed man. His ambition to be king led him to commit murder. Of course, the ambition to be an alderman is not quite the same thing as to be a king, but I must say that I have found myself wondering whether ambition has led to other less celebrated murders.'

Patrick nodded. He had a distant, shadowy recollection of *Macbeth* and thought he must have studied it for his leaving certificate, or for matriculation. Remembered learning off by heart some dreary speech about '*tomorrow, and tomorrow and tomorrow*' which was supposed to come up in the examination. He understood what the Reverend Mother was hinting at and his heart sank. Macbeth murdered an old man because he wanted to be king. James Musgrave might have been murdered because someone else wanted to be an alderman. It was not what I wanted, he thought. Not a murder with four powerful people as suspects, and the bishop standing over them, interfering in the investigation. This was not going to be an easy task. He had a moment of brief regret for an IRA suspect, but then squared his shoulders. He and Joe would get to the bottom of this.

NINE

The Reverend Mother hesitated. Indecision was not something that ordinarily afflicted her, but here, on ground not her own, it behoved her to be careful. A tactless intervention could do far more harm than good.

There was a small courtyard to one side of the convent buildings. In the centre of the space was a well, the original well which had probably guided the choice of the site – good, clean, fresh water springing from the limestone rocks of this south-eastern side of the city. Beside the well was a pump and a group of novices were energetically pushing up and down on the handle, filling pails with water. They were equipped for their charitable work, she guessed. Each girl wore an apron of sacking over her habit and there was a line of lidded baskets, probably holding bandages and medicaments, on the ground nearby. The sisters did good and charitable work among the poor and the diseased of the city; she knew that, but her eyes were on one figure, a girl with a bowed head whose shaking hands had already spilt some water which called down a sharp rebuke from the mistress of novices.

So when the shabby Humber car drove noisily through the convent gates, the Reverend Mother breathed a sigh of relief. She had been wondering what to do, wondering whether she was justified in interfering, turning over tactful forms of protest within her mind, but at the sight of Dr Scher her spirits were lifted. As an old friend, she was quite justified in going forward to greet him and hopefully to drop a few words in his ear before he went to see the superior of the Sisters of Charity, Mother Teresa.

He seemed to be, she was glad to see, his usual unperturbable self. Dead bodies were dead bodies to him and she supposed that the fact that this particular body had been in multiple pieces meant little to a man who spent most of his time at a dissecting table, working for the police as well as when he lectured on the subject to the students at Cork University. They would, she decided, as she walked towards the car, say little about that fragmented human body, although she would be available to answer any question which he might want to put to her. In the meantime, she had another task for him.

'James Musgrave's daughter, she's a novice here. I don't think she is up to this work. She should be resting upon her bed,' she said rapidly as Dr Scher pushed open the door and swung his legs onto the ground.

'Which one is she?' Dr Scher didn't waste time on greetings but straightened himself with a hand upon the door frame, his eyes on the group of novices by the pump.

'That very thin one. Look she has just spilt some more water. Her hands are shaking. Do something. Her father was blown to pieces almost in front of her eyes just yesterday.'

'I'll try, but I find nuns exceedingly difficult to deal with,' said Dr Scher. He reached into the back seat, took his hat, placed it upon his bald head and then pulled out his medical bag. 'Hope they're not going down to the city. There's diphtheria down in the Douglas Street area,' he said as he left her.

The Reverend Mother did not offer to accompany him. Doctors were privileged and could call upon their medical authority. Her eyes were on the girl's white face. Poor child, she thought and resolved to ask Mother Isabelle what age her former pupil would be. She looked younger than the others. She was extremely thin, and her skin still had the blotches of adolescence. There was, thought the Reverend Mother, a certain unfinished look to the features of her face and her shoulders were bowed. Not a strong-looking girl, she thought, and wondered whether it was the death of her mother and perhaps the emigration of her two brothers that had made the child search for security in convent life where there was a structure and a substitute mother.

But why the Sisters of Charity? She would have expected most fathers to refuse permission to a young daughter who wanted to join such an exacting and rigorous order of nuns and if that daughter had lost her mother, why then it doubled the unsuitability of such a huge decision being made at such a young age.

Dr Scher, she saw, was now speaking to the mistress of novices, waving his hand in the direction of the city which lay below where they stood. So far, he had not gone near to the orphaned Sister Mary Magdalene but had turned the full battery of his volubility upon the person in charge of the girls. After a few minutes, a novice was sent scuttling off in the direction of the convent, doing her best to be quick, but not to run. The Reverend Mother smiled to herself. These ridiculous rules for girls hardly past childhood. She was glad that she had instituted the custom in her convent that novices would polish the convent corridors every morning by sliding up and down the wooden expanses, wearing cosy sheepskin slippers donated by a furrier in the city. It served, she hoped, to release some of their inner energy and exuberance. However, these girls were not her responsibility and so, propelled by curiosity and a worry for the children of her own school, she made her way over towards the group.

'Did you say diphtheria, Dr Scher?' she enquired. Diphtheria was a worry. A terrible disease. In the foggy, marshy city of Cork, coughs and wheezes were widespread, but ever since the first epidemic which she had experienced among the poor children who came to her school, she had formed the habit of asking a child to open its mouth and say 'Ah' when they complained of feeling unwell. The sight of that thick grey membrane covering the throat and tonsils still had the power to make her heart stop for a few moments. She would have to harden her heart and send the sick child and its brothers and sisters home instantly in order to save the others. There would be little hope of saving the sick child; most would die, she knew, though she found the thought almost unbearable. The weak and the fortunate would succumb quickly to a high fever, but the stronger child would die in agony, choking as the membrane grew, strengthened, and eventually strangled the tonsils.

She would have to get back to her own school instantly, she thought. She would have to talk to all the children and warn them of the danger. Tell them to keep to their own street and not to wander, especially towards the Douglas Street area. They were not too near to Douglas Street, she thought, and prayed that they might be saved, that strict rules about sneezing and coughing into a handkerchief were observed. Sister Bernadette and the other lay sisters were trained never to waste any old sheets or pillowcases. The novices used to cut them into handkerchiefs for children to use in school. They were collected in a basket at going home time and set to boil on top of the kitchen range. For a while, they used to hem them, but that was a useless waste of time, the Reverend Mother thought impatiently, as unhemmed handkerchiefs were just as useful and keen needlewomen among novices and nuns were set to work on turning salvageable, though threadbare, habits into skirts for little girls.

But all the handkerchiefs in the world would not be enough to stop the deadly spread of diphtheria once it got into her school. Her eyes scanned the black-suited forms who moved around the sunlit ground. Where was the bishop when she needed him? She must instantly get back to her school, but she would have to see him first and make a pretence of getting his permission.

'Have you seen the bishop, Brother Ignatius?' she enquired as one of the Presentation Brothers drew near.

'I think he is in church, Reverend Mother. I saw him and Mr O'Connor, the builder, go in there about fifteen minutes ago.'

Better wait until he comes out, thought the Reverend Mother, though cynically she doubted whether bishop and builder were praying while they sat, side by side, within the dark privacy of the little church. Mr O'Connor had, she presumed, moved back into the position of prime favourite after the unfortunate demise of Mr Musgrave, the stockbroker. For a moment, she was diverted from her worries about diphtheria. Her own words about Macbeth, and about ambition, which she had spoken to Patrick, now came back to her. She looked across at the three other candidates who were wandering gloomily up and down the terrace. She doubted, also, that they were praying. How badly did they seek power? Not enough to increase the number of bodies in the orchard cemetery, she hoped. The bishop, by his obvious interference in profane matters, had perhaps stirred up a feeling of desperation in the mind of one of those four people. But was it conceivable that any one of them was responsible for the explosion that killed a man and blew his body into small particles? And if such a deed was possible to envisage, well, then who was the most likely to have done such a terrible deed? Her mind went over them as she surveyed the three who were, metaphorically speaking, left out in the cold.

Pat Pius? Well, he cared enough to have given her a substantial bribe, so goodness knows what he might be willing to do for the bishop's favour if he hadn't felt that he was wasting his money, or that the bishop's price would be too high for him to afford. That fifty or even a hundred pounds, which he might offer, would mean little to the bishop in comparison with a lifetime of favours from the wealthy builder or from the even more wealthy stockbroker.

The same, she thought, could be said for Wee Willie, the Northern Ireland owner of a stocking factory. Small businessmen, both, both probably leading a hand-to-mouth existence.

Nevertheless, when Macbeth murdered for the crown, the thought of obstacles, of Duncan's sons, had not deterred him.

Then there was the young lady. The Reverend Mother, with an impatient look at the church door, went across to the terrace and accosted Miss Maureen Hogan.

'I feel as though I know you, as my former pupil Eileen has spoken with such admiration of you. I think you are a role model for her,' she said with a friendly smile.

Miss Hogan did not smile back. She looked sternly and coldly at the elderly woman and made no reply for a few seconds. Oh dear, thought the Reverend Mother. Someone who doesn't like nuns. It was a pity, she thought, that despite the piety of some of the 1916 martyrs such a Padraig Pearse, that the later rebels tended to be very anti-religious and especially prejudiced against members of the holy orders. Nevertheless, she stood her ground. *If you are going to be a successful solicitor, then you will have to learn how to hold an amiable conversation even with someone who doesn't belong to your political organization*, she said to herself as she bestowed the friendly smile upon the young lady. *Well, if you are going to be rude, two can play at that game*, she added to her internal dialogue and decided to enjoy herself by being outrageous.

'What sort of hope do you have of becoming an alderman? I don't suppose that you have much of a hope, have you?' she asked affably, and her mind went back to sixty years earlier when she and her cousin Lucy used to giggle about their elderly and extraordinary old aunt with shrivelled skin and a waspish tongue, who would say the most outrageous things. She would, she decided, select Aunt Maud as a role model.

'So kind of you to encourage me.' The spirited reply came so promptly that the Reverend Mother was taken aback for a moment.

Oh, well done! was her immediate reaction, but she contented herself with raising her eyebrows and waited with interest for a more detailed answer.

It was a good policy. The young solicitor seemed to be waiting for a verbal reaction but when none came, she proceeded to explain herself.

'Of course, it's the ratepayers who vote, but who are the ratepayers?' Without wating for an answer to that question, she proceeded, speaking with a fluency and a grasp of the monetary structure of their city which surprised and pleased the Reverend Mother as she listened to an explanation of how the rich were dependent upon the poor, that the factory owners would not be rich without the workers to slave for them, for very poor wages and even poorer conditions. The young solicitor had a good grasp on how the city was run and of the disproportion between the classes. What she lacked, thought the Reverend Mother, was any practical way of putting it right. She decided on a challenge.

'How are you going to get the ratepayers to vote for you, if what you want to do is make them poorer and those without a vote slightly richer?'

'It's a terrible system. The fate of the city is in the hands of a small, ruling class.' Miss Hogan raised her voice slightly and then lowered it as she noticed that the bishop was emerging from the church. The Reverend Mother noticed also, and was about to excuse herself and move towards the bishop when she saw that he had by no means finished his conversation with the builder. In fact, the two, skirting the ruins of the orchard cemetery, had moved further uphill towards the hedge that separated the garden from a view of the city.

'Planning his new churches,' said the girl with such a note of disdain that the Reverend Mother had to bite back a smile.

'People like churches,' she said mildly. It was true, she knew. The parish church near to her school was packed to the doors for every mass on Sundays and on saints' days. It must, she often thought, be a peaceful and quiet time for these harassed mothers, and somehow, sitting in spacious, clean and colourful surroundings with nothing to do but join in prayers was probably a little oasis of pleasure in their hard-working stressful lives.

'That's because they have the mentality of slaves.' The words were shot out in a most aggressive fashion with no pretence of politeness – not even using her name. The Reverend Mother wondered whether Eileen thought like this and was, perhaps, too polite to express such views in front of her erstwhile teacher.

'Would you be able to do anything to make life better for them?' the Reverend Mother asked, making her tone conversational and enquiring, rather than challenging.

'I'd try,' Maureen Hogan said after a moment.

'How?' That the young needed to be challenged was a doctrine of the Reverend Mother.

'Raise the rates!'

'You'd be voted down if you tried that,' said the Reverend Mother sadly.

The girl compressed her lips. 'There might be ways and means, of getting people to vote on the right side – and these city council votes are not secret,' she said. 'If people can't be persuaded by words, there are other ways.'

'We've already had two wars during the last few years,' said the Reverend Mother, though she guessed that the young lady meant intimidation. 'Two wars,' she continued, 'and the poverty in this city is getting worse, not better.' Her eyes were on Dr Scher who was coming back towards her with an irritated expression on his face. He had failed in his mission; she could see that. Like herself, he failed again and again, but he never gave up. Her companion's eyes were on him also, but she tossed her head. 'It's time for the younger generation to take over, Reverend Mother. This city is run by West Britons, all these people who yearn for the past when they could pretend to be British, even though they were born and bred in Ireland. That man Musgrave, what did he want except for stocks and shares, like the railway stocks, to climb back to pre-1914 prices?'

With that, Maureen Hogan tossed her head once more and walked off.

'Any luck?' asked the Reverend Mother, even though she knew from Dr Scher's angry face that he had not succeeded. She gave him a moment to recover as she watched the young novices march to the gate, each laden with a bucket in one hand and a basket in the other. At least their journey to the city would be downhill and coming back up the steep slopes they would have empty buckets and empty baskets. She wondered what protection these aprons would give them and hoped that they would have some means of washing their hands after tending to the stricken diphtheria victims in their overcrowded filthy rooms. Dr Scher would, she guessed, know the risks even more than she did.

'Stupid woman,' he muttered and spread his hands in a gesture of frustration. 'I tried to tell her. Diphtheria is serious for the young and the delicate, I said. All right for an old man like myself. I know how to keep safe. Some of those girls are far too thin. They don't make them fast in these convents, do they? Please tell me, Reverend Mother, that your god doesn't impose such things as fasting on girls at a delicate age. They all look as if they need feeding up, especially that poor Musgrave child. She looks ill. I'd like to take her home and give her some beef tea and a few bars of chocolate and sit her in front of a cosy fire.'

'You did your best, and none of us can do more,' said the Reverend Mother consolingly. 'As for God,' she went on thoughtfully, 'I've long held the opinion that none of us really knows what He wants. After all, he is always being interpreted through man – even the gospels are just words written down by a few men who purported to have knowledge that they may not really have possessed. Don't tell the bishop that I said that,' she added in an effort to relieve the look of anxiety and strain upon her friend's face. They had a series of private jokes about the bishop which she would trust to no one else.

'I'm worried about this diphtheria,' he said, ignoring her efforts to lighten his depression. 'It seems to be a very bad strain. Is that Pat Pius over there?' he exclaimed. 'Mind if I call him over? Don't want to talk about his private affairs in front of his fellow candidates.'

Pat Pius came eagerly to the summons. He had a much-practised phrase upon his lips, but it died when he saw the doctor's serious face. 'Nothing wrong with Frankie, is there, doctor. The school didn't call you, did they? He hasn't had another attack, has he?'

'Where does he go to school?' Dr Scher was not going to waste any time.

'Turners Cross, I moved him there as soon as you said that the Model School was bad for him being as it was so near to the river. What's the matter? Has he had an asthma attack?'

'There's an outbreak of diphtheria in the Douglas Street area.'

'Should I take him out of school?' Pat Pius looked with trust at the doctor and the Reverend Mother saw with pity how the man's face had gone white.

'No, what would you do with him? That factory of yours is unhealthy for him with all the dust. And he's too young to be left alone. He might be best off where he is.'

'He slept at my sister's place last night. She's collecting him after school. She lives in Turners Cross. Oh my God, I don't know what to do. Perhaps he shouldn't be with other children. Perhaps she should keep him out of school, at home with her, but she won't like that. Likes to go off selling vegetables at the market. What'll I do, doctor? That last attack he had, I thought he'd die. He couldn't get his breath.'

'I've told you what to do. Get him out of this city. It's a death trap for children like Frankie. Get him out of here. Sell off that factory of yours and take him to live by the sea. Be a fisherman or something like that.'

Pat Pius said nothing but stumbled away. The Reverend Mother looked after him for a long moment while conscious that Dr Scher had shifted uneasily.

'I know, I know, I shouldn't have said that. The man is probably deep in debt for machinery and rent for that stupid factory of his. He's tied to it. But I'm not a god, not a god of the Old Testament, nor of the New, don't believe in religion, or even in gods, whether it's the god of Abraham, Isaac and Jacob, or the god of Jesus and the bishop. I'm just a poor hack of a doctor who knows that children like Frankie are going to die, either of an asthma attack or of diphtheria, or of a hundred and one other diseases and illness before they are seven years old.'

'He gave me a bribe, I can only describe it as such, though, of course, he cloaked it under the heading of a charitable donation,' said the Reverend Mother in a low voice.

'Did the same to me; told me that it would pay the fees of a few poor people who could not pay for themselves,' said Dr Scher impatiently. 'I told him to put his money back in his pocket and save it to take his son to the sea the next time that the asthma was bad. The money he was offering would have paid train fare and lodging for a few weeks somewhere like Youghal for the pair of them.'

'I must confess that I took the money,' said the Reverend Mother, feeling a certain amount of shame. 'Perhaps, Dr Scher, despite your words, you have a better trust than I in the Almighty, that provision will be made for the poor.'

'I'm less ambitious than you, I suppose. Not much is asked of me. The university pay me a good fee to teach those block-heads the elements of anatomy, the paying clients don't mind a little extra on their bill when they are feeling better after an illness. I do well for myself, live in the lap of luxury, even if I do, from time to time, bestow a bottle of medicine and my valuable opinion, or stitch up a knife wound, for nothing. It doesn't cost me much. I have my books, my collection of rare

silver, my housekeeper to pamper me. No, I do little in comparison to you. I don't go out looking for good works, just do a
few good works from time to time when they arrive on my
doorstep.' Dr Scher paused a moment before saying, 'Pat Pius
has a little book, you know, one of those little notebooks for
writing addresses in, and he has the names of what looked
like all the ratepayers in the city written into it. He opened it
at the letter S and I could see my name there and names like
Sheehan, Sweeney, Slattery, and loads of others, and the
amounts written beside them. Can't spell, poor fellow, not too
much education wasted upon him, just a drive to make money
and a good brain.'

'And a warm heart,' said the Reverend Mother. She thought
that she would be haunted by the expression of terror on the
man's face when the danger to his little son became apparent.
Pat Pius might not be educated himself, but he wanted the
best for his son. Not too many fathers, in her experience, were
so devoted. 'How old is Frankie?' she asked.

'Just about seven,' said Dr Scher. 'Nice little fellow. Bright,
too. Reads well. I got him a book, just spotted it in a shop,
cost nothing much, a bit old fashioned now. *Huckleberry Finn*.
I used to like it as a child, thought his father would read it to
him, but he tackled it himself. Told me that he skipped the
hard words, and the boring bits, but it was a great story. You
should have seen the look of pride on his father's face when
I pretended to faint with astonishment. He'd do anything in
the world for that boy.'

'Including murder,' said the Reverend Mother, her eyes on
the ruins of the orchard cemetery and then, when he did not
answer, she said, 'Of course, we all delude ourselves; we
justify our deeds with the phrase "it's in a good cause". I'm
as guilty as anyone. When I present a tissue of lies in my
accounts for the scrutiny of the bishop's secretary, I use that
phrase, telling myself, when burying the expenditure on buying
sweets and cheap clothing for children and packets of tea for
their mothers under the heading of educational supplies, that
the cause justifies the lie.'

'No doubt you confess your sins to your chaplain,' said Dr
Scher.

'No, I don't,' said the Reverend Mother in decisive tones.
Not even to Dr Scher would she confess that her opinion of
the elderly chaplain was that he was a meddlesome gossip.
She rapidly changed the subject. 'How important would it be
to get little Frankie out of the city?' she asked.

'Vital,' said Dr Scher. 'You are a Latin scholar, Reverend
Mother. You know the origin of the word, *vital*.'

'So, life itself, may – no, according to you, does – depend
upon a father being able to get funds together to move the
child well outside the city, even, perhaps, to pay for someone
to care for him by the sea while the father travels up and
down to the city.' There would be, thought the Reverend Mother,
her mind busily working on the problem, several fishermen's
wives who would be willing, for a fee, to board and lodge a
well-behaved boy and his father. The child could go on with
his schooling at the village school in Youghal. Her eyes went
to the gate. Pat Pius had disappeared through it, and she could
see the top of his head bobbing above the well-trimmed hedge.
He would run all the way back to the city. Take his child to
his unwilling sister, bribe her, perhaps, to forego her earnings
from the market and to keep the child at home from school
and in isolation from the deadly diphtheria.

'You haven't asked the question, but yes, I do think that
Frankie's life would be of far greater importance to Pat Pius
than the life of a gentleman like Mr James Musgrave.' Dr
Scher's eyes had followed hers.

'On the other hand, with James Musgrave out of the way,
there remain four more candidates. As for Pat Pius, I would
not, myself, have put him in the second place,' said the
Reverend Mother quietly. She now looked towards the bishop
and the builder as they both surveyed the flat landscape of the
city of Cork that lay beneath them. Where was the new church
to be situated, she wondered and endeavoured to banish from
her mind a speculation as to its cost.

Dr Scher's eyes followed hers. 'There's an architect that I
know, lives in Cobh, told me that he estimates the cost to be
about thirty thousand pounds – a lot of money, that. Might
be more if he wants a lot of fancy statues and stained-glass
windows.'

The Reverend Mother shelved the figure of £30,000 in her mind and decided that, at her next meeting with the bishop, she would ask the cost of building a road of council houses to rehouse the slum dwellers from the narrow lanes behind North Main Street. She wondered whether the solicitor candidate, Miss Maureen Hogan, might have such a figure memorized, and if not, she was sure that she could get the information from either her pupil, Eileen, or even from Mr Philip Monahan, the city council manager.

'I suppose that the figure of thirty thousand pounds includes the fee to the builder, the architect and the cost of the materials,' she said thoughtfully, her eyes still upon the squat, almost square figure of Mr Robert O'Connor. 'Bob the Builder' suited him as a nickname, she thought and wondered whether he had any worries about his safety. Even Patrick, careful though he was, had seemed to think that the murder might have had something to do with the politics.

'Do aldermen on the city council get paid a good salary or stipend, Dr Scher?' she asked.

'Pretty good, I'd say,' he replied. 'Certainly, Pat Pius has worked that out. He knows that the extra money would mean he could afford to take a house by the sea in Youghal and to travel up and down by train. Great things, trains, he was telling me. And the little fellow has drawn a map of the railway line going from Kent Station to Midleton and onto Youghal. He got him to show it to me. They'd been talking about it together. Clever child, little Frankie. Very well done for a little fellow of seven.'

Dr Scher's voice held a note of sadness. He identified very strongly with his patients and the Reverend Mother knew from his tone that he had little hopes for the survival of this clever, but delicate little son of Pat Pius. Not unless his father could get out of the city. She sighed heavily. There were so many problems in the world, so many children who could not be cared for, or who were neglected. She wished that she were back where she belonged and made up her mind that as soon as Lucy came she would make her apologies to the bishop, tell him about the diphtheria epidemic, and then beg a lift back into the city.

In the distance, she saw a car, shining in the sunshine, making its way slowly through the gates. She recognized the dark-green paint of Mr Rupert Murphy's stylish Bentley car and the sight of it cheered her. She turned to Dr Scher. 'My cousin is arriving. She is – was – a near neighbour of the dead man, Mr James Musgrave. The police need to have a word with his daughter who is now left without any near relative, but I persuaded them to wait until Mrs Murphy arrived. She knows the girl well and will, I hope, be able to support her, as well, of course, as giving the police any information about the family. Will you come with me, Dr Scher and be present during the interview? I'm anxious that the child will not be taxed beyond her strength, and I suspect that the mother superior is not too sympathetic. As soon as she comes back from that ill-advised expedition to the stricken poor of the city, you might be able to persuade Mother Teresa to send the girl to bed or even, perhaps, allow her to go home with a neighbour and prepare for the funeral. My cousin Lucy, I know, is practical and sensible and has granddaughters of the same age as Sister Mary Magdalene.'

'What's her real name?' asked Dr Scher. He had a note of distaste in his voice at the sound of the name and she wondered how much of the New Testament someone of his faith would know – but, of course, the word Magdalene was synonymous with prostitution. She herself, despite the ultimate sainthood status of Mary Magdalene, found that the name of a former prostitute, no matter how much she might have repented, was, perhaps, rather an odd choice for a young girl entering the convent.

'I have no idea what name she had before she entered the convent,' she said now, 'but, here comes someone who will know,' she added, as the green Bentley purred its way through the gates, opened by the gardener. 'Come and see my cousin Lucy,' she said as she went forward.

However, there was a disappointment for her. Only the chauffeur sat in the roomy car. He got out immediately when he saw her and stood beside the door, waiting for her to approach.

'I'm very sorry, Reverend Mother,' he said. 'Mrs Murphy is

not able to come today. One of the little ones in the family is ill and her mother wanted Mrs Murphy to come. She tried to telephone you, but apparently the person who answered the phone said that it would be impossible to find you. Mrs Murphy sent me to explain and in case you wished to return to St Mary's of the Isle this afternoon.'

TEN

Eileen aligned her sheet of paper in the typewriter and carefully rolled it to the correct position. She bit her lips to suppress the smile of sheer pleasure upon her lips, the feeling of satisfaction at a piece of work well done and appreciated by experts. The chief reporter had been very complimentary about her piece entitled THE DESECRATION OF THE ORCHARD CEMETERY; had liked the way she had framed it as if coming from the gardener's thoughts; it had, she hoped, an immediacy as if penned within minutes of the atrocity, and he had invited her to do another piece for the following day's *Cork Examiner*.

An idea had come to her as she had walked back to her desk and now, quickly, she typed the headline: WHO PLANTED THE BOMB? and then carried on, typing fluently, allowing the words to go straight from brain to fingertips. She would, she knew, subsequently correct, adjust and polish, until it was as slick and professional as any full-time reporter could produce.

This is the question on everyone's lips today, she typed. *As you walk down Patrick Street and visit –* she stopped for a few seconds – *the Oyster Tavern.* The *Cork Examiner* prided itself on being local, and knew that advertising revenue flowed after the mention of a place of business, and she intended to weave in names of public houses, cafes and shops as a source for her quotes. It would give the impression that she had been out and about, garnering opinions. Quite a good technique, she thought, as the smile came back to her lips.

'All this rubbish about the IRA,' said a voice behind her. She knew from the Northern Ireland accent who it was. John Fitzpatrick was the paper's foreign correspondent. He had been brought up in Cork, but worked for about ten years on the *Belfast News* and then moved back to Cork when partition had made him unacceptable. He had never lost his northern accent, though, and the harshness of his speech formed a strong contrast to the soft, singsong voices of Cork. Eileen suspected that he had deliberately retained his Belfast way of speaking with its strong vowels and sharply enunciated 'r' and 't' to intimidate those softly spoken citizens of what had been his native city.

'*Y're* on the wrong track, me wee girl,' he said now. 'Never saw so much rubbish in my life.'

'Mind your own business,' she snapped. He had made her lose track of her thoughts and her hands dropped from the keyboard as she turned to glare at him.

'Very hoity-toity, aren't we?' he said. 'Can't get over having been praised for a girly piece like that rubbish about the gardener and his hedge? Catch yourself on! I could tell you something interesting if you want to listen.'

'I'm listening,' she said. It took her quite an effort to get the words out in a reasonably polite fashion, but she knew him to be clever, astute and what was even more important, she knew full well that he had plenty of sources of information. It was rumoured among the reporters that his telephone bill was enormous, but that the owner of the *Cork Examiner* paid it without protest as his information was always so good. 'I'm listening,' she said again and turned slightly away from the typewriter. He dropped to his knees beside her.

'Ever wonder what Wee Willie Hamilton is doing all the way down south here?' he said, not whispering, but speaking in such a low voice that she had to strain her ears to catch his words. 'Ever wonder why, if he wanted to leave the Protestant north of Ireland, he didn't go to Donegal, Cavan or Monaghan; ever wonder who paid for him to be set up in business down here in this god-forsaken country? Or who is putting him forward to go up for alderman? And how he is going to make use of the job if he gets it? I'll tell you something, my wee girl, there's a crowd around down here that are not happy with the way things have gone, that think we were better off in the good old days when King George ruled over us. You ask a lot of people with money and they'll tell you how it's only their British shares that are worth anything, that land has lost its value and their standard of living has fallen because of all this fake nationalistic, independence stuff.' He had dropped the strong Belfast twang which had so distinguished him among his fellow journalists and now he spoke with the language and accent of his upbringing. Someone had told her that John Fitzpatrick had his schooling in the Presentation Brothers fee-paying school and then went onto Cork University where he had attained a first-class honours BA in English sometime in the early years of this century, before wandering up north to work on the prestigious, almost two-century-old *Belfast News*.

Eileen felt that slight tingle that she had become used to now while investigating a news story. She had no idea how she could handle this, no idea how she could find out details, but she knew in her bones that there was an exciting story there to be discovered behind his cryptic words. Without a pang, she unrolled the page from the typewriter, put it aside and then took up her handbag from the floor beside her. She was not too badly off at this moment. She would be paid for that story in the *Evening Echo* and she still had time, especially if she stayed up all night, to produce something that might make tomorrow morning's *Examiner*.

'I'll stand you lunch,' she said, endeavouring to make the words sound as though she uttered them every day. She had heard many of the journalists say that to an informant; it would be fish and chips for some, the Oyster Tavern for those further up the line. Lunch was, she knew, the road to getting information.

'You couldn't afford it,' he said with a slight laugh in his voice. 'I'm a man with expensive tastes. Get your hat. No, I suppose that you don't bother to wear one, do you? You can leave the motorbike, though. We'll walk.'

She half-hoped that he might take her to an expensive hotel, even perhaps the Imperial, but he didn't. He took her to a small dark restaurant in Academy Street where the waiter greeted him by name and escorted them immediately to a table by the window, spread with a snowy linen tablecloth and already adorned with a carafe of rich, dark, red wine. The table had been laid for one, but within seconds, one waiter had taken Eileen's leather jacket and the other had laid a second set of cutlery, and a pair of crystal clear drinking glasses, one a wine glass and the other a tumbler.

'I don't drink wine,' said Eileen defiantly.

'Don't tell me that you are a teetotaller,' he said.

'No,' she said. 'Just poor and ignorant. I wouldn't know if it is good or bad so it would be wasted on me. I've read about it in books, though.'

'Well, let's not leave you in a state of ignorance. This is a good St Émilion, but for the moment, let's just have a Beaujolais for comparison's sake.'

Without being asked, the waiter brought an extra glass for both and carefully poured a small measure into each.

'Which is the best one?' She asked the question, half knowing the answer and he did not surprise her.

'No such thing. Which tastes best to you? Bite a bit of that roll, in between sips.'

'I like the Beaujolais, best,' she said after a few minutes. She hoped that it would annoy him. He had obviously chosen the St Émilion for himself.

'Try again when the soup comes,' he said. And then when the waiters had disappeared into the kitchen, he leaned across the table and said in a low voice, 'We are discussing a man called Tom.'

Eileen nodded seriously, but within she was filled with the desire to laugh. This was like a spy story, a bit like *The Scarlet Pimpernel*, or John Buchan. She began to feel quite excited and gulped down some more of the Beaujolais wine. 'Here's to Tom,' she said carelessly, but then saw that she had annoyed him. He had his back to the window, but he sat so that the curtain obscured him from the passers-by on the street before him. There was hardly anyone but themselves in the restaurant, nevertheless, his eyes wandered ceaselessly around the small room, stopped for a second at a man sitting by himself at the back of the room and always returned to the curtain which hung over the door to the stairs as if he were on the alert to check every newcomer. He said nothing, though. Just crumbled a roll, sipped his wine and drank down his soup when it arrived. She began to feel that she might have disappointed him, and an inner caution prevented her from reopening the conversation. The soup was good, but she drank it without comment and tried a few sips of the stronger wine in between gulps. It was only when the main course arrived, a highly flavoured version of a stew which her mother used to make, that she began to appreciate the St Émilion. Her mother's stew was made from scraps of meat left over at the butcher's shop on Saturday nights, and some battered vegetables from the market stalls, but this was immensely succulent and she guessed that it was made with more expensive ingredients. Cautiously, after a few sips, she kept to the lighter wine and allowed him to drink his carafe on his own. Alcohol, she knew after three years at university, could do odd things and so she drank in moderation, in between mouthfuls of food and waited for the conversation to open. It was only when a noisy crowd of lawyers came in and occupied the largest table at the front of the restaurant, beginning instantly to discuss a case and the judge's verdict in increasingly loud voices, that he began to relax.

'Tom, I reckon, must have been very well paid,' he said, holding up his glass to the light as though occupied with assessing the quality of the wine. 'After all, the place from where he came was an infinitely better-off area. And what an immense expense it must have been to move lock, stock and barrel, a journey of about two hundred and sixty miles, I'd reckon, wouldn't you?'

'Nearer three hundred,' said Eileen. She hadn't the remotest notion about how far Belfast was from Cork, but she thought that she should keep up the appearance of a conversation. He rewarded her with a nod and emboldened, she took another sip of the second wine. It really was a good meal, she thought, and the wine was beginning to grow upon her. She wondered how much it cost and whether, if she got a second article accepted by the *Cork Examiner*, she should try to buy a bottle for her mother and herself to share over their Saturday night meal.

'Whatever it was,' he went on, still speaking in a normal, though low tone of voice, 'whatever it was, we can take it that our friend Tom must have had a strong purpose behind coming here. Money behind him, wouldn't you say.'

'The labourer is worthy of his hire,' said Eileen. She was about to take another sip of wine but thought she should play it safe and match alcohol for water, drink for drink, as one of her IRA friends had once advised her to do.

'They meet in a place in east Cork, greyhound racing, training the animals, not a sport that is too popular in Cork. Limerick, yes, Cork no,' he said with the air of an expert. 'Wouldn't be your idea of fun, would it, Eileen?'

'I like horses best myself,' said Eileen. She wondered about this place in east Cork. Quite a good place to choose, east Cork. There was a time when west Cork was swamped with safe houses for the IRA, young men on the run, hiding from the British soldiers and then from the police, but east Cork was full of well-groomed farms and large country houses. A place for the rich, and where the land was so good that in the time, when the English still ruled, no cottage went neglected and abandoned, but each was filled with a willing labourer and his offspring. Now all that was changed and if she read between the lines correctly, it seemed as though the positions were reversed.

'So the *craic* is good, is that it?' she queried, copying his tone of voice, keeping it light and casual and taking care to eat between sentences and to lean back in her chair when she sipped her Beaujolais. The Irish word for gossip usually figured in most conversations in Cork where the opening sentence was usually: 'What's the *craic*?' And the closing words: 'Well, that's the *craic* for you.'

John Fitzpatrick did not answer for a moment and she wondered whether she had been indiscreet, but then, quite suddenly he laughed. 'Now here's a little puzzle for you,' he said. 'When I went to Belfast first, I was just a lad, about your own age, I suppose, straight out of university with my shiny new BA and a picture of myself in gown and mortar board, off to my first job. Well, an old fellow on the staff of the *Belfast News* gave me a bit of advice and now I'm going to pass it onto you – in fact, he wrote it down on a piece of paper for me and told me to keep it in my pocket and to look at it every day. He didn't write it all out, just three letters and three full stops.' Deliberately he took his notebook from his pocket, tore a page from it, printed the three letters and the three full stops and then passed it across to her.

P.I.P.

She read and smiled. 'I'm more used to R.I.P. with all those funeral notices in the *Cork Examiner*,' she said, but then put her brains to work. The first had to be 'politics' . . .

'*Politics is* . . .' she said. And then, triumphantly, '"Politics is Power". Is that it?'

He said nothing, just smiled with an air of appreciation, drank a little more of his wine, holding the glass up briefly in her direction as a salute. She had the impression that he was trying to make up his mind about something, and when he suddenly replaced his glass and leaned across the table so that he was very close to her, she knew that she had passed the test.

'I was in London last week,' he said softly. 'Doing a piece about the Locarno Pact, I met a friend of mine who used to be on the *Belfast News* and then moved to the *Telegraph* in London and he said something quite interesting to me. And this is what he said: "I hear that there is a great need for a new stocking factory in a small town outside that little city of yours." Interesting that.'

Eileen stared at him. The words, '*what did he mean?*' were on her lips but she suppressed them. He had told her all that had been said between the two men. The one in London had heard something in confidence, didn't want to break that confidence, but wanted to give an old friend a hint that there was something exciting going on in the city where he had chosen to work. John Fitzpatrick, she thought, had been handi-capped by his Irish origins. He, too, might have moved to London, moved onto a job on the *Telegraph* or even on the prestigious *Times* newspaper, but with the tension between England and Ireland and the disappointment that Ireland had broken the hundreds of years of subservience to the United Kingdom, no southern Irish journalist like John Fitzpatrick would get a job in London. She began to understand now his air of weary superiority which annoyed so many of the young reporters on the *Cork Examiner*. He felt that his position as foreign correspondent on a provincial newspaper was very much second-best. He had a hint about a story, but it wasn't his province and now he was passing it over to her. Stocking factory must mean Willie Hamilton – and Willie Hamilton had been present at the retreat in the convent of the Sisters of Charity when a bomb had gone off in the orchard cemetery.

'I wonder,' she said casually, 'whether a clean sweep was intended.'

'I hear you are very much in with Reverend Mother Aquinas,' he said and instantly she understood his meaning.

'I owe everything to her,' she said. 'She was a great teacher. Got me through the Honan Scholarship. She and I trust each other.' That, of course, did not mean that she had access to all that the Reverend Mother knew. That was quite a different matter and she had always been careful not to ask too many questions. She pondered over his mention of the name and guessed that this mystery was somehow tied up with the rich and privileged citizens, people who spoke in the way that the Reverend Mother spoke and people who treated even the mention of her name with huge respect.

'Set you on the road to success,' he said mockingly, and once again raised his glass in her direction.

'I'm going to study law, to be a solicitor,' she said proudly. She would disabuse him of the idea that she was intending to earn a livelihood by picking up bits of journalism – 'a hand-to-mouth existence', to quote one of her mother's favourite sayings. Nevertheless, it would be quite a feather in her cap if she made a good story out of this, and perhaps even helped the police in finding the murderer. That would make Patrick regard her as a sensible adult rather than a small girl who had played around the street when he was studying for his leaving certificate. 'If they had all been in the orchard, then it would have been a straight road for *your* man,' she continued.

'Last man standing – and a nice little scapegoat, named IRA, sitting on the fence,' he said. 'Now why don't you try another sip of the Bordeaux. You'll get to like it; I assure you. Bit stronger than the Beaujolais but you should develop your taste buds – can't be a little girl all of your life.'

She ignored him. *I've more important things than wine to think of*, was her brief reflection before she moved back to considering his words. Willie Hamilton was sent down from Belfast to do a job. His cover was the stocking factory, but that was a most expensive cover, and what was more, it seemed to point to a long-term job, not just a one-off assassination. She looked across at John Fitzpatrick. He was tugging at something in the back pocket of his trousers of the rather elderly suit which he always wore to the *Cork Examiner* offices. When the object emerged, she could see that it was a rather worn and crumpled map of the county of Cork. He unfolded it carefully and spread a section out for her to examine.

'Watergrasshill, great place for racing. Many a point-to-point I went to in that place,' he said in slightly clearer and louder tones than he had used previously. From the corner of her eye, she could see that one of the lawyers had looked across, attracted by the map.

'Watergrasshill,' she repeated. His finger was not on that well-known village, but on something with small writing, about ten miles distant, she thought and memorized the name and the correct spelling while John Fitzpatrick reminisced over all of the money that he had lost at these point-to-points in Watergrasshill.

'Good land around there,' she said, making sure that her tone was casual.

'Great land,' he echoed. 'Get great mushrooms there, we used to say when I was a young lad. That's always the way. These rich and titled people have horses on their land, the horse manure feeds the mushrooms, and the mushrooms feed the hungry young lads. I can remember that myself and a friend used to bring an old frying pan and a box of matches and we used to gather a bit of wood and when all was ready for our meal we used to steal into the fields, pick the mushrooms, and then fry them in butter. Never tasted anything better in my life,' said John Fitzpatrick as he took the last bite of what was probably going to be a most expensive meal.

Eileen thought about it. Yes, even a cursory glance at the map had shown her that the land around the village which he had indicated was filled with well-known country estates, no castles, nothing so ostentatious, but lots of beautiful big houses. Most of the wealthy Anglo-Irish in west Cork and in north

Cork had been burned out of the country; some assassinated, many frightened out, and a few bought out with sums that were hugely below the value of the land and of the buildings. But these country estates in east Cork had been, up to now, left largely untouched. She wondered why. There must be some reason. She looked across at her lunch companion and he nodded as though he had traced her thoughts from the expression on her face.

'That's right,' he said in a low voice. 'Not much talk has there been, don't you think? Well outside the city, that part of the county, isn't it? And, you know the old proverb, "out of sight; out of mind". And, of course, they made sure that they had power. Easy enough. Great friends with the local police, subscriptions, and donations to the local churches, some even swapping religion, marrying Catholics, well, you know how it goes. And, of course, they were a long way out of the city, out there in east Cork,' he repeated. 'No one troubled too much about them. And the word had got around that bad things happened to anyone who made any threats or planned any raids. They had a network of men, you see, a network of protectors, all of them employed in some way so that they would not be noticed. Respectable people, small business-men, librarians, schoolteachers, quite a few schools, they had – you'd be surprised.'

Protestant schools, he meant, thought Eileen, and yes, she was surprised. The schools would probably have been built in the last century, on estates or in villages near to estates, well built, too. That was a time when big money was being made from the rich lands around the northern and eastern parts of Cork, in the places where Cork tipped up against Tipperary and Waterford – the Golden Vale, she remembered hearing that it had been called – rich, rich grass that reared splendid horses and cattle. The landowners had been given vast stretches of land by Cromwell and other English leaders, before and after his reign of terror in Ireland. They had brought their own servants with them, of course, had brought farm workers and gamekeepers and woodland keepers.

She looked across at John Fitzpatrick and he nodded as though he were able to read her thoughts.

'That's right,' he said. 'Still plenty of them around, all descendants, but not military men, not men to use violence. Peaceful crowd, though, but all of them willing to defend their masters and their own families. But not people for the shot in the dark.'

'Easy for them,' said Eileen, thinking of the wrongs of the Catholic tenants and workers, and for a moment, despite her caution, her voice rose slightly, and he looked a warning at her. Defiantly she stuck her fork into a succulent chunk of meat and thrust it into her mouth.

'Be that as it may . . .' He left a pause after the words, and then repeated them. 'Be that as it may, they were willing but unorganized; reacted to an emergency but didn't plan ahead. And, of course, the . . . the *boyoes*, our heroes . . . Well, they had learned their lesson in a hard world, they had been trained and drilled. Big Mick,' he said, using the nickname for the patriot Michael Collins, 'Big Mick, God have mercy on him, well, he was a great commander and he did what all good leaders should do: he trained men to train others and to pass on their skills. Did a great job, so he did! A great piece of work it was – who would have thought it – the elephant defeated by the mouse. But to come back to our friend, Tom. Well, he's another man who is, who was, a great trainer of men. Did sterling work, according to his principles, in certain areas up north until he made it too hot to hold onto him . . .'

'And now,' said Eileen. Her excitement was rising. The moment had come for his revelation, and she got ready for it with a quick gulp from the wine that he had called a Bordeaux. It was strong but it sent a fire down her windpipe and she felt her cheeks glow and a mixture of excitement heightened by fear. She sat up very straight.

'And now,' he said, copying her phrase and leaning across the table until his head almost touched hers and she could sense a certain warmth coming from him as though he felt an excitement from his own words. 'Well, some people don't like being frightened out of home and land, so a counterforce is being built up with our friend Tom in charge. He's got a cover; and you know what that is, he's got a business, he's established in Cork. He knows how to organize, how to train some willing workers. But, of course, to be potent, to serve these people in every way, he needs a bit of power, he needs to be doing something more than the work of a small factory, wouldn't you agree?'

Her plate was empty, except for a small smear of the rich brown gravy. Deliberately, she licked her finger, traced out the letters P.I.P. and then she sat back and admired the chalk-white of the china plate as it shone through the smears of gravy. She left it for a moment and then broke off a piece of roll and mopped up the remaining gravy and chewed it in silence.

He sat back. 'Well, I must say that you are a pleasure to take out to lunch,' he said. 'God bless you, but you have a fine appetite. Fancy a pudding or a dessert, as they are calling it in polite society, these days?'

She shook her head. 'Just a coffee,' she said in a careless manner. The meeting was over, now. She knew that. He had, without betraying any confidences, given her an excellent hint and now she had something with which she could follow up the story and find the perpetrator of the murder in the orchard cemetery and discover the reason behind it. These Protestants, they needed organizing, but also, they needed powerful protection. They needed alterations to the hastily drawn up laws of the new republic which allowed tenants the rights to purchase rented farms from owners who had held them from the time of Cromwell, or even earlier. Their tenants would be enabled to purchase back the land for what was claimed to be a fair price, but which was known to be anything but a fair price – its acceptance mostly insured by a mixture of threats and illegal blackmail. This Willie Hamilton had been sent down from Belfast, had been given the money to move his stocking factory which was to form a screen for his true activities. It was going to be important for him to be a businessman, a man known in the city and then to be elected as alderman and from alderman to progress, next year, to the post of lord mayor of the second biggest city in Ireland.

The coffee was black and very bitter, not at all like a comfortable cup of tea, but she drank it down without comment.

The coffee should sober her up. She had no desire to go, half intoxicated, back to her desk and even less inclination, with the wine running through her veins, to ride her motorbike out to Watergrasshill and beyond.

He read her thoughts as they both drank their coffee. When he had paid the bill, he took her leather jacket from the waiter and put it around her shoulders.

'Back to the office then.' He said the words loudly. It was, she knew, a command, and it was probably nothing to do with the fact that she had been drinking wine and was not used to doing that at lunchtime. No, he was being ultra, ultra cautious and wanted to have no link from himself to any journeys she might make into the heartlands of wealthy landowners in east Cork. In any case, what could she find out by walking around and asking questions? She would certainly arouse suspicion and when it came down to it, although she wouldn't mind giving poor old Patrick a bit of a nudge in the right direction, basically what she wanted to do was to write a good article for the *Cork Examiner*. The university term had finished. Her place was ensured for next year's work and now the four months of holidays scrolled out ahead of her. She would study, that went without saying. Study was a part of her life and a day would seem wrong without it. She would study, and perhaps be able to get a bit of experience in a solicitor's office, but she and her mother needed to eat, and she hoped that she would get a pound or two every week of work from the *Cork Examiner*.

As they walked together up Academy Street she said aloud, 'Innuendo.'

'I beg your pardon!' She had startled him out of some thoughts of his own.

'Innuendo,' she repeated. 'It's a great way of stirring up interest.'

'Thank you.' He took off his hat and bowed towards her. 'I shall remember that interesting word, so thank you for your most kind advice,' he said with solemnity.

'And thank you for such an extremely good lunch,' she replied graciously, with a slight nod of her head. She was beginning to feel a slight fizzing in her brain and had the supremely confident feeling that she was about to write a magnificent article for the *Cork Examiner*, all filled with questions and with innuendos. It would be a masterpiece of fine writing, something that would even garner a few words of praise from the notoriously grumpy professor of English at UCC.

ELEVEN

' I 'll interview the lady solicitor, Joe.' Patrick had finished writing and now he looked up at his sergeant. 'You pop into the kitchen and just check that this Sister Mary Agnes did suggest that the gardener dig a grave to be ready for the old nun when she dies.' Joe, he knew, would get on well in the kitchen and he preferred not to have him around while he was talking to Miss Hogan.

Patrick had an instinctive dislike of people like Maureen Hogan. By now, though having been brought up in the slums of Cork, he had achieved a manner which made him feel quite comfortable in the presence of the wealthy professional and businessmen of the city. He never pretended to be other than he was. Cork was a small city, and everyone knew the origin of everyone else – 'breed, seed and generation' was a great Cork saying. He had slightly modified his accent, toned down the sing-song tones of his boyhood, took some care to make sure that he bore in mind the second letter in the digraph 'th' and assiduously tried to widen his vocabulary by studying one of the classics, dictionary by his side, for half an hour every day when he wasn't too tired.

But Maureen Hogan did not fit in. For one thing, she wanted to be too matey, too much as though she had met him in a public house, rather than being a respectable solicitor who was being questioned by a police inspector, after the brutal murder of a respectable citizen.

'Let's go and sit on that wall,' she said in a friendly fashion. 'And, for heaven's sake, stop calling me Miss Hogan, Patrick. You're making me nervous. Don't be so stiff.'

Resentfully, he followed her. He didn't mind her sitting on the wall, though he did dislike the way her skirt was so short that when she perched upon it, she displayed most of a pair of shapely legs. No stockings either, he noticed. And he certainly resented the way in which she called him 'Patrick' as if he were one of her drinking pals.

'I won't keep you long, Miss Hogan,' he said as briskly as he could manage. He debated whether to sit on the wall also – then he could avoid looking at her legs, but he felt that would gravely threaten his dignity and so he compromised by putting his notebook on the flat stone which topped the gate pier and keeping his eyes fixed upon it. He occupied a few minutes in asking her name, address and occupation and noting the answers before proceeding to his more probing questions. He had settled on asking everyone their movements after the midday luncheon at the convent and to ignore their movements during the morning when mostly they all seemed to have been occupied in a group with religious matters. The chances were that the makeshift bomb had been planted in the very early morning or even overnight, but it would, according to the bomb expert, have had to be ignited shortly before it exploded as there was no trace of an alarm clock or timer. The gardener reported the prepared grave had been covered by him at the end of the previous day with a few planks, supporting a heavy, dark-green, canvas tarpaulin, which, in turn was decorated with a few pots of flowering plants. No one, whether the usual inhabitants of the convent or any of the visitors, would have had any reason to uncover this tactful display. The gardener himself had made it plain that he would not touch his handiwork until the morning of the funeral.

However, since no timing device had been found, the makeshift bomb would have had to be ignited with a flame of some sort, so it was important to know whether anyone had approached the place during the gap between lunchtime and the explosion.

'Could you tell me whether you spoke to Mr James Musgrave after lunch, Miss Hogan?' He hoped that he was giving the impression of reading the question from his notebook and that gave him an excuse for not looking at her.

'I can't remember,' she said unhelpfully.

He repeated the answer aloud, enunciating the words

carefully and in a neutral tone of voice. She gave an impatient sigh and kicked the wall with the back of her shoe.

'I didn't go up and set fire to a bomb beside his seat,' she said in an irritated tone of voice. 'You know what I mean, Patrick. This place was oozing with all those clerics and there were just five of us lay people. Mostly we tried to be friendly to each other – "let the best man win" and all that sort of stuff. I can't, for the life of me, remember whether I said anything to him – "lovely day", I suppose would be the level of conversation that I would have had with James Musgrave.'

That gave him his opportunity, but he planned the phrasing of his question while he wrote down her answer. His short-hand was rapid – well-practised, but he took his time. That note of irritation in her voice could have betrayed an anxiety – this type of reaction had been underlined during his training at the headquarters in Dublin. Always keep your temper during cross-examination and remember that you are winning if the guilty person is beginning to lose theirs, was a great maxim of the experienced RIC man who had been responsible for training them.

'You didn't have much in common with the late gentleman, did you?' was his next question and he delivered it in a neutral tone of voice.

'That didn't mean that I murdered him!' The retort came quickly but he took a while to write it down and did not make any comment upon it.

'I believe that lunch finished at about half past one o'clock,' he said with a quick look at the clock over the convent door and a confirmatory glance at his own watch. He was most proud of that watch. He had bought it with the proceeds of his first week's salary as a policeman and was scrupulously careful about winding it every night and having it serviced by a watchmaker a couple of times in each year.

'I'll take your word for it, Patrick,' she said. She yawned, very vigorously and without bothering to put her hand in front of her mouth. 'The last few days seemed like a never-ending and utterly pointless sea of boredom for me.'

He wrote the words down, though he normally didn't bother about answers which were obviously irrelevant.

'You have been disappointed with the results of the three-day expenditure of your time,' he said when he had finished the last word. It was an assertion, but she could take it as a question if she wished. As he turned to a new page, he wondered whether she would take up the challenge.

There was a silence and he waited impassively. Then she gave a sigh. 'Time spent on God is never wasted, isn't that right, Patrick?'

He did not write that down. It sounded to him like something that a nun or a priest or a Christian Brother would say.

He saw her glance at him, and he bent his head to focus on his pencil. There was a moment's silence and then she spoke again and this time she had lost the languid, unconcerned tone of voice.

'To be very honest, Patrick,' she said, 'I only came because I thought that it might do me some good in the coming election, or, I suppose I guessed that it would do me harm if I didn't come, would set me aside as a kind of pagan. I had nothing in common with all of those people. James Musgrave was a bit of a chump, but OK, I suppose. Quite polite and everything like that. Not my type, probably harmless. Robert O'Connor is a *chisler*; Wee Willie too good to be true, I'd say, myself, that he was some kind of fraudster; Pat Pius – well, I don't know much about him, can hardly understand a word that he says . . . bit wet . . . gives me the heebie-jeebies, to be honest, so I'd say he's not as pious as he pretends.'

Patrick wrote down everything; she was trying to confuse and embarrass him, he thought, and he would have to consult Joe about some of the words, like 'wet' and 'chump' and 'chisler' which she used, but he was certainly not going to give her the satisfaction of asking her, so he kept his face impassive until he had finished. When he looked up, he saw that she was examining him in a speculative manner, wondering, perhaps, how gullible he was. He knew enough Americanized slang to realize that she had, despite her careless manner, pointed out that she liked the dead man and that every one of her opponents had some moral failings.

'Did you talk to anyone during the hour which elapsed between the end of lunch and the explosion, Miss Hogan?'

He asked the question in a deadpan way and without looking at her, giving her no opportunity to practise these grimaces with which she tried to imply that they were both young people and that he was on her side.

There was quite a silence and he had a feeling that she was turning over in her mind which answer would serve her purpose best.

'No,' she said after what he would have calculated was a minute, but since he had once been ridiculed because he had gone to the trouble of sitting with his watch in one hand and watching the second hand tick through sixty seconds, he nowadays avoided using that aid and put within brackets the letters (LP) which he now used to indicate that there had been a long pause.

'And where were you in that time, after lunch and before the explosion?'

Again, she paused, and he told himself that she was concocting a lie, or else testing her words before she uttered them.

'I went to my bedroom,' she said.

He wrote without comment, but she seemed to feel that an explanation was needed.

'I wanted to think,' she said then. 'You see, I had decided that I was wasting my time. I knew that the bishop was antagonistic to me. I had made a mess of explaining to him what I wanted to achieve. I think he had decided that I was probably some sort of communist, or something like that. And so, I thought to myself that I was doing more harm than good by hanging around. I thought I would tell him that I was unwell, hope that he might immediately jump to the conclusion that it was "women's problems" – well, you know, Patrick . . . And then, while he was still gulping with embarrassment over that, I would jump into the jalopy and be back home before he could say a word.'

Patrick wrote down four words: *resolve, leave, excuse, ill.* Once again, he suspected the young lady was cleverer than the image which she had tried to project. On the other hand, he could think of no real motive for her to be involved in the killing of James Musgrave and somewhat unlikely that she had planned the killing of a group of people, and so he thanked her and checked that he had her home address and confirmed that she was at liberty to leave whenever she wished.

'Can't make her out,' he said to Joe five minutes later after receiving the report that it was, indeed, Sister Mary Agnes who had mentioned that the elderly nun had not much time left.

'Or so she said.' Joe sounded cautious. 'Seemed to me that she was fond of him. Like a mother to him. He'd be the right age to be a son for her if there wasn't this rule about nuns marrying.'

'Perhaps I should have a word with her . . . What do you think?' With an effort, Patrick switched his mind from the lay sister to the lady solicitor.

'The bishop wants to see you,' said Joe unhelpfully. 'Don't suppose that he has anything to say, but I suppose that you'll have to see him. Everyone seems to kowtow to him, so he'll probably take it amiss if you don't pop over there immediately. He's been pacing up and down while you were talking to the lady solicitor. Asked me twice whether I had told you that he had something to say to you.'

'I'd better go,' said Patrick. Joe, he thought, did not understand. The bishop would have expected a sergeant to walk straight over to inform his superior of the bishop's wishes, whether he was interrupting an interview or not. Now he would have to spend some time soothing down the bishop before they got to the reason for his request. Perhaps his lordship thought that he should have been the first person to be interviewed. Possibly it had been a mistake to have immediately dismissed him from the list. Obviously, the bishop was not the person who crammed a bag of fertilizer into a rusty old downpipe, poured diesel upon it and then ignited it. But the bishop would have been expecting to be kept in the picture during every step of this inquiry. As he walked over, Patrick uttered a muffled curse. It had been stupid of him and now he was going to have to waste a huge amount of time calming down the man and making sure that he contacted him at regular intervals during the rest of the day. Probably the whole affair was of great interest to the bishop. His views on violence and on Sinn Fein and on the IRA were very well known throughout the city and it was a mistake not to allow him every opportunity to vent them at great length. The superintendent, though a Protestant, would never have made that mistake, as he was a man who understood the echelons of power and would be bound to feel moved to reprimand Patrick if the bishop chose to make a complaint.

TWELVE

As Patrick hurried over towards the bishop, conscious that he had kept his lordship waiting, he was anxiously selecting from several apologetic phrases when a cold, clear voice sounded in his inner consciousness. *Don't be such an eejit, Patrick. Don't be always apologizing. If you're late, it's because they're early. If you haven't seen someone yet, it's because you were too considerate of their busy life, too unwilling to interrupt the important business which they are engaged in. Take my advice, Patrick. I know the world!*

Patrick grinned a little to himself and slowed down his strides.

Of course, Eileen was right. No one had much *meas* – as they said in Cork – on you if you didn't have a good opinion of yourself. He slowed his steps, imperceptibly, mentally practising his opening words and managed to arrive in a dignified manner at the bishop's side.

'How good of you to spare the time to see me, my lord,' he said. 'I won't take up more of your time than I can help. Perhaps we could stroll together for a few minutes?'

That went down well. The bishop looked at him with an air of friendly approval and crooked a finger at him to walk by his side.

He thought, and indeed hoped, that the bishop would suggest joining the Reverend Mother as she stood alone and slightly to the back of the terrace in front of the convent. The bishop, however, turned his back on the convent and proposed a walk towards the church. There was no one there; all avoided the ruined and ploughed-up orchard cemetery. Patrick found himself hoping that the old and dying nun would postpone her death until a moment when everything could be tidied up and restored to normality. One thing was certain: that grave had been well and truly dug. It would be the deepest grave in this orchard cemetery. Not a pretty sight now but within months all would be covered over, new grass seed sown, and the regular lines of the trees restored to their tidy formation; a place once again for prayer and thanksgiving for lives well spent. Just now the nuns avoided the ugly crater.

The bishop, however, chose to stop there and to contemplate the cavernous hole with a gloomy look.

'There is something that I would like to mention to you, Inspector,' he said. 'Obviously, of course, I would not like my name to be mentioned in public, in the courts or in the newspapers . . .' He paused, looking enquiringly at Patrick.

Patrick bowed his head in a graceful acknowledgement of his lordship's communication. There had been a time when he would have broken into the conversation with anxious apologies and explanations about why this would be impossible, but now he said nothing. If the bishop, with all his education, and all his knowledge of the ways of the world, felt that any relevant evidence that he might give about the murder could possibly be kept anonymous, well, that was tough luck, he said to himself and subdued a smile as he realized that he made use of another one of Eileen's favourite expressions.

The bishop was having a certain amount of difficulty in proceeding. He cleared his throat twice, and then took out a spotless and brilliantly white handkerchief and flourished it around the area of his nose.

'It's just a matter of being sure that I am doing the right thing?' he explained, spurred on by Patrick's silence into an unusual degree of loquaciousness.

Patrick decided that now was the moment to speak. The bishop, he thought, needed a little bit of friendly encouragement. 'I'm sure, my lord,' he said tactfully, 'that the whole city relies on your judgement.'

It worked.

The bishop gave a determined nod as a signal that he was prepared to go ahead.

'It's just that, before lunch, when the late Mr Musgrave and I were discussing matters purveying to the diocese, that he mentioned to me that he wished to discuss something troubling his peace of mind.'

'Peace of mind,' repeated Patrick slowly. It was, he thought, an odd phrase. After all, if the late Mr Musgrave had been worried about a spiritual matter, the more appropriate phrase would have been 'troubling his conscience', or even, perhaps, 'troubling his soul'. But 'peace of mind' for a stockbroker sounded like something else.

'To do with money matters, my lord?' he ventured, seeing that the bishop had, once again, come to a full stop.

'No, no, not money matters, nothing to do with stocks and shares, or anything like that. It was actually,' said the bishop slowly, 'apparently something to do with one of his fellow candidates, something that would render this person totally unfit for high office and should, he felt, result in the removal of that person's name from the list of approved candidates.'

'"Person",' repeated Patrick and turned an enquiring eye on the bishop.

'Yes, that was what he said.'

'All the time? He used that one word "person"? Throughout your whole conversation?'

The bishop reflected for a moment, staring straight ahead with a troubled expression upon his face.

'All the time,' he repeated.

Patrick reflected for a couple of moments. The bishop was an odd man and could easily take offence if there was any possibility or any suspicion that due reverence was not being paid to the dignity of his position as bishop of the second largest city in the holy Catholic country of Ireland. And so Patrick waited, cap respectfully retained in his hand and his eyes fixed deferentially upon the bishop's face.

After a long minute, he knew that it had worked. The bishop gave a little nod, a nod apparently meant for himself. He turned and paced up and down, and Patrick followed a few inches behind him like a very well-trained dog, available if needed but preserving an air of aloofness until he should be called upon. In the distance, he saw the Reverend Mother's eyes rest upon the two figures and guessed that she wore an enquiring expression. He wished that she would come and join them and extract from the bishop whatever information he had and which was obviously troubling his lordship so much, but he knew that she was far too tactful a woman to do such a thing. Now it was up to him.

Suddenly the bishop stopped. And he spoke; spoke so low that Patrick had to bend his head to catch all the words.

'Mr Musgrave had proof – and that was the word that he used to me – had proof that this . . . this person, one of the candidates for the high office of alderman had been responsible for the murder of a man.'

Patrick reflected upon this matter. There were two words in the bishop's statement which intrigued him, and he took the easiest first.

'He, Mr Musgrave, definitely used the word "man". He referred to the murder of a man but with no other details – is that correct, my lord?'

The bishop looked at him with an air of slight annoyance. 'Quite correct,' he said firmly.

Patrick reflected. In these troubled days, the most likely scenario for a hidden murder was that it was sectarian, in which case the word, Catholic or Protestant, would have been used. He murdered a Protestant, or he murdered a Catholic would have been a more normal expression.

Perhaps, though, the very absence of such a word might also be of significance. He moved onto his next question.

'And Mr Musgrave used the word "person" all of the time, did he, my lord?' he enquired.

'All of the time,' said the bishop firmly. 'He never mentioned the person's name.'

'And he did not make use of the words "he" or even "she", is that right?' suggested Patrick.

The bishop looked somewhat startled. He did not rush into an answer – something that gave Patrick a better opinion of him. *Quite a shrewd old buffer,* he thought. He knows what I am getting at.

'No, said the bishop eventually. 'No, I am certain that he never said "he" – of course, if he had said "she", I would have been instantly alerted.' Once again, he looked hard at Patrick. There was no getting away from it. There was certainly a very human look of curiosity upon his lordship's face. Patrick, however, preserved silence, and knew, from experience, that his face would show nothing. It had been one of the first lessons that he had learned when he returned to his native city to take up the position of constable. There were no end of people, men who knew him from boyhood, men that had once been in school with him, girls, now women, that had played in the streets with him when he was little, or who were friends of his mother. Half of Cork would have claimed acquaintanceship with him if he had allowed them to do so. But he had walked a solitary path. Did not socialize, kept away from making any new close friends with either men or women, learned to wear a polite, but blank mask which betrayed nothing of his thoughts.

The matter of the use of the word 'person' by the dead man was, he thought, extraordinarily important. However, one started a conversation about someone, by using the word 'person', surely it was only human nature, soon or later to slip into using the word 'he' instead of a gender neutral – as they used to say in his Latin classes – a word like 'person'. There could perhaps be an urgent necessity which would have made Mr Musgrave very scrupulous about his speech – and that was because he was at that stage discussing something relating to four people, only one of whom was a woman. Until he had made up his mind to divulge all, presumably with certain safeguards offered to him by the bishop – until he felt that he could tell what he knew without risking a shot in the dark or even, perhaps, more fancily, a bomb at midday – then Mr Musgrave might not have wanted to particularize the sex of the person he was accusing of a murder.

And the lack of pinpointing a religion for the murdered man was also possibly of significance. Patrick's brain, behind a calm and expressionless face, was racing through the possibilities. Only one person of the five had any overt connection with a military organization, and that was Miss Maureen Hogan. And only one person from the five was not from this part of Ireland, in this place where people liked to know who you were and where you came from: breed, seed and generation.

The name of Wee Willie Hamilton had come to his mind, and with it a certain question mark which had always clung to that person since he had arrived in Cork. Who was he really? And why had he come from the prosperous city of Belfast in the north, down to the extreme south, to live among people who did not speak as he spoke, who had no decent reserve like the people of the north and more important still did not have the money to buy the product which he was marketing? Yes, it was understandable that a Catholic might wish to leave the north, but why not go to Monaghan or Cavan, two counties just over the border from the north of Ireland?

I must see Wee Willie, thought Patrick as, with a nod, the bishop left him and went to join a group of Christian Brothers.

However, standing by the door of the church was Joe, making conversation with Bob the Builder, and the turn of Joe's head in his direction sent an unmistakable signal and Patrick went across to join them.

'Mr O'Connor has something rather interesting to say, Inspector, and I thought you would like to hear it for yourself,' said Joe with his usual politeness.

Patrick turned an enquiring glance upon the builder. A big bruiser of a man! Rich, of course, but how did he get to be as rich as that in a time of recession? Was there something dodgy about him? Come to think of it, thought Patrick, put side by side with the mild-mannered Willie Hamilton, most people would choose Bob the Builder as a more likely killer.

'Very good of you to assist us, Mr O'Connor,' he said, and watched the man preen himself.

'It's just this, Inspector,' said Bob. 'You see, builders know a fair amount about digging – a site has to be prepared, drains put in, foundations laid, before ever you start building walls. You mightn't know about that, Inspector.'

Patrick nodded curtly. He had no intention of allowing this big brute of a man to patronize him.

'And, of course, I was brought up the hard way, brought up on a farm, buried many a stinking dead corpse of a sheep, you have to bury them deep, you know, once they start to smell. Get disease on the farm otherwise.'

Patrick nodded again.

'I'm telling you all this, Inspector, so that you know I'm a man who knows what I'm talking about,' said the builder with the air of a man who is willing to go on and give multiple examples of his competence.

'Mr O'Connor made an interesting observation about the hole which was meant for a grave,' said Joe. 'He thinks that—'

This was too slow progress for Bob the Builder, and he took the story out of Joe's unqualified hands.

'I'm telling you this, Inspector, and I'm a man who knows what I'm talking about, but that was an almighty big hole for one man to dig by himself, in an evening, too.'

Patrick nodded impassively. Was it? He didn't know. He had been brought up in a tiny cabin with a road in front of it and a lane behind. Had never put a spade in the earth as far as he could remember. He relied on Joe, though. A man who had been brought up in a house with a garden in the front and at the back. Joe would have got rid of Bob if he had not thought there was something in what he had to say.

'Yes,' he said.

'What would it be? Six by six and six foot deep. That's a couple of hundred cubic feet of soil – a hell of a lot to shift in one evening, Inspector, pardon my language.' Bob cast a guilty glance at the church door.

'He might be good at digging,' said Patrick mildly. There was more to come; he knew that. Geometry had been his favourite subject in school, but the Christian Brothers were not ones to waste time on practical work. He had not the faintest idea of what a couple of hundred cubic feet of soil would look like.

'Well, let's say for argument's sake, that the skinny young lad is a world champion at digging,' said Bob affably, 'but why were there two heaps of soil, one at either end? Looks like two men dug that grave – if it was intended for a grave . . .' Bob allowed his voice to tail off artistically.

'Got the sun in his eyes,' suggested Joe.

The builder smiled at him. I was waiting for that one, his expression said. 'One heap on the north side and one on the south; take my word for it, that hole was dug by two men on that evening. Take it or leave it, but I'm telling you that I had a good look at that hole before anyone put a bomb into it.' He finished with a nod at both policemen and went off.

'I suppose he knows what he's talking about,' said Patrick reluctantly. 'Know anything about digging, Joe?'

'Dug out the odd dandelion for my mam,' said Joe. 'And I must say that I wouldn't like to shift a couple of hundred cubic feet of solid earth that hadn't been dug for a hundred years or so.'

'We'd better have a word with young Martin,' said Patrick.

'Saw him go into that shed of his a few minutes ago. Saw one of the nuns bring a cup of tea and a slice of cake out to him,' said the observant Joe. He led the way and Patrick followed reluctantly. If anyone other than the IRA had to be accused of this murder, he would have preferred that it would have been someone like the self-assured Bob the Builder.

A nervous lad, he thought a minute later, allowing Joe to do the talking while he eyed the thin face. Not tall, narrow chest and shoulders. Wouldn't feed them too well in those orphanages like Greenmount, healthy looking, otherwise. And they did have a lot of energy at that age, nevertheless, there had been a decisiveness about Bob the Builder that had convinced him.

Time to take over, he thought.

'So, who was it helped you?' he said quietly. 'Not one of the nuns, was it?'

Joe smiled at the feeble joke, but the boy's face went white.

'Just tell us the truth,' said Patrick gently. 'No sin in getting a bit of help. How did it come about?'

The boy hesitated for a moment and then, as if suddenly coming to a decision, he pointed to the plate on the wooden bench. He had taken a few bites out of the enormous hunk of cake, but the rest remained untouched. 'It's Sister Mary Agnes,' he said. 'She keeps giving me all that food, thinks that I'm too thin and that she must fatten me up. I don't have the stomach for it. Give it to the birds sometimes, but there was this fellow standing on the road, looking over the wall and he asked me if I could spare a few crusts because he had been tramping the road for days. Had a funny sort of accent, he had. So I took him in here and showed him the plateful of food and told him he'd do me a favour if he'd finish it up so that I could bring a clean plate back to the kitchen. Finished it up in a flash!'

'About your age, was he?' asked Patrick.

The boy thought about that. 'A few years older, big fellow. Big broad shoulders, nearly as tall as that window there.'

About six feet, thought Patrick. Some of those IRA men were fine fellows.

'I asked him if he'd like some more of the fruit cake and he said he'd love it, so I went back with the empty plates and Sister Mary Agnes was so pleased when I asked for more cake. She had a lot left over – a bit soggy, I thought it was. So I brought a big hunk of it back and Franz, that was his name, was so pleased that he asked me if he could help me with any job, said he was very good at digging and that he enjoyed doing it. And it was then I thought about the digging of the hole for the grave and he was dead keen. Knew a lot about soil, too. Went around with the pickaxe, testing places, chose a good site, too. Never saw a man work as hard as he did, loosened the whole piece of earth as soon as I had marked it out. I was following him with a shovel, but he kept on with the pick until he loosened all of the top soil. I can tell you he had some muscles, that German lad. Wish I had.'

'You'll grow them,' said Joe in a friendly way as Patrick shut his notebook. 'Did he stay the night?'

'Naw, I wouldn't do that, not without permission. Don't think the mother superior would think much of that,' said the gardener hastily. 'Had to have all sort of references before I got the job here. Nuns are very fussy. You won't tell on me, will you? There was no harm in it. I saw him go up the road when he left.'

'So, he went up the road, not down towards the city where he might get a night's lodging,' said Joe, once they were outside the small hut. 'That's interesting. Sounds as though he has friends in the neighbourhood. Or else he doesn't mind sleeping rough in the fields. I'd choose that myself rather than down there in the city.'

'You noticed that he was alone in the shed when the young fellow went off for more cake. He had plenty of opportunity to see where the fertilizer was, and probably the old metal downpipe as well.'

'And to see that there was a key in the door,' said Joe.

'I looked on the shelf, to see if there was a spare key, but I didn't notice anything. I think that I'll have a word with the Reverend Mother about references and things like that for a new gardener, and I'll ask her whether she might have noticed that lady solicitor talking to a young fellow, about six-foot high, at the gate or over a hedge, or anything like that,' said Patrick. 'You could wander around and have a word with anyone you meet and ask the same questions. We won't make too much of a fuss. I must say that there are more than Miss Hogan who want the job of city council alderman and I'm not ruling them out by any means. And, of course, we have her link with the IRA, but then the IRA might have had a reason to kill the man that has nothing to do with Miss Hogan. They are responsible for a lot of murders in every city and town of Ireland. But at the moment, between ourselves, Joe, my money is on the lady.'

THIRTEEN

When, on the following morning, the green Bentley appeared again at the convent gates, the Reverend Mother was hugely relieved to see that, this time, Lucy was in the back seat of the car. She had feared that something serious had happened to a very beloved little great-grandchild.

Angela was the eldest of Lucy's grandchildren and, Reverend Mother always suspected, the favourite. After the death of her own mother in a late pregnancy, Angela had taken her position of eldest daughter to her grandparents. She was of huge importance to Lucy and to Rupert, caring in her efficient way for her grandparents as well as her own sisters and for her own child. Something serious must have happened to cause her to summon her own elderly grandmother to her aid and the Reverend Mother scanned Lucy's face anxiously as the chauffeur helped her out of the car.

'All is well. It was not diphtheria, after all. Angela panicked. Not like her, but this little one is very precious to her.'

'What was it?' The Reverend Mother was not surprised. The dreaded word diphtheria was probably in every mother's mind.

'Just tonsillitis – tonsillitis and a temperature. I felt I had to go to her. Her sisters all have concerns of their own. None would want to run the risk of bringing diphtheria into their homes. Poor Angela!'

Lucy's face was, as always, delicately and carefully made-up, dusted with a faint pink powder which mimicked perfect health and a slight flush of rouge on the cheek-bones. Normally, Lucy would pass for a woman twenty years younger than her real age, which the Reverend Mother, as they had been bought up together, knew as well as she knew her own. Today though, she thought, Lucy looked her full age. She slipped an arm affectionately around her cousin's waist and leaned forward to kiss her.

'I'm all right,' said Lucy, answering the unspoken sympathy. 'It was a bad night, though. Terribly high temperature. Angela kept on taking it and getting whiter and whiter every time. In the end I persuaded her to try the old-fashioned remedy and put the poor little mite into a cool bath. Worked well – she fell asleep afterwards. Makes sense to me – cool the blood – but nowadays the mothers want everything scientific and she could not be at rest until the doctor came back again. To give him his due, he turned up at eight o'clock in the morning. Shone a torch down her throat, said he was sure now that it was just tonsillitis, said that we had done the right thing to cool her down, prescribed some medicine or other. Everything is very technical, these days, not like when you and I were young, but I slipped down into the kitchen and luckily the cook had some carrageen moss, so I got her to boil it up with some brown sugar and squeeze a few lemons into it. The poor little thing drank it down, said '*werry* good' and off to sleep she went. Did her far more good than the doctor's medicines, I'd say, but of course, you try anything. Her temperature was down by the time I left. I told our man to drive me straight over here in case that you wanted to get out of the place.'

'You should have waited, gone for a sleep,' said the Reverend Mother, touched at her cousin's concern for her.

'I'm fine,' said Lucy, looking across at the devastation in the orchard cemetery. 'But how are you? Terrible, isn't it! I'm so upset about James Musgrave. Such a nice man. You would have liked him so much when you got to know him. He was so religious, went to mass every morning, early mass and took communion, very strict with the children about it also. Thinking of getting married again, too, poor fellow. Mind you, I'm not a fan of Kitty O'Shea, but there's no doubt that she's extremely rich. He met her when giving advice about buying stocks and shares with her spoils from her first marriage.'

The Reverend Mother smiled at the acid note in Lucy's voice and wondered fleetingly whether the extreme religiosity of the late Mr James Musgrave might have been instrumental in driving his sons to exile in Australia.

'Be careful what you say,' she said in a low voice, seeing the rigid form of Mother Teresa emerging from the convent door. 'The lady is a relation of the mother superior.' She nodded in the direction of Mother Teresa. 'Visited her cousin twice during the first couple of days of the retreat,' she added.

'Sixth cousin once removed, if you ask me,' said Lucy tartly. 'Come to play one off the other, is my bet.'

'I'm sorry you went to the trouble of coming all the way over here, Lucy,' said the Reverend Mother, lifting her voice slightly. 'I'm afraid that you've had your journey in vain. I would have liked to go back to St Mary's of the Isle, what with this outbreak of diphtheria and the unpleasant affair of the bomb, but the bishop is adamant that nothing should be allowed to interrupt the progress of our retreat. However, I do need your help, so I am glad to see you here.' Lucy, she noticed with amusement, had raised her tidily plucked eyebrows in a silent dissension from the bishop's verdict, but before she could say anything more, they were interrupted.

'Mrs Murphy!' The harsh tones, the over-loud voice, was immediately recognizable as the builder's and Reverend Mother said, 'Good morning, Mr O'Connor,' without even turning to face the intruder. She looked with concern at the dark shadows beneath Lucy's eyes and knew that her cousin had probably spent most of the night away, supporting poor Angela as she hung over the precious child and kept feeling the hot forehead. However, she needed Lucy. It was important to have her cousin with her when Patrick made another attempt to question the unfortunate daughter of the dead man. Lucy was used to girls, had her own daughters, then her granddaughters and now, despite her age, was the first port of call when a tiny great-granddaughter was in peril. She would handle Sister Mary Magdalene with her own unique mixture of coaxing and firmness.

There was, however, no stopping 'Bob the Builder' once he got going.

'So glad to see you, Mrs Murphy, and looking so well, too. You've heard of the terrible business here. The IRA, of course. Will we ever be free of them? A scourge on this distressful land, that's what they are, a scourge. No other word for it,'

he said, his eyes looking significantly across at the tall slim
figure of the lady solicitor and resting there long enough to
make it plain that this scourge on the land had even found its
way into the hallowed precincts of a convent graced by the
bishop's presence.

'Well, if you'll excuse . . .' began the Reverend Mother, but
Mr O'Connor was not to be dissuaded.

'I'm so glad to see you, Mrs Murphy. I was going to pop
in and see your husband, but I know what a busy man Mr
Murphy is – has all the cares of the most important people in
this city of ours – has all the cares resting on his shoulders.
Yes,' he said emphatically, 'I said to him one day, "What you
want, Mr Murphy, is a nice little conservatory built onto the
south side of your house and then you could sit out there in
the sun, stretch out and enjoy yourself and even have a nice
little nap, and with proper glazing you'd be able to use it
winter and summer." And he said to me, "You are quite right,
Mr O'Connor!", and you should have seen the way that his
face lit up at the very thought of it – you should have seen it,
Mrs Murphy, and you too, Reverend Mother. Poor man, God
love him, he works too hard.'

The Reverend Mother thought the moment had come
when she needed to get rid of this wretched man. Lucy looked
too exhausted to do her job forcibly enough.

'I fear we must leave you now, Mr O'Connor,' she said
firmly. 'Mrs Murphy and I need to see the mother superior of
this convent.'

He babbled on a minute, uttering some disjointed sentences,
but she ignored him and, taking Lucy's arm, marched her
firmly in the direction of the convent.

'Dreadful man,' said Lucy in an undertone as the words
'good discount' came floating after them. Lucy gave a slight
giggle and held her handkerchief to her lips. 'No wonder he
says Rupert looks harassed whenever he sees him. He's been
pestering the life out of him about this wretched conservatory.
He managed to build one, at huge expense, for the Crosbies,
and the wretched building is nothing but a nuisance to them.
You know what winds we get up there on Montenotte, and
every time there is a north-westerly, a pane or two of glass

falls out and a few more plants die. An ugly-looking thing it is, too. Rupe dives back into the office every time he sees that wretched man coming!'

'"Good discount" is interesting, though,' said the Reverend Mother thoughtfully. 'You know, Lucy, it strikes me that there must be a very considerable advantage, over and above any salary, to be got from this position of alderman. People seem to want to pay for the privilege.'

'Well, a non-stop flow of bribes would come their way once they are in office, according to Rupert,' said Lucy cheerfully.

The Reverend Mother raised her eyebrows but decided that bribes were none of her business and she dismissed the subject of the builder from her mind. At least his loud voice had made Mother Teresa move well away. 'I'm so glad that you managed to come, Lucy,' she said. 'That poor girl, James Musgrave's daughter, is in a wretched state. The police, of course, will have to interview her, a very short interview Patrick assures me, but neither the mother superior here, nor the mistress of novices, seem to be on sympathetic terms with her and so I thought if you, as a neighbour and close friend of the family . . .?'

'Yes, of course, poor little Nellie.' Lucy was immediately concerned. 'Yes, she was quite a friend of my youngest grand-daughter. I was amazed when she entered the convent, but that is always the way. Those who seem the least suited for the life often surprise you by taking it all so seriously. Mind you, if she had been my daughter, or granddaughter, then I'd have got her to wait for a few years. Girls change their minds so quickly at that age! They go through these religious phases and then they're boy-mad and then they want a career, and then they change their minds again and want to get married. You just have to keep an eye on them and know the moment when to talk sense to them. And, of course, that poor girl lost her mother at around eight years old. Missed her terribly, poor little thing.'

'Here's Mother Teresa, the superior of this convent,' said the Reverend Mother. She would have liked to have had some time to brief Lucy, but her voice, she knew, held a warning note. She and Lucy knew each other well enough for that warning note to be picked up. She would not need to give any instructions. Lucy was always so adroit.

Her cousin went forward now, both hands held out, her face filled with sympathy. 'Oh, Mother Teresa,' she said. 'What a dreadful thing to happen! And on consecrated ground, also!'

'My dear Mrs Murphy! How well you understand. That is what makes it all such a nightmare.'

Would it, wondered the Reverend Mother wickedly, have been better if the bomb had exploded on unconsecrated ground, in a shop, or even on a road full of people? At least, with this bomb, only one life was lost, and she was thankful for that. She listened with admiration to Lucy's flow of commiseration.

Mother Teresa visibly thawed. She bowed her head with the air of a martyr and looked upon Lucy with favour. Nuns, thought the Reverend Mother, with a moment of exasperation, are such terrible snobs. She wondered whether she, also, was affected by the disease. Perhaps, she admitted, her courting of the well-off in the city, the smile of approval she bestowed on such who were liberal contributors to her school and its associated charities, or those who, she guessed, had the potential to be turned in that direction – perhaps that also was a form of snobbery. Lucy, as the wife of one of the wealthiest and the most esteemed citizens of Cork, was given the full sunshine of the mother superior's smile.

'Terrible, terrible,' said Lucy with practised ease. 'He was a neighbour of ours, of course. His poor wife, God have mercy on her, was one of my best friends. And, of course, the little girl, you have her here in your convent, I understand; well, she was in and out of our house so much during her years of growing up; went to school with one of my granddaughters. Her mother was dead, died when she was eight years old, and those brothers of hers were very wild, up to all sort of mischief, so, poor little thing, she would come in and play with the little girls in my garden whenever they visited. I must say that I was as fond of her as I was of my own,' said Lucy with a sentimental sigh and a sharp sideways glance at Mother Teresa. It wasn't working, thought the Reverend Mother. Her sister in

Christ, the mother superior of the Sisters of Charity, had a stiff look about her. Not stupid. Beginning to suspect.

Nevertheless, Lucy ploughed on bravely. 'How fortunate it is to think that she is here under your care, with the other sisters to bear her company, instead of being left alone in that empty house. It brought tears to my eyes when I drove past it this morning. I had to stop and go in and tell the servants to lower all the blinds and to close the shutters. Worrying about whether they would get paid! That's what they were doing! Would you believe it, Mother Teresa!'

That worked! Mother Teresa gave a sigh at the wicked, self-seeking nature of lay servants as the Reverend Mother spared a moment's compunction for the delinquents who were more interested in their weekly stipend than in closing curtains and lowering blinds. Who was looking after matters? she wondered. As far as she knew, the dead man did not have a partner; secretaries and other office workers, she supposed, but nobody to take charge automatically.

'Such a dreadful thing to happen, and here in the most peaceful spot in Cork.' Lucy, having established a common ground between herself and Mother Teresa, wisely went back to sympathy. 'Now is there anything that I can do for you, Mother Teresa. My cousin, Reverend Mother Aquinas, tells me that you have the additional burden of the police hanging around and wanting to question everyone.' Here Lucy threw a disdainful glance across at Patrick and Joe, conferring in low tones over shared notebooks. 'You'd think that the police would move back down to the city, now,' she said in lowered tones. 'They must have seen everything that they need to and must have had enough time to interview everybody,' she went on, and then gave an exasperated shake of her head. 'Oh, I suppose that they haven't been able to interview little Nellie yet. She has collapsed, has she? I remember her well. Used to alarm her poor father with these floods of tears. "Leave her to me, James," I used to say to him, poor man. Of course, as you probably know, they were without a woman in the house, except servants, of course. "Leave her to me, James. I've had a lifetime of experience of girls of this age – what between all my daughters and all of their daughters, I could write a

book on how to handle the tears and the hysteria. Stand back!"
I used to say to him. "Take yourself off. Go for a walk, or
better still, take your golf clubs and go off for a game." And
it will be no surprise to you, Mother Teresa, with your experience of young girls, but by the time that he came back, there
she was, all the tears gone, good as gold, in my kitchen, baking
him a little cake for his supper.'

Mother Teresa was beginning to look impressed. 'Of course,'
she said confidentially, addressing herself to the Reverend
Mother as well as to Lucy, 'at that age a lot of the tears and
the hysteria are nothing but attention-seeking, don't you
agree?'

'Just what I always say,' said Lucy with the air of one who
was vastly impressed by the sanity of the mother superior.
'You've found out through experience, of course. All those
girls going through your hands and becoming calm and useful
members of society, doing such wonderfully good work for
the community.'

'Well, I did allow her to go to bed, but now, I think—'

'You're so right,' said Lucy admiringly. 'The secret is to
pick the right moment, isn't it? Would it help if you said that
I was here and would like to see her? Of course, as a lay
person, I would not wish to intrude upon the inner sanctum
of the convent . . .' Lucy allowed her sentence to falter on a
slightly indecisive note while the Reverend Mother held her
breath. Either way, she thought, Lucy had probably won.

Either Mother Teresa would have to admit that her convent
was not sacred in any way and that any casual visitor could
go tripping up the stairs to invade the young novices' dormitory, or else, and certainly preferable, that Sister Mary
Magdalen should be extracted from her bed, made to dress
herself and to come downstairs and out into the open air. She
thought that if gambling were not a sin, that she would like
to put a most substantial bet upon the latter solution.

'Yes, I thought I would give into her for just some time
as she fainted while carrying out her duties, but by now . . .'
Mother Teresa said as she looked up at the clock on the
convent wall. 'Well, she has had an hour or so to recover
– time for her to get up and come out into the fresh air. After

all, she had already given up all family ties and therefore, though obviously she has had a shock, she should – well, I always say to my mistress of novices, "Teach the girls to have moderation in all things".' Mother Teresa beckoned to a lay sister who was picking some herbs from a pretty circular bed and said in her authoritative way, 'Ask Mother Carmel to send Sister Mary Magdalene to me immediately.' And then she relaxed with a self-satisfied manner.

The Reverend Mother gave Lucy an appreciative glance and then lifted a beckoning finger towards Patrick, whose eyes had strayed in her direction quite a few times during the long conversation. He, she noticed, had a quick word with Joe but, she was glad to see, did not invite his assistant to come with him, just advanced bare-headed and alone to greet Mother Teresa in a quiet and restful tone before turning to Lucy and telling her to thank her husband for his message and that he would be going into the South Mall as soon as he had finished all of his interviews here at the convent. Lucy received his communication with an approving nod and the mother superior of the Sisters of Charity convent looked at him with the air of someone who had, perhaps, misjudged the import- ance of a visitor to her convent. It was obvious that Patrick, with his easy acquaintance of not just the wife of an important solicitor, but also with the Reverend Mother from St Mary's of the Isle, had suddenly gone up in her estimation. She gave Patrick an approving glance which seemed to give him permission to question her further.

At that point he opened his notebook and read out the names of all at the convent whom he had seen and invited Mother Teresa to mention any others whom she felt that he should interview.

What a lot of trouble this ridiculous woman is causing, everyone is having to pussy-foot around her, thought the Reverend Mother impatiently, though she preserved a peaceful silence and knew from long experience that her rather-expressionless, pale face and heavily hooded green eyes, would reveal nothing of her thoughts.

Her thoughts were mixed. There was sorrow for the unfortunate, doubly-orphaned girl, but also a pride in Patrick

– thousands of children from the slum area of the south side
of Cork city had gone through her hands. Some were memor-
able for a variety of reasons; some she had lost sight of;
some she had continued to take an interest in, even when they
were grandmothers; some, like Eileen, she had picked out,
from the start, as being exceptionally clever, the only one that
she could recollect, who had come to school already able to
read and to write. Patrick, however, she remembered for his
perseverance, his hard work, though he had not stood out in
any way as being clever. It would have been difficult, she
often thought, these days, with a certain measure of almost
maternal pride, to have predicted the evolution of this calm,
competent, quite well-spoken police inspector from the
tear-stained, rather dirty and ragged little boy whom she
remembered at the age of five as enduring a hard time from
his teacher because of his persistence in accomplishing a
self-appointed task of counting the number of ants going into
a hole in the school playground before he obeyed her instructions to go back into the classroom. Now she watched with
interest to see how he managed this unhelpful woman.

'Ah, yes, Sister Mary Magdalene.' Mother Teresa pronounced
the name in a rather non-committal voice.

'You would wish to be present?' said Patrick, addressing
her in a scrupulously polite fashion.

Mother Teresa hesitated. Lucy made a sympathetic face.
Such are the trials of high office, her expression seemed to
say. And then a flash of inspiration came across her expressive
face.

'Could I help in anyway?' she asked with a humble note
in her voice. 'You must be so busy. My cousin, Reverend
Mother Aquinas, has often made use of me in lay situations.
Of course, she knows how experienced I am with these
young girls.' Lucy bestowed a smile upon the Reverend
Mother, who preserved a discreet silence and tucked her
hands into her sleeves.

'Do you know,' said Mother Teresa, after a few moments
of rather tense silence had elapsed, 'I do believe, Mrs Murphy,
that someone like you would be the right person to talk to this
girl. In confidence, and between us three,' she said, lowering

her voice and turning her back to Patrick. 'Yes, in confidence, I have to say that she has not been the most satisfactory of novices. If it were not for her father's conviction that she had made the right decision, I would have hesitated to allow her to progress from the position of novice to professed sister. And of course, now, she is left upon our hands.' Mother Teresa paused for a moment and then bestowed a smile upon Lucy. 'Yes, well, it's extremely kind of you, Mrs Murphy, and I think that given the fact that you have known the girl from an early age and will have been to a certain extent, like another mother to her, well, I do think that if Inspector Cashman is happy, that might well be the best solution. Not that I can see that the girl can have anything of use to say to you, Inspector,' she finished in a slightly snappy fashion.

Patrick was busy making a few small marks on a fresh page of his notebook and did not raise his head for a moment.

'Sister Mary Magdalen did not speak to her father alone on any occasion, then?' he said with a note of query in his voice.

There was a moment's silence and then Mother Teresa succumbed. 'Now that you mention the matter, Inspector,' she said, 'well, no, that is not correct. Sister Mary Magdalene did speak alone with her father. It's not usual, of course, but given the circumstances, given that Mr Musgrave was here as a guest of the bishop, well, I did consent to her being alone and not supervised in any way. She was coming near to the time when she would take her final vows, and so I always think it wise that, in certain circumstances, the families have private access to the girls in case there are any problems afterwards, any suggestion of undue coercion or influence by the convent. Their decision, their final vows, Inspector, need to be taken in full and certain knowledge that this is what they want and that it is their choice to devote their future lives to the service of God.'

Patrick's face did not change in any way and he made another note in his notebook. The Reverend Mother admired, in a detached way, how adept he was at shorthand and wondered rather mischievously whether those cryptic symbols were a blueprint for the stepping stones that a novice had to undergo before becoming a fully-fledged nun, or related to some quite different matter. She was pleased that permission had been granted, though. It was, after all, quite possible that James Musgrave, a man who lived alone and appeared to have no close friends, had expressed some worry, some threat even, to his daughter.

The child looked terrible when she came hesitantly through the convent door and out onto the terrace, approaching her mother superior and companions with a face which, oddly, seemed to show an expression of intense fear. Even alarmed at the sight of Lucy, whom she must have instantly recognized, because Lucy, in her cousin's opinion, had not changed in any particle during the last the twenty years or so – the hair, tinted ash blond, the perfect make-up, the youthful figure clad in the most expensive clothes that could be purchased in Cork or Dublin, all of these things could not have changed during the months since the girl had left her father's home.

Lucy, on the contrary, did not hesitate for a moment. 'My dear child,' she said warmly. 'Let me look at you.' Impulsively, she bent forward and kissed the girl on the cheek, and then, with a swift movement which could have been forethought, she tucked her arm inside the girl's and without a moment's indecisiveness, marched her to where the sun shone over the four-foot-high wall between the convent grounds and the road leading down to the city.

An excellent choice, thought the Reverend Mother. Standing side by side, neither needed to look at the other, no feeling of being scrutinized and enough random, unrelated objects to look at, such as horses pulling hay wains, countrymen walking from field to field; enough sounds to listen to such as birdsong and the distant mooing of cows separated from their calves, and the raucous squawks of a shouting match between two rival cuckoos – plenty of distractions to fill an awkward silence for a girl who did not know what to say. And, of course, by her side, a woman whom she had known for her entire home life.

Patrick gave them a couple of minutes, and then he, too, strolled over and went to stand on the other side of the girl. The Reverend Mother hoped that he had rehearsed his questions. There was something about the utter rigidity of the thin form of the girl that worried her immensely. She cast a quick glance over at the car and at the chauffeur standing leaning on the bonnet, smoking peacefully. Could Lucy work her magic to get permission to take her neighbour's child home with her, to shelter her, at least until the funeral was over?

There was a slight stir in the distance and for once she welcomed the sight of the rotund figure of the bishop issuing forth from the small church, surrounded by the four remaining candidates for the coveted position of alderman on the Cork city council.

'I think that my lord bishop may be looking for you, Mother Teresa,' she said, salving her conscience with the knowledge that the bishop almost invariably was looking for someone and that he rarely allowed other conversations in his vicinity without drawing his flock beneath his sheltering wing. She herself took a few steps forward, smiling graciously, and at the sight of her the three men and the one woman fell back a little as if acknowledging her superior claim of access to the bishop.

'Mother Teresa and I have been discussing the question of poor Sister Mary Magdalen attending the funeral of her father, my lord,' she said, and stopped there in the sure and certain knowledge that the bishop was bound to have an opinion on the matter and if, by luck, his opinion colluded with her own, it would then be most difficult, almost impossible, for Mother Teresa to express an opposing point of view.

The bishop was in an amiable mood and had, as usual, a keen eye for the important citizens in his diocese. He looked with pleasure at Lucy's trim figure and expensive clothing.

'Mrs Rupert Murphy,' he stated and raised an amiable hand in what was half a greeting and half a blessing.

'My cousin has come to bring, if she can, some comfort to the unfortunate daughter of the late Mr Musgrave,' said the Reverend Mother as rapidly as she could. 'Of course, Sister Mary Magdalene has no family left to support her in this most sad time. I understand that her two brothers are out in Australia and so the arrangements for the funeral . . .' She allowed her voice to tail off at that point and hoped that his lordship's brain had not been slowed by the very excellent and enormous breakfast that she had seen him consume.

'Of course, the funeral.' The bishop sounded worried about this complication and she hastened to reassure him.

'I think that Mr Rupert Murphy, and his wife, my cousin, will take the matter into their own hands, my lord,' she said reassuringly. 'I understand that the late Mr Musgrave's monetary affairs, the will and other matters, will be dealt by the South Mall practice.'

'Of course, of course.' The bishop, who, like Shakespeare's Richard II, did like to talk of wills, noticeably cheered up at this point. 'Poor child,' he said compassionately with his eye on the thin, pale face. 'How sad to lose such a father. The chaplain was telling me that the novices were cleaning the church just as the bomb went off. What a dreadful thing for a daughter to witness. Such a worthy man.'

'A most religious man, my cousin was telling me. Always a daily communicant and a contributor to charity, I believe,' said the Reverend Mother.

Luckily, that brought the bishop's mind back to the possibility of a substantial donation to the church that might be revealed once the dead man's will had been opened and read. It also, judging by his expression, made him look with even more compassion on the girl, who, as she was a member of a religious order, could not inherit any of the late stockbroker's substantial fortune.

'Come, Reverend Mother,' he said graciously, 'let us go and greet your cousin and see what she thinks would be best for the poor child. Perhaps it would be easier for her to attend the funeral under the wing of a neighbour and a close friend.' The bishop was in an amiable mood and had, as usual, a keen eye for the important citizens in his diocese.

The Reverend Mother followed him obediently. She was pleased with the success of her scheme, but there was, however, something troubling her, some puzzle in her mind. When the bishop had artlessly repeated his chaplain's words in his clear and carrying voice, there had been a sudden change in the atmosphere, and she could not quite lay a finger on what, exactly, she had noticed. Not a gasp, nothing as overt as that. It was, she thought, almost as if one of the attendants on the bishop – either Mr O'Connor, the builder; Mr Hamilton, the factory owner; Mr Pat Pius, the provider of shoes for the indigent citizens of the city; or indeed, the young lady solicitor, Miss Maureen Hogan, the person who had spent years in an entangled relationship with the IRA, who could well have laid the bomb for her, sometime in the dead of the night or at dawn, and left her with the task of igniting the makeshift fuse – one of them had suddenly caught a breath, had ceased to move, had in some way which she could not even explain to herself, reacted to that news that the daughter of the dead man may have been within an inch of seeing his murderer at work. It could, thought the Reverend Mother, have been any one of them, as, indeed, it could have been any one of them who had slipped through the orchard cemetery and ignited the lethal bomb.

The bishop was full of affability as he shook Lucy by the hand and enquired tenderly after all her daughters and granddaughters. Passing over, with grace and charm, the fact that he could not produce a single name of any of them, he professed to remember every single occasion when he had conferred the sacrament of confirmation upon the numerous young ladies.

From time to time, the bishop, now in a most benign mood, looked with pity at the white face and the red-rimmed eyes of the young novice. After a minute or two, and with gracious words to be conveyed to the highly esteemed husband of Mrs Murphy, he allowed Lucy to kiss his ring and strolled back in the direction of Mother Teresa, who was standing rather stiffly on the terrace outside the convent. The bishop opened the subject instantly, looking to the Reverend Mother for her support.

'The young novice looks quite ill,' he said abruptly.

Mother Teresa bowed her head, but she made no comment. Her face was stony and would have been discouraging to anyone other than the bishop.

He, however, went ahead as smoothly as though he had received an enthusiastic endorsement. 'I would feel, and I'm sure that you must agree with me, Mother Teresa, that it would be better for her to spend a few days away from this environment in which her father was so savagely murdered. What do you think, Mother Teresa?' Though he had a note of query in his voice, he didn't wait for an answer, but swept on, smoothly enunciating the words in the rather God-given manner which he adopted from time to time.

'Yes,' he said with an air of impartially approving of his own judgement, 'yes, I do think, though it might not be quite orthodox, that a few nights in the home of her father's best friends will help her to prepare for the ordeal of his funeral. There is, of course, no possibility whatsoever of contacting the brothers in Australia in time for their return. What do you feel, Mrs Murphy?' he said addressing Lucy who, on cue, arrived holding the hand of the stricken orphan.

Lucy will have her hands full; that girl looks on the edge of a nervous breakdown, thought the Reverend Mother, while she bowed her head in acceptance of the bishop's verdict. She wished that Dr Scher were here. A strong dose of a sleeping draught would be the kindest thing. That girl needed help in distancing herself a little from the appalling tragedy of her father's death.

Mother Teresa also nodded her acquiescence. She could do no more. The bishop was in supreme charge over them all. He took his power from God and they owed perfect obedience to him.

The four candidates had stood a little back, but four pairs of eyes were fixed upon the girl. Was it pity in all of them or did one of them wear a slightly different expression? Yes, thought the Reverend Mother, bowing her head so that her veil cloaked her face, yes, oddly enough it was not one of the men, but the lady solicitor who looked with such scorn, almost dislike, upon the face of the devastated young novice. Did she, perhaps, despise one who had all the advantages of wealth and education and yet who had not chosen to study for a profession, whether for law or medicine, or even teaching, but who had instead retired from life and taken refuge in a convent. Was that, wondered the Reverend Mother, the reason for that rather strange expression on the young woman's face? Or was there, perhaps, a more sinister reason?

FOURTEEN

Eileen stared at her motorbike with an expression of blank fury. Just when she had a lot to do and just when she needed it, it was not going to start for her.

'Give it a bit of a kick,' advised one of the messenger boys. Eileen rewarded him with a cold look. She was in a bad mood. The room had been too noisy for her to put her thoughts into words. Everything seemed to distract her and the words which normally flowed easily to her fingertips, just did not seem to come, almost like a stream that had dried up. After half an hour of struggle, she got to her feet, took her bag, and walked out. Although, welcome to use a spare typewriter, she was not an employee of the *Cork Examiner*; she did not need to keep office hours or to make any explanations.

Usually when she came into the office and began pounding on the ancient typewriter model now semi-officially reserved for her usage, she had an article already outlined in her mind, just as clearly as if her brain was a sheet of white paper where all the words, all the punctuation, all the arguments were already outlined and could flow from brain to fingers without the slightest hesitation. Somehow, though she was excited by the hints that had been dropped and by the whole story that her brain was building up, there wasn't enough material there – she had not fully understood the matter well enough to write a good article. It was all very well for her to announce dramatically that she was going to take 'innuendo' as her watchword. That was the right way to handle it, and she had seen the quick nod of approval and the slight glint of perhaps admiration – certainly of interest – in John Fitzpatrick's eyes when she had announced her intention, but now she realized that she did not have enough information. She needed to visualize the whole article before she started to write it. It was no good,

she knew, asking John Fitzpatrick for more meat to cover
the bones of the story; he had given her all that he was
prepared to give – had not wanted to be involved – after all,
why had he not written the story himself if he had thought
it would be right – would be safe – for him to do so? No,
he had made her a present of a little information and he
had paid her quite a compliment when he done so. Now it
was up to her to flesh out those bare bones and to write a
piece, an article which would get the whole of Cork talking
over their breakfast toast.

But now her motorbike wouldn't work, and her plans were
ruined.

There was a repair garage nearby, but she had no luck
there, also. Yes, they'd send someone up to collect the motorbike, but there wasn't a hope that anyone could look at it
before tomorrow morning at the earliest. He shook his head
at her and went back to stripping down the engine of a van.
She walked away in a bad mood. There was nothing for it but
to go home, have her tea and hope that inspiration would
dawn. If not, she would just have to be content with the
payment for the article about the gardener.

And then, just as she was about to emerge from the dark
little street and join the crowds on Patrick Street, there was a
sharp beep of a horn. She stopped, looked around and then
saw Maureen Hogan.

'Want a lift?' The young solicitor stuck her head through
the window in a friendly fashion and Eileen was grateful for
that. She had feared that since she had turned down the offer
of an apprenticeship they might be on bad terms, but Maureen
wore a friendly smile, so she guessed that it might just be a
spur of the moment offer, and that Maureen probably knew,
as well as she did herself, that it would not afford a new
recruit much experience.

Eileen had dropped a hint that there might be an offer of
an apprenticeship from a solicitor on the South Mall, and
that had very much impressed Maureen, who had served
her own apprenticeship in the office of her father, who was
a man with a small practice and not much of a reputation
in the city.

'Lovely day,' she said now in a friendly fashion. 'Are you busy, or what would you say to a drive out into the countryside?'

'Love it,' said Eileen enthusiastically, and she went around to the other side of the car and pulled open the rather rickety door. 'I thought you were saying your prayers, with the bishop, no less,' she said, climbing into the front seat of the shabby, second-hand Baby Ford. 'This car is a bit of a mess, isn't it,' she said, with a glance at the back seat which looked as if someone had taken a knife to the leather. 'Want a hand to fix it up a bit?'

'Who cares if it's a mess! That's how I managed to afford it,' said Maureen carelessly. 'Well, what do you say? Shall we go to the sea? Look at that sun! Never known a summer as good as this.'

'Let's go to Youghal,' said Eileen with a sudden inspiration. Youghal was a seaside resort in east Cork – bound to be crowded with trainloads of people on a day like today. Two girls would not be noticed going there and they would probably soon be tired of it – Maureen got tired of things very quickly – and then she could propose a circuitous route back through the east Cork countryside. Eileen could get a feel for the place, even have a look around and perhaps walk through the small town where Wee Willie had his stocking factory. It was, she realized with a flash of excitement, perfect. She would worry if she had betrayed Fitzpatrick. He had, she remembered guiltily, told her very firmly to go back to the office and had made, now that she came to think of it, a remark about not wanting her on her motorbike to be making herself conspicuous in that area.

'Come on! What's the bishop going to say if you are caught mitching?'

'Got tired of it all,' said Maureen, in a careless fashion. 'Don't think I have a hope of getting any votes from the bishop or from his priests or from anyone under his thumb.'

'Most of Cork, in other words,' said Eileen. She wanted to keep Maureen in a good mood and open to her suggestions, but she did not believe her. As the car was being manipulated around a tricky bend, she glanced curiously at her companion. Didn't look her usual cheery self! Maureen was very pale and when she was not talking, her lips had tightened to the degree that small lines had appeared on either side of her mouth. Something was wrong. She was sure of that. People didn't go out of their way to offend the bishop. He had the reputation of never forgiving a man or woman who went against his views and his influence in the city was enormous. Of course, Maureen may have decided that if she were going to endeavour to bring IRA policies and socialist viewpoints to the city council, that she was going to incur his enmity, inevitably, but that would be a different matter once she was elected. Then it would be one councillor, one vote. And if by a lucky chance she managed to get elected as lord mayor in the following year, then she would have considerable power in her hands.

'Does he know that you walked out?' she asked curiously.

'Oh, for goodness' sake, stop cross-questioning me,' said Maureen crossly. She had a look of strain upon her face and Eileen began to get suspicious. Of course, the bishop would not be the only power up there in the Convent of the Sisters of Charity.

'You look worn out,' she said sympathetically. 'Patrick Cashman making a nuisance of himself?' she enquired. 'I suppose that he's very suspicious of you. That fertilizer bomb would shout IRA to him.'

'Nah – I can handle men like that.' Maureen's words sounded as though she were unperturbed, but there was a line between her eyes and the hand on the steering wheel seemed to grip it rather tightly.

Eileen glanced at her, and then glanced away. She had her own fish to fry. If Patrick suspected Maureen Hogan, well, then it was up to him to find the proof. He would not like her to interfere in any way, was never one to take a friendly word of advice from her, but she did wonder whether Maureen could have rigged up that bomb. It sounded a very amateur affair. The gardener had told her all about it – about the rusty old downpipe, about the lack of a timer, he had warned her not to mention that in her article, and she hadn't as she did not want to get him into trouble, but that did

sound very amateur and very 'hit-and-miss'. Whoever shoved
that fertilizer and diesel into an upright drainpipe, and then
took the terrible chance of dropping a match or a lighted
screw of newspaper down upon the lethal mixture of ammo-
nium nitrate and fuel – well, that had been a terribly
dangerous thing to do. The work of an amateur, she was
sure of that. None of the lads with whom she had worked
during her teenage years in the IRA would have done
anything so haphazard. A bomb like that would have been
as likely to blow up the man or woman who planted it, as
it would have been to kill the chosen victim.

Would Maureen have been so keen on being an alderman
that she was prepared to blow up one, or perhaps the entire
bunch, of her rivals?

Youghal turned out to be a failure. It was a Wednesday
afternoon, half day for most of the schools in the city and the
train from Midleton and from Cork, puffing vigorously, had
just drawn into the station as they drove into the town. It
seemed as though thousands of women and children, almost
like the whole population of Cork, streamed off it and went
shrieking and shouting, and waving small buckets and spades,
large picnic baskets and sun hats as they made their way to
the beach.

And what was worse, the tide was in, right in, covering the
whole of the half a mile of sand and the waves were crashing
over the wall and onto the pavements.

'God! I can't stand this place. We'll have to go somewhere
else. Those screaming children will give me a pain in my head.
There was I thinking that we could lie on the sand and have
a nice sunbathe.' Maureen's lips were tight with fury.

Eileen looked at her with interest. Well, yes it was
crowded, but there was no harm in it. They could have gone
for a walk along the seafront and the weather was so hot
that it would have almost been pleasant to duck in and out
of the spray of fresh sea water. Nicer than the streets of
Cork, anyway, where in hot weather the River Lee stank to
high heaven and a green scum formed over the stagnant
waters of the river. Something, she decided, had upset
Maureen. Must be Patrick, she thought and smiled to herself

at how much she would tease him about upsetting an important solicitor like Miss Hogan.

'Let's go for a drive,' she said with a shrug of her shoulders, as though to indicate that she had no preferences, and then, as if inspiration had suddenly struck, she said, 'What about going up to Watergrasshill? We can pick some fresh sprigs of watergrass. You can have it for your tea.'

'I haven't a clue as to how to find the place, so I hope you are good at reading signposts.' Maureen gave an indifferent shrug. She was very much on tenterhooks, thought Eileen. She continually looked over her shoulder, and when a policeman in his Garda Siochana uniform arrived, Maureen gave a terrible start and turned very pale.

'Guilty conscience,' said Eileen gaily, but was sorry for her joke when Maureen rounded upon her angrily and asked her what she meant.

'Sorry!' said Eileen. 'I forgot that you've had the rozzers on top of you, up there at the convent. Have they found out who killed the fella, yet?'

'Who cares,' said Maureen in such a surly tone that Eileen decided to avoid the subject.

She had an aim for this afternoon, she reminded herself, so she sat very quietly and soaked up the atmosphere and looked eagerly through the window as Maureen directed the car away from the Midleton area and towards the rich lands of east Cork.

'Well, Anglo-Irish settlement or not, you have to say this is a nice part of the countryside.' Maureen sounded to be in a better humour. 'Wish I didn't have to do law,' she said, after a few minutes of driving quietly through the well-tended farms with their small patches of woodland here and there, looking intensely green in the June sunlight.

'What did you want to do?' asked Eileen. More than ever, she was glad to have been talked out of joining the Maureen Hogan Practice. She, herself, was full of enthusiasm for the law, dying to be qualified, to be sitting at a desk, scanning leather-bound books and leafing through parchment copies of deeds. She wanted to know the law so well, that she could stand up for the poor, for the patriotic and for those threatened with injustice. 'What did you want to do if you didn't do law, Maureen?' She repeated her question, but it was a while before Maureen answered. And before she did so she stopped the car just where there was a break in the hedge that lined the fields. They sat there for a couple of minutes in silence, looking out through the car windscreen. The hawthorn had been recently trimmed and lowered to a neat bank, barely the height of cow's shoulders, and over the top of it they could see the house that stood in the background.

'Just look at that house,' said Maureen, and there was a strange note in her voice. 'Just look at it. Isn't it perfect? They call that kind of house a Queen Anne, it's a style of building from the time of Queen Anne. I don't know whether she had any interest in building or not, but the houses built in that time are just so perfect. Look at them. See the way everything balances, look at the way the windows are set. And the height and the width – it all fits together. Even the slant of the roof is perfect.'

Eileen leaned back in the car seat. She found that she was quite enjoying herself. It appeared that Maureen had wanted to be an architect, had wanted to design beautiful houses, to start a new age of perfection and make the Irish landscape beautiful instead of flooding it with ugly concrete and brick, to make sure that builders used the lovely limestone which was so plentiful below the surface of the fields they were looking at.

After a while, they drove on, but Maureen never ceased to talk and as she talked, Eileen found herself, for the first time in her life, to be experiencing a certain sympathy for those intruders who had, as she had always been told, stolen the land from the Irish people. Stolen, yes. But nevertheless, these men, soldiers, commanders of regiments, had built some beautiful homes, had landscaped the ground, had planted orchards and woodlands, had filled the countryside with stately oak and chestnuts and beautiful orchards of pears and apples. They had needed houses, of course, but they had taken care that these houses would fit well into the landscape. And they had built them from local stone, that

crisply silver-white limestone which lay beneath the surface
all through the counties of east Cork, Limerick and Tipperary,
the Golden Vale of Ireland. An easy stone to cut and to
shape to a purpose, Maureen told her, and she could see for
herself that there was a perfection about the curve of the
small stone bridges that arched above the many rivers. Even
the lodges at gates, the schools for children of the workers,
built here and there, though small and old fashioned, were
little jewels of perfection. Through Maureen's worshipping
eyes, Eileen saw it all, was led to understand how beautifully and symmetrically built were the stable yards, framed
by the stone stables for the horses, and paved flagstones
surrounding small pump houses in the central yard.

It was only when they came into the town, whose name and
spelling she had so carefully memorized when eating her lunch
with John Fitzpatrick, that she saw ugliness.

There were still a few traces of what she now could identify
as buildings in the style of Queen Anne: a clergyman's house,
with its regular pattern of windows; an old Protestant
church with a single yew in the churchyard and a beautifully
shaped spire piercing the blue sky; a library, whose Queen
Anne windows were disfigured with some notices and a few
ugly replacements.

But marring all, standing out in its sheer ugliness, was
Hamilton's Stocking Factory, made from ugly corrugated iron,
already beginning to rust. And when Eileen gazed upon it,
suddenly she knew that she had found the theme for her article.
She would paint a verbal picture of all those lovely houses,
carefully memorizing the words that Maureen had used; would
give dates for as many as she could and then she would come
onto this ugly factory. The title of her article would be THE
STRANGER IN OUR LAND, and the theme would be that
good and bad had come with those strangers. Nothing to alarm
even the Cumann na Gael fellows, but she would speculate
on the reasons for a factory to be moved from Belfast down
to this obscure village in a rural area of east Cork. No reason
not to give the man's name, not even any reason why she
should not state that this man, a stranger to Cork, was trying
to get onto the city council. And, she would argue, should not

the new buildings, so desperately badly needed for the unfortunate citizens still living in rat-infested, crumbling
buildings, in conditions of dreadful poverty, should not these
new houses for the unfortunates be built so as not to disgrace
the beauty of the countryside.

'Yes,' she said in answer to a question from Maureen. 'Yes,
let's get back. I have an article to write for the *Cork Examiner*.
Hope it gets into tomorrow morning's edition.'

FIFTEEN

The Reverend Mother missed the pleasant calm of the orchard cemetery. Everywhere she went she seemed to be accosted by people wanting to have her opinion or to discuss politics and so she edged her way around the gardener's shed and made her way towards the clump of woodland at the far side of a field of potato plants.

I'm getting old, she said to herself as she stumbled on an uneven path. The ground was rough and her shoes unsuitable for anything but walking upon paths. She was about to go back when she noticed, well inside the shade of the woodland, a small seat, made from elm, she guessed, by the look of the wood. It bore an unused appearance, just the stump of an old tree with straight willow rods inserted into the earth behind it, carefully interwoven with some slim wands giving the seat an inviting appearance. Perhaps some huge old tree had been felled in a storm and the gardener had carved this seat from its remains.

Or perhaps not the gardener, not that young man who mowed the lawns and cared for the potatoes and for the apple trees. There had been a gardener at work here, but not a professional gardener. Just one who loved plants and who had gathered them and planted them in this secret spot. Here and there were clumps of foxgloves mixed with the frail white flowers of wild garlic and a dog rose had been trained to make an arch, artistically spanning the slight gap between the elm trees and framing the view of the distant city of Cork.

There were signs, discovered the Reverend Mother, as she looked closely at the stump and at the barely covered heap of crumbled wood on the ground beside the seat, that hands had recently scraped off, from time to time, rotten wood from the stump turning it into a slightly sunken seat. The crumbs of this decayed wood had been colonized by thick cushions of moss, forming a circle around the seat, and some

careful hand had framed these small verdant islands with
clusters of primrose and violet plants which must have been
very pretty in the spring. There were also, she found, as she
looked around, a couple of beds, edged with stones of limestone gravel, filled with montbretia plants, often seen
growing wild in their orange and green exuberance on the
roadsides, but here as neat and pretty as in a well-cared-for
house garden. A similar bed of some purple loosestrife, taken
from beneath the hedge of the potato meadow, perhaps, and
mixed in with clusters of creamy meadowsweet, was scenting
the air. A very carefully nurtured clump of wild white orchids
was growing within the protection of a rusty cartwheel and
all in all, it appeared as though someone, without recourse
to nurseries, or without the money to buy plants and seeds
had, nevertheless, made a little secret garden to beautify this
hidden spot.

One of the novices, perhaps?

Her mind went to Lucy's words about little Nellie, now
known as Sister Mary Magdalene. 'Nellie was just eight when
her mother was killed,' Lucy had said, 'the day before her
eighth birthday, poor little thing. Used to be a little shadow
to her mother, always out in the garden helping her with
planting and weeding. I can just see the two of them.'

The Reverend Mother paid the little wildflower garden a
silent tribute of admiration.

She found herself quite glad to be at a distance from it all.
She led such a busy life with demands upon her from early
morning to late at night, that the annual retreat where not a
word could be spoken, had been, she had often thought, balm
for the soul. Now that the bishop had abolished that rule of
silence, the day seemed to be filled with non-stop chatter and
with the tension of dissenting opinions. Carefully she swept
stray crumbs of moss and crumbling wood from the seat,
placing them carefully to encourage another small island and
then sank down upon the seat, allowing her mind to wonder
about the maker of this private garden.

But her peace did not last long. A heavy footstep, an
abrupt rending of a branch. Strong hands by the sound of
the splintering wood. Not Mother Isabelle whose presence

might be tolerable, though this place was made for one person only.

The Reverend Mother tightened her lips with annoyance and took from her pocket her enormous set of rosary beads.

'Ah, Reverend Mother, you're like myself. You like the shade.' Oddly, he didn't seem to notice the beads for a moment. Not good eyesight, perhaps. Kneeling, they would have made a better show, perhaps. Still, seated as she was, they were so large that they coiled in her lap like a jewelled snake.

It was Mr Hamilton – Wee Willie to the people of Cork. Although his factory was outside Cork, he was a frequent visitor to the city streets, in and out of drapery shops, offering samples of his stockings. The Reverend Mother heaved a quiet sigh but did not repulse him. She was, after all, in his debt for many pairs of low-priced black stockings and for the release of the nuns from hours of darning the remains from their trousseau.

Nevertheless, she did not get to her feet, or make any move to engage in conversation with him. She saw him look around, as though for a seat, or even a tree stump, but if ever there had been a time when other stumps had littered the clearing, by now they were gone leaving little trace.

'What can I do for you, Mr Hamilton?' said the Reverend Mother, with an air of decision, bearing, she hoped, the demeanour of a very busy person, who had no more than a few minutes to waste. *Why on earth, don't they have a placard around their necks, saying 'Vote For Me'*, she thought crossly and waited resignedly for Mr Hamilton to tell her how very concerned he was for the poor of the city and how he would make it a priority to bestow sums of money upon any charity which the Reverend Mother Aquinas might wish to nominate.

'I was wondering if you could be induced to approve me as a candidate, Reverend Mother,' he said in a straightforward manner that won her respect.

'You'll have to give me a few good reasons,' she replied, meeting frankness with frankness. 'I don't mean stockings,' she added with an attempt at humour which, to give him his due, he appreciated, and paid the compliment of a quick flash of a smile. He would be, she thought, somewhere in his early forties, well-cared-for hands and, as far as she could see, he had all his own original teeth and they had been well-cared-for, also. A reasonably prosperous family, she guessed, and wondered whether his father also had a factory which manufactured stockings. 'And your fellow candidates, in what way are you more worthy of election than them?' she enquired, though she knew that the question was an unfair one.

He took a few long seconds before he answered her question, and during that time, he eyed her sharply. '"It's not what we say, but how good we are as men, or women",' he recited.

The Reverend Mother bowed her head. She recognized the quotation. There was nothing wrong with the sentiment. 'By their fruits, you shall know them,' Christ had said, and that phrase she thought would rise more rapidly to the lips of a man who was supposed to be a Roman Catholic. The quote that he had given was from John Knox, the Presbyterian preacher. Only one in ten thousand of the denizens of Cork city would recognize that quotation, let alone have it so readily on the tip of the tongue. She, herself, had recognized it, because she had, at one stage, resolved to collect Knox's views on women and write a thesis refuting his work. She had only got about a quarter way through it when she decided that the whole business was a waste of time and unworthy of her, and so she had thrown it in the fire and began to draft a document about the teaching of reading to young children who had no background of literate parents. It was a summary of all that she had observed and learned and had been, she thought, a better use of her talents.

But how very strange to quote John Knox down here in Cork where such a tiny proportion of the population were of the Protestant faith, she said to herself. It was, she thought, almost as if he lived among a fraternity of fellow Protestants. And then as she looked at him with curiosity the bell clanged for the noon recital of the Angelus.

Automatically the Reverend Mother made the sign of the cross.

And he copied her. He touched the index finger to the centre of his forehead and then to his breast.

And when she touched her left shoulder, he touched the shoulder opposite to hers, but it was, of course, his right shoulder.

He realized his mistake almost immediately. Bent down hastily as though bitten by an insect on the ankle, but she was not deceived. She had seen enough four- and five-year olds, being taught to make the sign of the cross, make mistakes like this – the instinct was to do a mirror image of the instructor. In fact, she had instituted a fun practice in the first days of schooling when the little new recruits were taken through this ceremony by recruiting enough older girls to have one standing behind each child and moving their arm to the correct position while chanting, 'In the name of the Father, the Son and the Holy Ghost, Amen.'

No adult Catholic could ever possibly make a mistake like that after a lifetime of signing themselves four or five times, at least, during each of their days.

But if Willie Hamilton were a Protestant, why on earth did he leave the prosperous north of Ireland and risk life and fortune here in Catholic Cork?

Her face, she hoped, showed little of her thoughts. She murmured a prayer, smiled upon him and made her way towards the church. Perhaps there she would have some peace during this very secular holy retreat.

As she mechanically recited the Angelus, there was another matter on her mind.

That little secret garden in the centre of an area of felled woodland had worried her. Though filled with wildflowers, there was something about the neat, almost suburban arrangement of the flower beds, the climbing wild rose tamed over a makeshift garden arch, framing a view of the city and the small, neat paths made from purloined gravel, that seemed to hint at another garden in the mind of the maker.

Was that girl in need of rescue? In need of time to reflect on what she wanted from life?

SIXTEEN

Patrick seldom read the *Cork Examiner*. He told himself that he had neither the time nor the interest, but he knew in his heart that if he didn't have Joe to point him towards matters of interest, then he would have to order the wretched thing to be delivered to his room in the barracks and then would have to make time – to cut precious moments out of his extremely busy day – in order to keep up with the news in his local city. Everyone in Cork read it and you could hardly go down the street without someone asking whether you had seen some article or other. Without Joe he would have appeared very ignorant.

Nevertheless, he always feigned a little impatience when Joe put his head around the door, waving the paper in his hand as he did this morning.

'Yes,' he said, finishing transferring some details to a card. He had a brand-new box on his desk, full of unused cards and he was starting a collection of the details of everyone who might have been involved in that murder among the apple trees. Bit by bit, the cards were filling up and they satisfied some need in him for an orderly approach to solving the mystery. He thought that once he had a respectable number of words written on all of the cards that he might show his system to the Reverend Mother. She might like to adopt a similar method to keep track of the pupils in her school. He would, he thought, be glad to present her with a replica of the box on his desk.

'Article by Eileen,' said Joe cheerfully. 'Read the first few lines, but I didn't bother reading the rest of it – seemed like a lot of boring nonsense about old houses, but my mother read it as there was something in it about a house where a cousin of hers was working when she was a girl, a place out in east Cork, one of those big houses. She read it right through and then she told me to read it. Not stupid, my mam. She's got her wits about her and she straightaway picked out a name that we would be interested in.'

Patrick looked at the article impatiently. His eye skimmed down it without interest. '"Queen Anne, Palladian", oh, for God's sake, Joe!' he said. He had a lot to do. There had been trouble on the docks last night, a break in at the Imperial Hotel and, looming above all, the very strange case of the murder in a convent cemetery. 'What on—' he began, but Joe held up an admonishing finger.

'Read it, Patrick,' he said. 'It's not what it seems. Not altogether about pretty houses and fine stable yards and old churches.' And then, with a look at Patrick's impatient face, he took the paper back. 'Let me find the bit, yes, here it is. About our friend Wee Willie Hamilton. Wonder whether Eileen has had a tip,' he said. 'Worth some minutes of your time, I'd say.'

Patrick read the end of the article and then went through it carefully from the beginning. Typical of Eileen, he thought. So keen to be clever. And yet, and yet . . . Wasn't it what he had thought himself the other day when he was with the bishop – something a bit odd about Willie Hamilton?

'I'd say myself that she has had a tip-off,' said Joe eagerly. 'She's had a tip-off, but she's scared to give her source, or else she has promised someone that he won't be involved. You know Eileen. She's in with all sorts of people.'

'Bring her in for questioning, then,' said Patrick badtemperedly, but he had to laugh at himself when he saw Joe's eyes widen. 'I don't mean that we should arrest her, or anything, but you could send off that lad you are training to see if he can find her and ask her whether she would spare me five minutes of her valuable time. Nice fine morning, the lad will enjoy a spin on his bike going around the city and you'll have a rest from him asking you what he should be doing, or how do you fill in a form.'

'Wonder where he'd find her. The university is on holiday,' said Joe thoughtfully.

'They don't really have holidays like schools,' said Patrick impatiently. 'A lot of them spend the summer holidays reading in the library or chatting to each other on that quad

– you know, the big square of grass in between the buildings.'
He detected a slight note of envy in his own voice. Would he
have liked to have gone to university? A couple of boys from
the North Mon. – as the Christian Brothers' monastery school
in the north of the city was always called – yes, even two of
his own classmates had got scholarships and had gone to
university. Wouldn't have suited me even if I had been good
enough to get a scholarship, he decided and turned back to
his card index box.

With a feeling of pleasure at its neatness, he leafed through
and when he came to the letter 'H', he extracted Willie
Hamilton's card and stared at the meagre few lines outlining
name, date of birth, previous residence. He had an instinct
to take the car and to go and question the man in his own
workplace. But it was in a god-forsaken village, far outside
the city and the whole business would take up too much of
his time. He could send Joe to fetch him, but then it would
waste Joe's morning and really, apart from this business of
Eileen's article, he had nothing to go on. No, better to get
hold of Eileen and see what she had to say for herself. The
card gave a neat summary of the interview, which was like
all the others. All the lay members of the retreat, in just the
same way as the religious school leaders, walked around
the extensive grounds, mostly on their own, though a few
of the school leaders, probably old friends, went in the
company of another. Willie Hamilton had been on his own,
but there was nothing of significance to that. He, as a man
from Northern Ireland, had little in common with the other
members. He had, he said, spent some time at the wall that
bounded the convent grounds, looking down over the city.
He had not been seen by anyone in the spot which he had
named, but that was not surprising as he had chosen to sit
in the shelter of a large, flowering bougainvillea. Next to
the name of the bush Patrick had inserted a small capital
'J'. That meant, according to his system, that there would
be some information about this bush in Joe's notes, which
he always, according to the system Patrick had set up, did
with a carbon copy. He leafed through them, found the Willie
Hamilton page, and read it through. As he had remembered,

the detail was there regarding the wall and the large bougainvillea. Patrick had never heard of the bush or tree, but Joe
had written an interesting note:

> People plant bougainvillea to stop passers-by sitting on
> their wall or climbing over it. They have it in the terrace
> where I live. The gate is closed every night by the lodge-
> keeper and there is a padlock on it, but apparently there
> used to be trouble with people – drunks, usually –
> climbing the wall and so they planted this bougainvillea
> all the way along the inside of the wall. Makes a great
> show – all red flowers right through the summer, but it
> has enormous thorns. I went to have a look and I do not
> think anyone would have chosen to sit on the wall at that
> spot. They would be torn to pieces by the thorns. He
> only disclosed that when I asked why it was that no one
> had seen him during that time.

'Well, well, well,' said Patrick aloud and then the door opened.

'I've sent off the young fellow to get hold of Eileen,' said
Joe, and then saw his carbon-copied notes on the desk. 'That's
what I came in about,' he said. 'What with that article
mentioning the name of Willie Hamilton, well, I just remembered feeling a bit dubious about his account of himself.'

'You did well to spot that about the thorny bush,' said
Patrick. Joe, he thought, was an excellent second-in-command.
If this case was solved satisfactorily, he must remember to
write a note praising the assistance that he had got from him.
'Did you have a look at the position where he said he spent
that time?'

'Yes, I did. Just the way that I remembered the wretched
stuff – many a sharp scratch I got from it when I was
a youngster trying to retrieve a ball. Looks pretty from a
distance, but it is lethal stuff to be among. Anyway, there's
not much of a view to be seen from there, mostly just the
road.'

'So, he was probably telling a lie. Saw the bush from a
distance but didn't know about the lethal thorns.' Patrick

felt immensely cheered. He'd probe Eileen, see what he
could get out of her, and then he would interview Willie
Hamilton again. 'Listen to this,' he said, leaning out to push
a chair forward for Joe and then picking up his notes from
the bishop.

'Listen to this, Joe,' he repeated. 'It looks as though we
have another reason for the murder of Mr Musgrave if he
knew about one of the candidates killing a man. I must say
that apart from the IRA lady, it didn't seem too likely that
someone would murder the favourite candidate just to give
himself a chance at being alderman.'

'Does seem a bit far-fetched to want the bishop's vote that
badly,' said Joe obligingly. 'I must say that I was thinking
that the only one who might fall under real suspicion
with that motive would be the man who was the original
favourite – that is the builder, Bob O'Connor. Most people
that I know seemed to be putting their money on him
getting the job when the names came out first. But of course,
as soon as the bishop let it be known among all the ratepayers
that he favoured the stockbroker – well, that would have
changed the stakes, wouldn't it.'

'According to his lordship,' said Patrick, 'Mr Musgrave
confessed to him, well, told him – don't suppose that it was
in confession – that he had been given information . . .'

Patrick was conscious of a certain restlessness from Joe
as he went through as accurately as he could – with the help
of his notes – his conversation with the bishop. Patrick had
trained himself into carefulness, into a rigorous adherence
to the words spoken by suspects, or by witnesses and from
time to time, he took his eyes from his notebook to refer to
his typewritten account of his conversation with the bishop.
Because of the explosive nature of the bishop's declaration
and because of the importance of the bishop himself, he was
being careful, and he spoke slowly and hesitantly weighing
up every sentence before he uttered it. He was somewhat
hampered by the silence in the room. It would, he thought,
have been more natural if he had been interrupted with a
few eager questions or even an exclamation of astonishment.

In the end, he drew to a silence, shut his notebook, replaced the sheets of typed paper in the drawer, locked it carefully and then he looked at Joe.

'Well, what do you think?' he asked.

Joe did not speak for a moment. That was quite characteristic of Joe. He was very sure of himself, but he was careful and meticulous. When he did speak, it was unexpected.

'I don't believe a word of it,' said Joe.

'What!' Patrick was genuinely surprised. Even the fact that Joe was a Protestant didn't seem to justify this dismissal of the testimony of the bishop, the most respected man in the city of Cork.

'It just sounds so far-fetched,' said Joe with an apologetic note in his voice. 'Why on earth would a sensible man like a stockbroker, say something like that to the bishop? You might confess a sin to a bishop, I suppose,' said Joe, with a slightly dubious note coming into his voice, 'but if you are talking about a crime, about suspecting someone of killing a man, well, then any sensible citizen would go to the police, report to the Garda Siochana. Why should he ask the bishop? He was a stockbroker – ran a business; wouldn't need the bishop's permission to report a crime. No, one or other of them was making up a story. Either the stockbroker was trying to put the bishop off the other candidates or else, the bishop was trying to make himself more interesting. And I'm sorry, Patrick if I sound unreligious, but I'm almost inclined to think it was the bishop trying to make himself interesting. Or perhaps,' said Joe apologetically, noting Patrick's stunned expression, 'the bishop, being a fairly elderly gentleman, misunderstood something that the stock-broker said to him, perhaps it got entangled with a dream that he had, or something like that, and in the end he thought that it might be the best thing to mention it to you. And leave the matter in your capable hands.' Joe finished, rather with the air of one who wished that he had never embarked upon an explanation.

Patrick thought about the matter. He had a good opinion of Joe and the fact that he was a Protestant had been, up to this moment, regarded by Patrick as more of an asset than a drawback. He would look at matters and people from a fresh point of view and Patrick made it a rule to never criticize or jeer at any opinion. A good leader was one who encouraged his men, he had worked that out quite a while ago, had even mentioned the thought to the Reverend Mother who had not only expressed approval, but had quoted a few examples from history so that he had been quite pleased with himself to be put on a level with famous historical personages.

'You may be right,' he said. It was a neutral phrase, one that he was rather proud of and he felt that it combined discretion with encouragement. It satisfied Joe, anyway. An eager look came into his eyes and he leaned back on his chair. To Patrick's horror, he tilted the chair and balanced it upon its two back legs and a slightly mischievous grin puckered at the corner of his mouth. He gave his superior a speculative glance. He wore, thought Patrick, the expression of someone who was wondering whether to venture upon an outrageous statement or to let well alone.

Patrick said nothing, just waited. This affair was baffling him. It was correct that the motive for murdering James Musgrave appeared to be a very flimsy one. It would be more feasible if there had been just two candidates. Given that there were five, then if one were murdered, the hopeful candidate would still have to get rid of three more in order to ensure victory. In fact, if there were four murders attached to this election then the chances were that the government in Dublin would stop the election of a new alderman and leave the position vacant for the moment. There may be, he thought, something else behind the bomb. Perhaps James Musgrave was an accidental victim and something else had been intended. He looked at Joe and raised an eyebrow.

'You know,' said Joe in a contemplative tone, 'we may have been approaching this matter from the wrong angle. We've been concentrating on the election and those five lay people involved in this election – but what if the bomb had been meant for someone else. After all, there were all of those Christian Brothers, priests, nuns . . .' Joe hesitated for a couple of seconds after that audacious statement, and then said quietly, 'And there was the bishop himself. What if one of them had been sitting on the seat when the bomb went off? It would be a chancy way of murdering someone, wouldn't it? Or what about a headmaster of a small school wanting a bit of promotion to a big school? Or a deputy bishop wanting to become the top man?'

Patrick thought about the matter. His head was spinning. He couldn't possibly do any more than he had already done with all of these religious leaders and the bishop himself. Everyone had made a statement of what they were doing between the hour after lunch and before the moment of the explosion. Most, had, he had noticed with interest, retired to their room in order to pray and meditate – something which Joe had remarked seemed suspiciously like an after-a-meal nap to him, but as to trying to find a motive for any of them to murder James Musgrave, or even one another, that seemed to be an impossible task.

'Or blackmail, perhaps,' said Joe, reading his expression, but Patrick shook his head.

'We're being stupid with this,' he said energetically. 'We're on the wrong track. Think about it, Joe. Think how he was murdered. No one slipped a knife into him, fired a shot at him, or even strangled him – any of those things could conceivably have been done by one of that crowd, but not planting a bomb and blowing up the man. No, it's the IRA or something to do with them. We just need to find a link. I'll check again about whether our victim ever acted as a magistrate or something. I couldn't find any sign of it, but everything was very disorganized between the end of the War of Independence and the Civil War.'

'Hang on a minute, Patrick,' said Joe with a note of excitement in his voice. 'What if the wrong man was blown up? What if it was meant to be Wee Willie after all? Eileen has obviously heard rumours about that fellow. Then that would make sense that the IRA did it. They suspected him of being an Orangeman, after all. Sent down here to organize the Protestant landowners. Defend themselves against the IRA by arming and training small groups of militia. Kill a few Catholics. Perhaps even the bishop himself. The Orangemen from the North have never got used to losing part of the British Empire. They are forever trying to stir up trouble. And then, you know, it would make very good sense to use a bomb. Make the whole thing spectacular, send a message to anyone connected to Wee Willie that they could not mess with the IRA. They got the wrong man, of course, but that's quite possible. Wouldn't be the first time that they made a mistake. A wild lot of lads, these fellas. Wilder lot now, than they were in the years when there was more justification for their presence, when more people were on their side. A lot of respectable young fellows, and girls joined them then, but after the war of independence and the civil war, most of the patriot types got sick of the whole business – look at Eileen, for instance. Lots of them went to college, or got a job, or even went off to Australia. But the ones that stayed members, stayed because they enjoyed killing, even killing innocent Protestants. Do you know, Patrick, I think we may have something? Remember that Wee Willie wasn't one of those who went off to their bedroom when lunch was over. By his own account he was sitting on a wall admiring the view – and even if he wasn't where he said he was, the fact remains that the man was out and about. He might have been waiting for the stockbroker to go away so that he could meet someone else there, could follow the directions that had been sent to him, a note pretending to be from one of his friends, but really sent by the IRA.'

'But why would anyone want to murder him,' protested Patrick. When Joe gave an impatient sigh, he said hurriedly, 'Still, it might be worth finding out whether Wee Willie had been sitting on that bench during the days before.'

'Good idea; take it slow and careful,' said Joe, and Patrick gave a nod of approval. He looked at Joe with gratitude. Somehow a talk with him always seemed to be a huge help to him.

The puzzle which had almost seemed beyond the power of man to solve, seemed now to be opening out to show several intriguing and possible solutions. There was no doubt that Willie Hamilton had been wandering around the grounds when most of the others had retired to their bedrooms.

Eileen's article seemed to hint at some connection between Willie and the Protestants. There had been a few shootings in that part of east Cork, all justified, IRA men caught trying to burn down a house. But, on each occasion, it had seemed as though the Protestant owners had known something was planned and had been waiting with a gang of well-armed neighbours. If Willie Hamilton was a spy of some sort, that could be the explanation. And if he were, the IRA would be after his blood.

Unfortunately for James Musgrave, he may have taken, by the bishop's command, the very bench where the man from the north of Ireland had planned to be sitting upon. And so, the bomb had killed the wrong man. Patrick felt immensely cheered by the thought. It would, he thought, be an acceptable solution for both the lay and religious powers in the city. 'I think you may have something there, Joe,' he said generously and then looked up at the clock.

'Where's that lad of yours?' he said impatiently. 'Surely Eileen should be here by now. It's only five minutes ride from the university to Barrack Street on that bike of hers.'

'Oh, he's back,' said Joe guiltily. 'I meant to tell you. She said that she was busy, but she would drop in on her way home.'

Patrick knew that he should say something, laugh it off, make a joke, but somehow he could not find the words. It didn't matter too much whether he talked with Eileen today or tomorrow or even left it for a couple of days. There was still plenty of interviewing to be done, there were plenty of people in the city who acted as informers, who had an eye on local members of the IRA. Either past members or present members, or even those who would ingratiate themselves by carrying out a commission. None of these had been interviewed yet and they should be. Eileen probably had little to divulge, but at the same time he felt furious with her. The trouble with Eileen was that she didn't take him seriously. From time to time, he had wondered whether he might have been better off looking for a position in Limerick or Galway, or even Dublin itself. Any place where he was not immediately recognized as a barefoot boy from Barrack Street, from a city where so many people had gone to school with him, played in the streets with him, knew everything about him and expected little because of his undistinguished past.

It was six o'clock in the evening before Eileen arrived. Patrick was just about to lock the door of the Garda barracks when he heard the familiar roar of her motorbike. He hesitated for a moment, key in hand, wondering whether to ignore her, but then told himself not to be stupid. It was pointless reacting to Eileen and her tricks. He had more important matters on his mind.

Nevertheless, when she drew up beside him, he could not forbear looking at his watch although he told himself that it was the wrong thing to do. Would make her think that he had been waiting impatiently for her arrival.

She looked amused when she dismounted, and he hated that expression of hers. Just as though she was well aware that he had been looking at the time continuously for the last couple of hours.

'Oh, are you shutting up shop?' she enquired with simulation of surprise. 'Never mind, another day, eh?'

He stopped himself from a retort. She could play that game better than he. He should impress upon her the seriousness of his work, not barter insults like a pair of youngsters. 'Come in, Eileen,' he said in as even a tone as he could manage.

She made a face; determined, he thought, to annoy him. 'That place of yours smells of Jeyes Fluid,' she said. 'Why don't you walk up the road with me to my mam's place. She's making something special tonight. One of her best stews. You can have something to eat with us and we can chat all you like, walk up to the top of the hill, like we used when we were *chiselers* and had secrets to tell,' she finished, smiling at him.

For a moment, he was tempted. There was no doubt but that he was lonely. Food was something that he stuffed into his mouth in order not to feel hungry, but he had no pleasure in his canteen meals in the barracks or solitary snacks in his room. And he liked Eileen's mother who always treated him with great respect and greeted him warmly whenever she met him. Still, it was not the right thing to do and important police business should not be discussed on top of the hill in the place where hundreds of Barrack Street children exchanged secrets.

'That's very nice of you, Eileen,' he said as gently as he could manage while still preserving an official demeanour. 'I think we'd better come in here, though. I have to do things by the rule book,' he added, in an effort to placate her. He would, he decided, make no mention of her late arrival and no mention of the young constable's opinion, voiced to Joe, that Eileen hadn't really been studying, just sunbathing on the grass with a crowd of lads.

She patted him on the arm with a condescending show of sympathy. 'I know *you* have to, Patrick,' she said and though there was an undue emphasis on the word 'you', an implication that he was timorous and that others would be more courageous, he did not rise to the challenge, but led the way back into his room and pulled out a chair for her. The building was empty. Everyone else had gone home. It was ideal, really, no fear of a shout from out in the corridor or of a door being opened when he was in the middle of extracting information from her. He checked the phone for messages and then left the receiver lying on the desk. He saw her eyes go to it in an amused fashion, but to his relief she made no comment.

'What can I do for you, Patrick,' she asked. He rather resented the brisk tone to her voice, as though she were the busy and important one, but he did not rise to the provocation. He just opened the drawer which was now devoted to the orchard cemetery murder and took out Joe's copy of the *Cork Examiner*. It had been neatly folded at the page where Eileen's article was placed beneath the title: 'Strangers in our Land'. She smiled at it, when she saw it, but he did not feel annoyed by that smile as he recognized that it bore a stamp of pride. Clever girl, he thought. Like himself, she had had to struggle out from her environment, from the dreadful poverty which both had experienced, but unlike himself she had been gifted with a top-class brain. Life had been more difficult for him, he thought. Perhaps he had less courage and more wariness. In the eyes of the world, so far, he would appear to have achieved more success, but he knew that Eileen, when she found her feet, would far outshine him.

'An excellent article. I found it most interesting.'

'Which part of it?' She asked the question with a half-smile on her face.

'Let's not play games, Eileen,' he said.

'No, no, you're a busy man. And probably a hungry one. I'm sure that you haven't had your supper yet.'

Patrick forced himself to sit still and to say nothing. The thing about Eileen, now and when she was five years old, in and out of his house, chatting to his mother, then, like now, she talked an awful lot and she found it hard not to break a silence. Deliberately he passed the folded newspaper over to her and then sat back in his chair.

She read the article through. Read it rapidly, taking no more than half of the time that he would have taken. He saw a smile of pride widen her lips and noted how she reread, at least twice, the part about the ugliness of Willie Hamilton's corrugated iron factory. He knew, then, that Joe had spotted something of significance. Perhaps he should have left Eileen to Joe, he thought with that self-doubt which constantly haunted him. Joe was cleverer and was more at ease. He would joke with Eileen, flatter her, read between the lines, not have to have everything spelled out for him. He sat in silence for a few minutes, miserably aware of his shortcomings, knowing that he had only one good point and that was an ability to work hard, to take enormous pains and to check and double check. It seemed to him to be a mediocre gift.

'You look tired, Patrick,' she said suddenly, looking up from the newspaper and scrutinizing his face in that easy-going fashion of hers.

He looked back at her helplessly. He couldn't play her games, couldn't produce repartee or wit without a lot of thought – something which robbed it of its edge.

'Give me a break, Eileen,' he said earnestly. 'This is serious. There's a homicidal criminal up there in that convent and . . .

and the Reverend Mother is up there. I'm worried about her.
She was good to me when I was young and still is. I couldn't
bear anything to happen to her through my lack of ability to
find a murderer in time to prevent another murder. And
there are all those nuns. Goodness knows, one of them may
have seen something and may be next on that villain's list.
I have to find him.' He spread out his hands and said no more,
feeling slightly ashamed of himself. For a moment he regretted
that he had exposed his inadequacy, but then he put the thought
aside. There were more important matters at stake. He put his
head on his hands and then ran his fingers impatiently through
the rough dark hair which he so carefully smoothed out every
morning with a brush well smeared with Brylcreem. He looked
across at her; now sitting very straight and restraining himself
from any more apologies or explanations.

She didn't look away. That was Eileen. Straight as a die,
always. And always full of courage. She didn't smile, didn't
pretend not to know what he was talking about, but looked
with that air of one who is weighing up matters.

'I have to keep faith in my sources, Patrick,' she said. 'I
had a tip, but I can say no more. I promised, you see.'

'That's fair enough,' he said, feeling his heart race with
excitement. He was a slow but meticulous reader and he had
read every word of her article, had noticed the emphasis on the
origin of those who had built those houses, who had worked
on those farms, had tended those horses, whose children had
peopled those schools. Protestants, every one of them. A colony
of them. And none of those lootings and burnings and none of
those assassinations of Protestants that had stained the name of
many villages and small towns in west Cork and in north Cork
had taken place in these peaceful villages of east Cork. It all
made sense, thought Patrick. He nodded at her. 'You've said
enough,' he said. 'I'll take it from there. Thank you, Eileen.'

'Good,' she said. She said it in a slightly unsure fashion,
and she got to her feet with a tentative air. For a moment he
wondered whether she would repeat her offer of supper with
herself and her mother, but she didn't. She looked across at
him for a moment and then said quietly, 'Good night, Patrick.
Don't work too hard.'

Then she was gone, and he cursed himself for a fool. Perhaps, he thought, it wouldn't hurt to drop in later in the evening, pay his respects to Eileen's mother, and perhaps they might go for a walk . . .

SEVENTEEN

Patrick had been late to bed after seeing Eileen the previous evening but, nevertheless, he was, as usual, the first person into the police barracks on the following morning. As he put his key into the lock, he heard the phone ringing and just managed to reach it before it ceased. Too early in the morning for a riot, it would be a burglary or a dead body, he thought as he lifted the receiver.

'Inspector Cashman,' he said.

'Ah, Patrick. Rupert Murphy, here. You're like myself, an early bird,' said the affable voice on the other end of the line.

Patrick felt a slight rush of pleasure to be on first name terms with the foremost – and the richest – solicitor in the city.

'Lovely morning,' he said and waited to see what was wrong.

'Something a little unexpected has happened. One of the sons of my late neighbour, James Musgrave, turned up last night. Spent the night with the son of a colleague of mine. Just met the man on the South Mall. Apparently, the boy got into Cobh last night, got a lift up to Cork. I thought you should know.'

Patrick pulled himself together. 'Very good of you to phone me,' he said. 'What's his name?'

'This one is Peter – they were Peter and Paul and I never knew them apart, but apparently, according to my colleague, they separated when they were in Australia. Peter settled in Broken Hill, near to Sydney; the other boy, Paul, went to the Melbourne area first and then moved away without leaving an address with his brother.'

'Odd that they separated,' said Patrick. 'Very big place, Australia.' About a hundred times bigger than Ireland, he seemed to remember, but it seemed a bit schoolboyish to mention that.

'Let me give you the address where he spent last night. It's in Tivoli. By the way, he does know that his father is dead. Someone in Cobh told him once he had disembarked from the liner. Would it be possible for you to drop in and see me in the South Mall before you go to Tivoli? I have a slight problem and I'd like to have a chat with you about it.'

Patrick was conscious of a warm feeling as he went to request the use of the Garda car from the superintendent. He hoped that he might be of use to the solicitor but doubted it. Murphy had the name of being immensely experienced and immensely astute. It was probably a polite way of requesting some action from the police. He would definitely go to the South Mall first. In fact, if necessary, he could send the constable to Tivoli to request the newly arrived son to drop into the police barracks. But he would certainly like to hear what the solicitor had to say as quickly as possible.

The chief clerk was waiting for him at the door at the top of the steps when he parked the car in the South Mall.

'Mr Murphy will see you immediately, inspector,' he said. 'I'll take you straight in. He's due in court at ten o'clock.'

Patrick nodded. A year ago, he would have felt guilty and promised not to be long, but these days he had learned that the less you said, the more people thought of you. He followed the man in silence and again just nodded his thanks when he was ushered into Mr Murphy's office and given a cup of steaming coffee poured from the great man's own percolator.

'I've been meaning to talk to you, Patrick, about the will of the late James Musgrave.'

Patrick sipped the coffee and then dropped three lumps of sugar into the cup, hoping that it might improve the taste and looked at the man across the desk from him.

'I'm in a rather awkward situation about this,' said Rupert. 'You see, only a week ago, James came in here and asked for his will. He said he wanted to take it away and to study it. I argued against that – never like to have wills knocking around in private houses – but he insisted. Said he wanted to have it and needed to study it. I offered to have it copied, but he was against that – said he didn't want any talk about it. I assured him that my staff were a hundred per cent reliable, but he wouldn't listen. Laughed at me and said that he would take very good care of it. Would guard it with his life.'

'And the will?' said Patrick.

'The Will and Testament that I handed to James Musgrave was made some time after the death of his wife, about eleven years ago. It had a large number of small legacies, but the major part of his estate was to be held in trust for his three children, if he died before they reached the age of eighteen, but otherwise to be divided equally between the three, the two boys, Peter and Paul, and his daughter Ellen, known as Nellie. I would guess that since Nellie was about to take her final vows that he decided to change his will, leaving the bulk of his estate to be divided between his two sons, and perhaps a small token of affection to his daughter. James was a good Catholic, but not to the extent of leaving one third of his estate to a convent!'

'I see,' said Patrick. 'And was that Will and Testament changed?'

'Not by this firm,' said Rupert.

'Would he have taken it to another firm?' The question had to be asked, although Patrick felt a certain compunction in uttering it. It seemed a bit of an insult to the man sitting opposite.

Rupert Murphy made no audible reply, but he pursed his lips and wagged his head from side to side. *Not without my knowledge,* the gesture seemed to say. Patrick guessed that these solicitors all knew each other and all confided in each other, but a nod and a wink usually took the place of words.

'You said that you were in an awkward position,' he said firmly. 'Is there a will in existence?'

Rupert Murphy gave a half smile and a nod.

'I've searched the Musgrave house from top to bottom,' he said. 'Not a sign of a will. We, my wife and I, keep a key to his house – and he had the key to our place. He had no locked safe or anything like that in the house, and his managing clerk reported nothing to be found in his office. I can only think that he burned it. He had an appointment with me on this very morning.'

'To change his will?'

'Yes, indeed. I would guess that is what he intended to do.'

'And what happens now if no will can be found – he died intestate, is that right?'

'It looks like that,' said the solicitor with a sigh. 'We will handle matters of course, but if a man dies without a will, then everything will go to the eldest son. That is Peter, of course, as he was born a few hours before Paul.'

'And everything would amount to quite a sum, I suppose,' said Patrick. He told himself not to show any surprise at the sum, but even so he could not help a slight start when the solicitor said carelessly, 'Something around the quarter-of-a-million-pound level.'

A quarter of a million pounds! Patrick took a deep breath but decided not to comment. Ideas were running through his head, but he decided to keep them there.

'So, everything goes to Peter and nothing to Paul,' he said slowly. 'And Peter is the one who is here in Cork, in Tivoli. That's handy, I suppose.' Patrick tasted the coffee again. Quite drinkable now if you just sipped it, he thought and looked across the desk at the solicitor. There was, he thought, an odd look on Mr Murphy's face and he waited. After a moment, the man smiled, slightly and then shook his head.

'My wife, Patrick, often accuses me of always borrowing trouble and I'm sure that she is right. But I thought of something as soon as I heard that the boy had turned up and I realized that the original will was nowhere to be found and had probably been destroyed.' He paused, not looking at Patrick, but doodling interlocking circles on the pad in front of him. And then he put back the pen and looked up.

'The devil of it is that I don't think that I could say, let alone swear, that the boy who came back from Australia is, in fact, Peter. I never knew them apart even when they were our nearest neighbours and running in and out of our house. Remember, I haven't seen either of them for more than about three years! Lucy never knew them apart. Nor did any of their aunts. The school, I heard, insisted on them wearing a nametag

– 'Musgrave major' for Peter and 'Musgrave minor' for Paul. Even so, they swapped them regularly and always accused the other of any wrongdoing. So, you see my point. If this is Peter, he gets it all, but if it isn't Peter, but Paul, why then I can't hand over the money to the wrong man. I'll have to scour Australia for the fellow who was a few hours older or younger than his brother.'

'Why did they go to Australia?' asked Patrick with a degree of curiosity. 'I would have thought that they would have gone into their father's business.' And it was odd, he thought. Well-educated, a rich father, the world at their feet and yet they went off on the boat, just like the lads from the Coal Quay and from the lanes around Barrack Street.

Rupert leaned back in his chair. 'Well, you see, Patrick, their father would have liked them to study accountancy, but neither had the brains, or the work ability. They both did very poorly in school. No profession would have been open to them. I think that James was relieved in a way when they got enthusiastic about this Australian farming business. Never got on well with them. Perhaps they would have been better if their mother lived.' Rupert looked at the clock and then checked his watch.

'I think, if you will give me the address, I will go out to Tivoli and have a word with young Mr Musgrave,' said Patrick, rising to his feet. He had the facts now and he needed to see the newly arrived man.

'Yes, you do that.' Rupert also got to his feet and accompanied him to the door. 'Oh, and by the way,' he said as he opened it, 'apparently Eileen gave him a lift back to Cork from Cobh – on the back of her motorbike! She was down in Cobh doing a piece for the *Cork Examiner* about the links between Ireland and Australia. If you see her, tell her to pop in and see me. I'd like to congratulate her on her brilliant results.'

Patrick wrote himself a note 'See Eileen and deliver message from Mr Murphy, solicitor.' He placed the piece of paper into his attaché case and then made his way to the address in Tivoli.

*   *   *

Nice house, was his thought as he parked the car outside the gate. Newly built, about six bedrooms, he guessed, looking at the rows of windows on the two upper storeys. Well-cared-for, neatly raked gravel covering the semi-circular drive and a pair of twin garages to one side of the house and a large greenhouse on the other side. There was a gardener mowing the lawn and he nodded briskly to him before ringing the doorbell.

He had barely removed his finger from the doorbell when the door was pulled back. Not a maidservant, as he had expected, but two young men, carrying golf clubs, one well-dressed in typical golfing clothes, plus fours, ornate socks, waistcoat and immaculately shining brown shoes, while the other was very bronzed with shabby trousers, threadbare around the knees, no tie and jacket and cap that were bleached by the sun and ragged at the edges. It was obvious, thought Patrick, which was which, nevertheless, he addressed both and removed his own cap politely.

'Inspector Patrick Cashman,' he said. 'I'm looking for Mr Peter Musgrave.'

'And you've found him,' said the man wearing the plus fours. 'What's he been doing? What have you been up to, Peter, my lad?'

Patrick ignored that and addressed himself to the other young man. 'Is there somewhere we could talk, Mr Musgrave?'

'About my father? I've heard that he is dead.'

Hadn't lost his accent. No trace of Australia about him. Sounded very tense. He looked around indecisively and then said, 'Could I pop into your police station later on?'

Doesn't want the other fellow present, perhaps, thought Patrick. 'Better come now,' he said briefly. 'I've a car outside the gate and I can give you a lift.' He did not wait for a reply, but went down the path, through the gate and opened the back door of the car.

To his slight surprise, the young man followed him. Did not protest, did not make a joke, just followed in his footsteps, down the path, through the gate and neatly seated himself on the back seat. Patrick slammed the door shut and went around to the other side, cranked up the engine and then set off.

'Had a good trip over?' He asked the question in a fairly perfunctory way over his shoulder as he was busy steering his way out into the traffic and the Ford car, the pride and joy of the superintendent, was a very awkward one to turn. There was no answer from the back of the car, not even a perfunctory 'thank you'.

Well, play it that way if you like, thought Patrick, and concentrated on making his way through the traffic. Late risers, the people of Tivoli. No shop workers, stall holders or cleaners here, mainly office workers – managers, probably, he decided – assessing the houses as he steered a cautious path. One valuable thing that his training course in Dublin had taught him was how to drive well and how to be always in the right, no matter how many others were in the wrong. Too many people spent money on a car but grudged the money to pay someone to teach them how to use it properly.

Not a word from the fellow in the back seat. As Patrick took the car onto the wide and straight stretch of the Glanmire Road, he began to wonder about him. A quarter of a million if your name is Peter and nothing if your name is Paul. And the one just born hours before the other. And if you had arrived a couple of weeks ago, the fortune would, after your father's death, of course, have been divided between the three of you, with just some small legacies to relations. But, of course, if his father had not been murdered, then this young man might have had to wait, twenty, even forty, years before he got any money at all.

The long, straight road gave him a chance to formulate some questions, but he had no intention of asking them until the young man was across the desk from him. So he said nothing more, until they reached the Garda barracks.

Patrick parked the car neatly, got out and nodded to the duty constable who was standing at the door to keep an eye on some ragged children who were gazing hungrily at the window of a small corner shop.

'Take Mr Musgrave into my room, Tommy, and tell Joe that

I'm back,' he said. He would have to see the superintendent and tell him the result of his conversation with the solicitor and about the complication of the will. Hopefully he could get through with it quickly on the grounds that the man himself was waiting in his room.

When he left the superintendent still exclaiming about the money there was in stockbroking and declaring that he was in the wrong job entirely, he found that his sergeant, Joe Dugan, was standing by the window in the corridor waiting for him.

'Just a word, Joe,' he said curtly, and led the way into the sergeant's room and sat on the corner of the desk. It wouldn't hurt to keep that young man waiting; Tommy would have bestowed a copy of the *Cork Examiner* upon him. Patrick could hear the old man's voice from within his room busily pointing out various articles of interest to a man from Australia.

'Musgrave's son has come back from Australia,' he said abruptly. 'His father has left him a quarter of a million pounds – that is, if he is who he says he is. The money goes to the eldest son and no one could ever tell the twins apart. Peter and Paul, apparently.'

Joe's eyes widened. 'A quarter of a million! Interesting!' And then after a moment's thought, he said, 'How long has he been back in Cork?'

'My thought, exactly,' said Patrick, though he wasn't sure that it had come to him as quickly as it did to Joe. 'So that's the first thing that we'll ask him. The solicitor said that he was in Cobh yesterday and that Eileen, of all people, gave him a lift back to Cork, but that doesn't prove that he arrived yesterday.' Patrick thought about that for a moment and then dismissed it from his mind. 'What next?'

'Well, I suppose this is more a matter for the solicitor, but I wonder whether he can prove that he is Peter.'

'I wondered that, too, and I was wondering whether he or his brother or both of them, could have had any connection with the IRA, what do you think?'

'We can ask,' said Joe. 'In fact, it might be a good idea to see whether you could get something like that out of

Eileen. They'd be about the same age, wouldn't they? A lot of youngsters were up to their necks in the IRA four or five years ago.'

'I'll think about that,' said Patrick cautiously. He wondered whether to ask Joe to see Eileen, but then decided that was his job. 'Let's go in,' he said abruptly. 'Tommy will be running out of steam. He's not exactly talkative, this fellow.'

No tea in front of the visitor so he had declined it. Tommy never forgot to offer tea and to get out some biscuits if it looked as though the person was of some importance, but there was silence in the room when they entered and the *Cork Examiner* was lying on the side of the desk. Tommy snatched it up and retired. Patrick went to his seat behind the desk and Joe took his shorthand notebook from his pocket and sat at a low table out of the sightline of the visitor.

'Just a few formalities, first,' said Patrick. He was damned if he was calling this fellow 'sir', he thought and then rushed onto the first question. 'Full name and date of birth, please.'

'Peter Swain Musgrave.' There was a slight pause and then he said with emphasis, 'My date of birth was Friday the first of February 1907 and I was born at six a.m.' He looked across at Patrick with an air of expectation. Patrick was inclined to deny him the pleasure of commentating, but he knew that a good policeman gets all possible information.

'Unusual to know the day and the hour,' he said without any particular emphasis.

'Well, when you are a twin, and an identical twin, these things are important.' He looked expectantly at Patrick, but Patrick did not respond.

'And you emigrated to Australia, you and your brother. When was that?'

'A couple of years ago,' said the young man carelessly. 'Goodness, it must have been about three years ago, this summer.'

'And your brother?'

'We bought some land and tried out some sheep farming, didn't go very well and then we tried some arable and that didn't go well either and then I got a job in a hotel in

Sydney and Paul cleared off. We both went to Broken Hill first, then he went to Melbourne, but then he moved on, apparently. Don't know where he went.'

'You didn't write?'

'Not too keen on letter writing. Sent a couple of wires. No answer.' The man shrugged, but there was a watchful look in his eyes which didn't seem to go with the carelessness of the gesture.

'I see.' Patrick eyed him sharply. He had never had a brother himself, but something about this didn't ring true to him. After all, these were twins, identical twins. From what he had heard, this pair of brothers had been very close, as thick as thieves, amusing themselves and getting in and out of trouble, according to the solicitor, by playing on their likeness to each other. And then they go off to the other end of the earth and separate.

'When did you arrive in Cobh, Mr Musgrave?' By now he had perfected the technique of looking at his notebook as he asked the question and then looking up sharply to catch an expression.

'Goodness, I'm not sure. Sometime yesterday afternoon, can't quite remember exactly the time.' His face had remained untroubled, but the hesitation appeared to be slightly forced. Patrick flicked a glance at Joe who immediately slid from the room. Good fellow, Joe. They had almost got to the stage where they read each other's minds. Joe would check with the harbour master and with the lists of arrivals from the ship. There was a very efficient man down there in Cobh who kept his records tidy and accessible.

'Have you been in touch with your sister? I believe that her name is Sister Mary Magdalene, is that correct?'

A flash of anger at the name. But that was understandable.

'She wrote to me,' he said after a long pause. 'Told me that she would be taking her final vows in the middle of June.'

'So, she had your address, is that right?' A bit strange that he was in touch with the younger sister, but not the twin brother.

'Got it from my father, I suppose.' There was a pause and

then he said, with a slight struggle, 'I wrote to my father asking for money, explaining that things had gone badly with me. You'll probably find the letter in his desk, in the drawer marked "Family", very methodical man, my father. The receipted bills from Clongowes Wood College are probably in there, too, and the ones from the Ursuline Convent. He probably looked at them from time to time, sighed over the sums of money that were spent and had brought no good results. I suppose even a successful stock-broker makes a few bad investments and my father wasn't one to bury his mistakes. "Learn by your mistakes" – that was one of his little pieces of advice, but you know what fathers are like,' he added with an obvious effort to lighten the tone of his voice.

No, I wouldn't, thought Patrick. Mine didn't stick around too long. He did not respond to the self-pity in his head, though, but briskly asked, 'And did your father send you some money?'

'Just enough to get both of us home – enough for two single first-class tickets, he said.'

The door opened quietly. Joe slid into the room, resumed his seat, took his notebook and indelible pencil from his pocket and gave Patrick the slightest of nods, just a lowering of head and of the eyelids. So, the young man was speaking the truth. It had been tempting to think of that fortune of a quarter of a million as an incentive to murder an unloved father, but the truth must lie elsewhere, if he had, indeed, only arrived from Australia yesterday. In the meantime, he could make some use of him while he was there.

'As you know, your father was brutally murdered by a makeshift bomb made from a sack of fertilizer and probably some diesel,' he said. 'I wonder whether you could assist us with any recollections of enemies: business associates, social contacts, even relatives – anyone that might have a grievance against your father. Everything you say will be kept in strict confidence. Go with the sergeant and see if you can come up with a few names.'

Joe was on his feet almost before Patrick finished speaking. He had read the signs and guessed that Patrick wanted to make a phone call. He ushered Peter Musgrave from the room with an air of firm friendliness and Patrick lifted the phone and dialled a number.

'I wonder whether Mr Murphy is back from court, this is Inspector Cashman,' he said, endeavouring to make his voice sound self-assured.

'I'll enquire.' The standard answer. Would know, of course, but would want to ascertain that the great man wanted to take a phone call from a lowly police officer. Patrick waited, going over the interview in his mind. Something a little strange about the fellow. No sign of shock or horror, no enquiries, and then that quarter of a million pounds – a huge fortune, an almost inconceivable amount of money – even divided between the three children, still huge.

'Patrick, Rupert here. Well, did you find our young friend?'

'Yes, indeed, thank you. Just found him going off for a game of golf.' And that, in a way, thought Patrick, was very odd. Didn't the news come as a shock? Surely, he should have been on his way to the convent to see his sister. 'I told him nothing, of course. He arrived yesterday in Cobh. We checked with the harbour master and the ship's clerk. He doesn't know where his brother is. They parted company. I wondered, Mr Murphy, whether you wanted to see him. I could get my sergeant to take him across to the South Mall.'

'That would be really kind of you. Yes, I would like to see him. I shall have to see him. Thank you, Patrick, and good luck with the investigation.' And then he rang off. No conversation about the identical twins and the problem that would afford. No promise to share any information gleaned from the young man.

Perhaps I should have asked, thought Patrick, and why the hell did I call him Mr Murphy when he has told me to call him Rupert? Feeling dissatisfied with himself, he went into Joe's office where the pair seemed to be chatting about Sydney and Melbourne and curtly told his sergeant to convey the man – he just stopped himself saying 'the prisoner' and changed it to 'Mr Musgrave' – to the office of Mr Rupert Murphy.

Hard to read what the young fellow felt about that. One of

those poker faces. Was he pleased? Anticipating hearing
something to his advantage? Apprehensive? There was a look
of tension on his face, perhaps. And if so, why?

Patrick walked back into his own office, took out his list
and went through the notes about Willie Hamilton again.

EIGHTEEN

The Reverend Mother woke early and her first thought, a happy one, was, 'Last day, thank God!' She was glad that it was all over. The last breakfast, the last sight of that terrible crater desecrating the beautiful orchard cemetery; the last couple of hours of enforced idleness, of making conversation, of listening to political speeches. Soon, her cousin Lucy would come to collect her and bring her back to where she belonged. The Reverend Mother thought of her school with a feeling of nostalgia.

She had not enjoyed this year's retreat, had found neither solace for the mind nor food for the soul. It was, she thought firmly, a huge mistake to mix politics with matters of the soul. It had been a poor excuse to talk about praying for guidance. Extraordinarily little praying, she guessed, had gone on either before or after all these tedious lectures and displays of power by the bishop.

And, of course, the death of a man had been a terrible affair. The Reverend Mother, at her advanced age, was well used to death and she did not fear it, neither for herself nor for those of her community who had finished long and useful lives. But the death of James Musgrave had been a dreadful carnage, a man blown to pieces by a bomb within the peaceful surroundings of the orchard cemetery.

Lucy would not be late. She would undoubtedly know that her cousin would be anxious to get back to her convent again. The outbreak of diphtheria had not been a severe one; many children, she suspected, may well have been immune since an earlier pandemic a few years ago. Nevertheless, the Reverend Mother could not wait to be at the helm again.

However, it was not just the prospect of getting back to her convent which pleased her. Between the two of them, she and Lucy had managed to manipulate the rather steely-hearted Mother Teresa to give permission for Lucy to take the orphaned novice home with her and to escort her to the funeral the next day. Of course, thought the Reverend Mother uncharitably, Mother Teresa had the consolation that otherwise the convent of the Sisters of Charity would have incurred a certain amount of expense and trouble of hiring a car so the girl could go to the funeral.

Mother Teresa, thought the Reverend Mother with a certain amount of sympathy, must be anxious to get rid of them all, bishop, priests, nuns and brothers, not to mention those lay members, the candidates for high office on the city council.

She dressed carefully, making sure that everything was in order, packed her modest suitcase and gave one last look around the room, which she had left neat and tidy, with a bed stripped of linen, towels added to the pile and nothing astray. Tonight, she would sleep in her own familiar room, but before that she would take up the reins of her responsibilities, would be welcomed back by members of the congregation – soberly, but with pleasure, she hoped. And, less soberly, but most enthusiastically, by the children of her school. Her lips curved into a smile as she imagined the eager questions. By now, all of the details of that bloody murder would have been spread through the city and her pupils, though coming from families who could not afford a daily newspaper, would have picked up all of the grisly details and be eager to hear her account.

Breakfast was a sombre affair. Patrick, rather unexpectedly, appeared just as the meal was drawing to its uncomfortable finish. His eyes went towards hers when he came into the room, and she was touched to see an expression of thankfulness in them before he looked around the room.

So, Patrick was on the alert for another murder. The Reverend Mother pondered upon the matter as she sipped her tea and nibbled upon the slice of dry toast which was all that she allowed herself at breakfast time. An astute boy, she said to herself, feeling fond and proud of him as he sat beside the bishop, and allowed himself to be persuaded into partaking of some tea and toast. This was no accidental death, nor was it, she had begun to think, one of those, sometimes haphazard, IRA assassinations. No, Patrick was alert for a train of events to follow on that initial death. And she could understand his thought process. Whosoever had dropped the flame into that pipe stuffed with fertilizer and soaked in diesel, whosoever had done that terrible deed had taken an equally terrible chance. It could have been a massacre. But it could also have resulted in the immediate identification and arrest of the culprit. The grounds of the convent were full of strolling members of the religious orders who had come to make their annual retreat and of the nuns and novices of the convent itself going about their daily duties. The windows from the convent buildings, at least from the prime bedrooms, all overlooked the grounds and the sight of a figure creeping through the apple trees might have been sighted by someone who had just woken from an after-lunch siesta.

There was an uncomfortable atmosphere of fear and suspicion. She was glad that within a few hours Lucy would arrive and her efficient chauffeur would whisk her cousin and that unfortunate child, Sister Mary Magdalen, away from the dangerous precincts of the Sisters of Charity Convent, back to the city of Cork and then up to the privileged heights of Montenotte where the funeral would take place.

Once breakfast was over she sat patiently listening to a long and rather rambling speech by his lordship who was, she decided, feeling that his idea of mixing laity and the leaders of education in the city had not turned out as felicitously as he had expected, and who was determined to justify his decision by pointing out what a huge success the seven days had been.

'. . . *apart le cadaver, bien compris*,' said Mother Isabelle in rapid French, and the Reverend Mother did her best to suppress a smile. The bishop, she guessed, would not like to dwell on the thought of that particular corpse which had been scattered in small particles all over the orchard. He, too, may have had that thought because he sat down very quickly and allowed Patrick to stand up and explain that he wanted to have a clear picture of who had sat upon that bench during the last few days – names and times, said Patrick solemnly, would be of great use and the sergeant was waiting in the hallway and would not detain them for more than a few minutes on their way to church.

'Just a word, Reverend Mother, if I may delay you for a moment.' Mother Teresa, accompanied by her mistress of novices, accosted her just as she emerged from giving Patrick as much information as she could remember about the occupancy of the favoured bench in the apple orchard.

'Certainly, Mother.' The Reverend Mother stopped but was not surprised when Mother Isabelle moved rapidly away. The French superior of the Ursuline Convent in Blackrock had already delivered her private opinion of Mother Teresa, firmly stating that she *'une femme assez intelligente'* was *'incapable de supporter les imbéciles avec bonne humeur.'*

'I am most sorry to have to tell you, Reverend Mother, that Sister Mary Magdalene will be unable to accompany you and your cousin when you leave this morning,' said Mother Teresa. She did not, the Reverend Mother thought, look particularly sorry. There was, in fact, a certain note of satisfaction in the voice that made the announcement.

'Oh, dear,' said the Reverend Mother. She waited for a moment for an explanation but when none came and the two women turned away, she deliberately stood in their path and enquired whether something was amiss.

'It's just the case that Sister Mary Magdalene finds herself unwell and she feels she is unable to leave the convent today.' Mother Teresa delivered the words in a very firm tone of voice and then walked off in the direction of the bishop. The Reverend Mother looked after her with a feeling of annoyance. It was certainly an unwritten rule that no one interrupted a conversation between the bishop and one of his flock, so she was unable to question her further. She turned back to the mistress of novices.

'What exactly is the matter with Sister Mary Magdalene?' she asked bluntly and held the woman with a stern eye. She was not going to be fobbed off with that rather vague statement.

'It may be just a cold,' said Mother Carmel. She had a worried look on her face. 'None of the other novices have it, so it may be nothing.' She frowned and pressed her lips tightly together. 'No,' she repeated, 'none of the others are unwell in any way. It is of course quite serious for the novices, because on Sunday they take their final vows. They, and the whole convent, have been so looking forward to the occasion.'

The Reverend Mother nodded. Noviciate day was always a happy occasion in the convent in her own community, Sister Bernadette would bake numerous cakes, all of them iced with a pure white icing to symbolize the purity of the new members of the community. The families of the new recruits were all invited to the ceremony, and whatsoever had been there of inner doubts during the last eighteen months, on this day every face would shine with happiness.

Yes, indeed, it was important that all would be well for this ceremony on Sunday. Poor Sister Mary Magdalene would have no members of her family present, thought the Reverend Mother – both parents were now dead and her brothers out in the far-distant land of Australia. It crossed her mind that Lucy and perhaps one of her daughters might be prevailed upon to take the place of an absent family and she resolved to have a word with her cousin later.

In the meantime, it was important to make sure that there was a valid reason why the girl should not attend her father's funeral.

She waited until the mother superior and the mistress of novices had retired from the dining room and then slowly and meditatively, threading her beads between her hands, she made her way up the stairs and towards the novices' dormitories.

When she had climbed the last staircase and had emerged upon the corridor at the top of the house, she was waylaid.

It was Mother Carmel, herself, who, obviously, had come up by a different staircase.

The Reverend Mother did not hesitate.

'I just want to give a first-hand account of Sister Mary Magdalene to Mrs Murphy; I feel that I should assure my cousin that all possible care is being taken of the girl,' she said instantly. 'Of course, you and I know, Mother, that the laity does feel that the girls are not cared for as they would have been in their own homes. I've often,' said the Reverend Mother with a sigh, 'had to prove to anxious relatives that we in the convent would care for their daughters as well as they could do, themselves, within the confines of their homes.'

Mother Carmel looked a little bewildered. She was, guessed the Reverend Mother, slightly baffled as to the exact relationship between Lucy and the girl known in the convent as Sister Mary Magdalene. 'I'd be glad if you would have a look at her,' she said and looked at the Reverend Mother with a worried frown. 'It's nothing, I'm sure,' she said. 'She's a worrier, always fancying herself ill. If it were anything, the others would have it as well.' She had the air of one who sought to reassure herself.

'Just a head cold,' hinted the Reverend Mother. She moved her veil forward, with a quick movement of her head. It was her summer veil, transparent and thin with age and through it she could clearly see Mother Carmel's face. It bore, she noted with misgiving, an air of anxiety, a certain expression where worry struggled with a desire to say that all was well.

'Yes, I suppose so.' The rejoinder was uttered slowly and with a certain amount of reluctance.

Not a very experienced mistress of novices, she guessed. A woman who was a little out of her depth and who was eager to shift some of her responsibilities onto another pair of shoulders.

'I haven't been too long in this office,' she confided with an anxious look around her. 'Previously I held responsibility for the grounds.' She heaved a sigh. Did not say that plants and trees were easier to care for, but the Reverend Mother understood that involuntary escape of air and smiled at her reassuringly. 'God gives us the gifts to care for all of his creation,' she said reassuringly. 'Now let's have a look at Sister Mary Magdalene.'

The girl was stretched out upon the bed. A pair of young novices were there in the room with her, but they were both standing over beside the window at quite a distance from the bed. They started guiltily when their mistress of novices entered the room.

'She keeps telling us to stand away from her. She says that she's infectious,' said one girl. She took a step forward, followed by her fellow novice and then both stepped back hurriedly as Sister Mary Magdalene half sat up in the bed and sneezed violently, grabbing a handkerchief at the last moment and scrubbing at the moist patch on the bed covers. The young novices looked at each other.

'She has a fever,' said one. 'I felt her forehead.'

'Just a head cold,' said Mother Carmel with an effort. She went forward towards the bed.

'Stand back,' said the Reverend Mother sharply. 'Stay over there by the window.' Carefully she extracted a couple of pins from her wimple and pinned the veil securely over her face, covering eyes, nose and mouth. She felt in her pocket and extracted a pair of smooth, almost paper-thin leather gloves and pulled them over her hands. They had been given to her by a leather merchant once as a Christmas present about twenty years ago. He had told her how to care for them and had given her a supply of wax and saddle soap and by now they washed as easily as cotton. She attributed some of her immunity to disease to their protective shield.

'Let me feel your forehead, my child,' she said, and went forward and placed a hand on the skin. It burned through the thin layer of leather within seconds. An exceedingly high temperature, she guessed.

'Open your mouth, my child,' she said, wishing that she had her small pocket torch. Nevertheless, strong sunlight streamed through the window and she had light enough to see the bad news. Sister Mary Magdalene's throat was covered with a thick grey membrane. Her breath came thick and fast and her nose ran almost continuously into the damp handkerchief.

'Close your mouth, sister,' she said gently. And then she thought hard.

Undoubtedly it was diphtheria. And diphtheria was highly infectious. Potentially the whole community was at risk. Diphtheria took, she remembered, about two days after exposure to make its appearance. Five days without any symptoms usually meant that you had undoubtedly escaped. She looked around the room. A big dormitory. It probably adequately fitted the eight young novices with a curtained-off area for the mistress of novices.

'What are your names?' she asked the girls huddled together at the window.

'I'm Sister Rose and she's Sister Monica.' Sister Rose of Lima had a complexion that matched her name and despite her fright, she had not paled. Sister Monica, a very tall girl, looked more delicate. The Reverend Mother hoped they might escape.

'Did she go to morning service?' she asked, and they shook their heads in denial. That, at least, was something.

'We didn't go either,' said Sister Rose. 'We had permission to stay with Sister Magdalene as she was crying and feeling very poorly. She told us that she kissed a little girl with diphtheria, kissed her on the lips. She shrieked at us to keep well away from her.'

'I see,' said the Reverend Mother, rapidly running through what needed to be done. These two might need to be isolated. The nuns and the visitors to the convent were probably safe. She was, she was almost sure, immune after her years of exposure to children in her school, and would stay to nurse the girl. Not for long, she thought, seeing the sunken eyes and listening to the laboured breathing. She turned to Mother Carmel.

'Inform your mother superior of the situation, Mother, please. And would you be good enough to phone Dr Scher and tell him that I think it is diphtheria and phone my cousin, Mrs Murphy, the number is Montenotte twenty-three, and explain to her that she must not come to collect me.' And then she took pity on the very white face of the mistress of novices and said gently, 'Don't worry. I'll stay here. You have not yet been near enough to catch the infection, so you must stay away now, and the rest of the novices will have to be accommodated in another dormitory. Don't worry,' she said again, and gave the woman a brisk nod. She would not waste any more time on her until Dr Scher arrived and put an official seal on all arrangements.

NINETEEN

'**N**ow, look here, Reverend Mother,' said Dr Scher. Punctual as always, he came to make his daily visit at precisely nine thirty in the morning. 'I'm the doctor,' he went on, 'and you are a teacher, a manager, a miracle worker; anything you like, but just keep it in your mind that I am the doctor and do what I tell you. And what I am telling you now is to get to your feet and come out into the fresh air with me. Stand a good six feet away from anybody that you meet, if you wish, but I'm one hundred per cent certain that, after all those years and all those outbreaks, that you are immune to diphtheria and immune, Reverend Mother, means that you can't pass it to someone else. But what you can do is run down your own health by getting no fresh air and sitting all day and half the night too, You are no chicken, you know, Reverend Mother!'

The Reverend Mother sighed. He was, she was sure, correct. Generally, she was able to balance the good of the majority against the individual need. It was important that she stayed vigorous and well. Obediently, she rose to her feet.

'What's the prognosis?' she asked, looking down at the white face of the girl. Divested of her nun's regalia, the young novice looked like a sick child.

'Not good,' said Dr Scher abruptly and almost angrily. 'What can you expect? The girl is malnourished and a good stone underweight. When I came in here this morning, there was a lay sister polishing the convent's treasures. Cups and plates made from pure gold! And they don't feed their novices. Sell the stuff and give those girls a few good steaks!'

The Reverend Mother had tried in the past to feed Dr Scher with the official view of the Church that nothing was too good for God, but he had been impatient with her explanations and silenced her with the argument that a loving God would prefer children to be fed and housed to having more than £30,000 spent upon the ornate church in Turners Cross. Now she merely said, 'The food was probably available, but the appetite was lacking.'

'Well, then you tempt her to eat, you get food that she likes, make her plate look attractive, and when all else fails, you get a doctor to look at her. You don't watch a girl get thinner and thinner, paler and paler. After all, they took her away from her family. What's the good of names like "mother" and "sister" when no one took notice of what she looked like? I knew that she was malnourished the first minute that I saw her.'

'Has she any hope?' asked the Reverend Mother in a low voice. And then, after a quick glance at his face, she added, 'How long do you think that she has got?'

Dr Scher made no answer but went to the door and rang the bell placed on the corridor windowsill. An elderly lay sister who had suffered from diphtheria a few years ago was acting as assistant nurse to the Reverend Mother and she appeared instantly, rather bored with her other task which was to darn worn towels and sheets from the linen cupboard. The Reverend Mother summoned her as little as possible because the woman was starved for lively conversation and a good five minutes were wasted in satisfying her desire for gossip. Now, disturbed by Dr Scher's verdict, she merely nodded at the woman, gave one last glance at the white, unconscious face on the pillow and then followed Dr Scher who was impatiently holding the door to the stairs open for her.

They descended the stairs in silence and neither spoke until they reached the terrace outside the convent building. From time to time, she was conscious that he had looked at her uneasily and when they reached the wall, he said apologetically, 'Forgive me.'

'There is nothing to forgive,' she said. 'Sometimes you shock me – and I'm sure that's good for me – but you never offend me.'

'Like that new vogue for electric shock treatment in my own profession,' he said with a half grin. 'If it doesn't kill you, it does you good, so they say.' He gave a tentative look at her and she rewarded him with a smile.

'Now tell me the answer to my question,' she said. 'Is she in danger of death?' Odd she thought, as she waited for the answer, the way she found it hard to pronounce the words 'Sister Mary Magdalene', but used the pronoun 'she' or the word 'girl'. What had possessed Nellie Musgrave, only daughter of a rich man, to choose that name? *Very wild, unsatisfactory*, had been her school's verdict. And her brothers? *Failed to take advantage of one of the best educations in Ireland. Went off to Australia to work on the land.* What had been the home life of those three children when their mother was killed in a car crash? Even the sudden dismissal of a cook who had been fond of the children and loved by them could have added to their maladjustment.

Dr Scher turned to face her. 'Yes,' he said bluntly. 'The answer to your question is yes, and I will go further and tell you that I believe that short of a miracle she will die within a few days. I've given her a sedative and it's about the only thing that I can do for her now. To put it bluntly, she will either die from heart failure or from choking. That's why I've given her a lethal dose and I will go on giving it to save her from agony. And don't give me any lectures about respecting human life,' he added savagely.

'I won't,' said the Reverend Mother. There was, she thought, a bleak note in her voice and she reproached herself for it. She had long schooled herself against the sin of despair and had concentrated on achieving the possible and shelving the impossible. Almost sixty years, she thought, and there have been many failures, but some small successes and it was on them that she needed to focus.

'I'm sorry,' he said quickly. 'These things upset me still – even after all of those years. Odd, isn't it?'

The Reverend Mother thrust her hands into her long sleeves and gazed unseeingly down at the valley where the city of Cork had spread its tentacles of streets and rivers across the original marsh. There was another question that she needed to ask Dr Scher, another service, perhaps, that he could arrange, but now, she felt, was not the moment to ask that boon of him. 'Thank you for telling me, and thank you for all you do,' she said quietly and then turned back as she saw a nun emerge from the door and beckon to her.

'A phone call, Reverend Mother. Your cousin, Mrs Murphy.' The voice called out the message from a distance and was reassuring and kindly, knowing perhaps that the Reverend Mother might have expected bad news from the sickroom.

'Sorry to get you out of bed at this unearthly hour of the morning.' Lucy's voice was blissfully normal and relaxed. The Reverend Mother smiled. This was an old joke between the two of them.

'Now that I am out of bed,' she said good-humouredly.

'Well, interesting news. I meant to call you yesterday evening when Rupert came back from work and told me but didn't get the chance. Guess what – one of the Musgrave boys, Peter, apparently, has turned up, just back from Australia. Arrived in Cobh on Thursday. Rupert wants to bring him up to the convent to see his sister. Is she well enough?'

The Reverend Mother felt sad. A few days earlier, before this deadly disease had taken grip of the girl, perhaps her brother's presence would have been hugely cheering for her, and who knows what decisions she might have taken for the future.

'I'm afraid not, Lucy,' she said. 'Apart from the question of infection, she is very seriously ill and drifting in and out of consciousness. She would not know him.'

'Oh, dear.' Lucy was silent. There had been a catch in her voice and the Reverend Mother guessed that she was holding back the tears with difficulty. Nellie Musgrave, she guessed, was very dear to Lucy, had lived next door, to her, had played with Lucy's daughters, And when she had lost her mother in such tragic circumstances, Lucy would have been concerned for the girl as she made the difficult transition from a child to an adult.

'I'll tell Rupert,' she said after a minute. 'He'll be disappointed.'

The Reverend Mother wondered why Rupert should have been disappointed, but she asked no questions. Lucy's voice had a cautious note in it and everyone in Cork knew that the ladies in the telephone exchange were prone to listen in to any conversation which promised to be of interest, and then to spread their knowledge among the eager gossips of the city. She was not surprised when after a brief pause, Lucy said, 'I'll pop up and see you. Be with you in half an hour. Have most people gone now? And the bishop?'

'Yes, indeed,' said the Reverend Mother. 'It's a tranquil and calm place again now.'

'Good,' said Lucy. 'I need not bother wearing my best new black silk stockings to do honour to the bishop. I'll just come in my old rags.'

And with that she rang off. The Reverend Mother, wondering a little about what prompted this visit, as Lucy had been warned of the sickness and that the Reverend Mother could no longer leave, went to promise Dr Scher that she would go for a walk when her cousin arrived, but in the meantime, she would relieve the lay sister from her vigil over the dying girl.

However, she had only spent ten minutes in the sick room when footsteps sounded on the corridor outside the door.

'Inspector Cashman would like a word,' was the message from the lay sister and she handed over her patient and went down to see him.

Patrick looked at her in a concerned way when she came through the door and she guessed that her elderly face showed the signs of strain and anxiety.

'You've heard the news,' she said to forestall any enquiries, and she took a few steps back as he stepped towards her.

'Yes. Will she be well enough to see her brother? He could stand at a distance. Just perhaps to say his name.' He read her expression and grimaced, pulling absent-mindedly at the middle fingers of his left hand. 'I've been to see Mr Murphy, Mr Rupert Murphy,' he said. And then continued, speaking slowly and carefully, 'He's a bit worried about the situation.'

'I see,' said the Reverend Mother, and she did, in fact, see, in a sudden flash of enlightenment. Lucy, also, had mentioned Rupert. A death. A wealthy man. She shook her head and Patrick nodded.

'That was yesterday, when I talked to him, yesterday

morning . . .' Patrick hesitated for the moment but then seemed to make up his mind to share his perplexities. 'Apparently,' he said, 'the dead man, Mr Musgrave, did not make a valid will; in fact, a will has not been found. He withdrew his previous will from Mr Murphy, his solicitor, with the intention of drafting a new will, in the light of changed circumstances, children growing up, one in the convent, the lessening of certain family ties, etc. And so, he had made an appointment in order to have the new will drawn up and witnessed.'

'But he died, and now, I suppose,' said the Reverend Mother, 'all will go to the eldest son.'

'Yes, indeed,' said Patrick, looking at her respectfully. 'I would have thought that since they were twins, that the money would have been shared between them. But you're right, it goes to the older even if there are only a few hours in the difference. You know more about the law than I do,' he added rather ruefully, and she hastened to reassure him.

'I remember reading a book by a French author named Dumas, when I was young, called *The Man in the Iron Mask* and it was all about Louis XIV of France and his twin brother, identical twin – all fiction, of course, but very gripping. So, yes, the heir to all will be the elder of the two boys. Which one has arrived?'

'It's the eldest boy, or so he says,' said Patrick, 'but that's not my affair. I wanted to talk to you about something different. It's just that I was talking to Eileen . . .'

The Reverend Mother turned an interested eye upon the flush of colour which came to his cheeks but waited in discreet silence while he gathered his thoughts.

'Well,' he said with a visible effort, 'you see she asked me to call in and to have dinner with herself and her mother, but, well, I couldn't spare the time, and so I dropped in when I had finished working at about nine o'clock and there was a neighbour there, talking to Eileen's mother, so Eileen and I went for a walk, up to the top of Barrack Street.' He smiled a little then. 'Funny the way everyone in Barrack Street goes up that hill for a walk. You can see the whole city and the rivers and the bridges; it's a great sight, Reverend Mother.'

The Reverend Mother bowed her head and thrust her hands into her sleeves, making sure she did not go too near to him. Six-foot distance, Dr Scher had said, and six-foot distance was, she reckoned, her normal communication space with all, except her cousin Lucy.

'Yes,' she said quietly; and reassured, he went on. He was not, she thought, a very articulate person, but he drew quite a picture of the busy city, of the gas lamps and of glitter on the dark waters of the river and movement of the people crossing and recrossing the many bridges and she could see how he was reliving the time spent there, shoulder to shoulder with Eileen, looking down over the streets and rivers of Cork. She experienced a moment's pride in them both. Eileen for the quick wits which had jumped to conclusions about the presence of the northerner Willie Hamilton in east Cork and his possible connection with several murders of Catholics in the area, and Patrick who had connected the story with the recent violent desecration of the orchard cemetery. She told him what little she knew for certain and then turned the conversation.

'I hear that Eileen gave young Mr Musgrave a lift back from Cobh to Cork the other day. How did she like him?'

'Not much,' he said, and there was a note of satisfaction in his voice. 'She had some story about him being rude to an old lady from that nursing home near the harbour who was just telling him how much better he looked without that beard. Poor old thing: Eileen said that she looked quite taken aback. Odd fellow. I didn't like him much, either.'

'Do you suspect him of having anything to do with his father's death?' Patrick, she thought, was perhaps a bit harsh. The Musgrave children had a complicated upbringing. Both. Patrick and Eileen had been deserted by a father, but both had a devoted mother, immensely proud of their only child.

Patrick shook his head at her comment. 'No, I don't suspect him of being involved. He couldn't have been. He definitely arrived a few days after his father's death. Joe's been down to Cobh and seen the harbour master records and the ship records before it sailed back. He will be returning to Australia to wind up his affairs and to endeavour to get in contact with

his brother; indeed, he had probably already left to join the
liner at Cobh,' he said. 'We checked and double checked on
his arrival.'

'No reason for you to ask him to stay, then,' said the
Reverend Mother, suppressing a smile. Patrick, she thought,
would always check and double-check.

Lucy's car was just coming through the gate, so she turned
her interested gaze from Patrick's face and went forward to
meet her cousin.

'Don't come too near,' she said, raising a warning hand as
the chauffeur helped his mistress from the car. 'Perhaps you
could make your handkerchief into a mask.'

'I never catch anything,' said Lucy. 'Sorry I'm a bit late. I
was calming down Rupert. He's in a state and I annoyed him
by saying that it was like *The Man in the Iron Mask.*'

'Yes, I was telling Patrick just now about the iron mask,
welded to the shape of the man's head, meant that Louis
XIV and his identical twin could never be confused,' said
the Reverend Mother. There was strong link of shared memories between herself and Lucy and she was not surprised
that her cousin, too, had thought of this fictional case of
identical twins.

'Oh, bother,' said Lucy. 'Why need you always be three
steps ahead of everyone else? I suppose you know all about
the twins, do you?'

'I guessed Rupert had a reason to be disappointed to hear
that the Musgrave boy could not be identified by his sister,'
said the Reverend Mother placidly. Unobtrusively, she had
tucked her veil across her nose and mouth. She would never
forgive herself if she gave the infection to Lucy. 'Are they
really so alike?' she added.

'I told Rupert that it's no good asking me, as I never could
tell them apart when I was seeing them every day, years ago,
not even when they were standing side by side.'

'And now it is important. No will,' said the Reverend
Mother, 'so all goes to the eldest son. Perhaps they should
have been marked at birth – not anything as drastic as an iron
mask, of course. Is there really nothing, no birthmark or
anything?' Her eyes were on Patrick who had accosted the

young gardener. Sister Agnes had emerged from the kitchen and for once was not bustling about but standing quite still and looking across at the two figures. And then the woman's eyes went to Lucy and she disappeared quickly back into her kitchen.

It would be a long time before the shadow of murder was lifted and the convent regained its pious tranquillity.

TWENTY

The Reverend Mother looked around the almost empty room. Under her direction, the young gardener, suitably gloved and masked, had removed the surplus beds and chests of drawers, had cut through excess paint so that the two windows opened easily and had, at her request, removed the blinds one night and returned them the following morning showing proudly how he had darkened their pale cream by a light wash of a deep brown wood stain. Now though the windows were open, the light was filtered. The floor and the remaining chest were wiped down every morning by the obliging lay sister who shared the nursing duties and the room was as cool and clean smelling as she could possibly make it.

But nothing helped. Step by step, the deadly disease took possession of the frail body, and by now there was no hope left in the Reverend Mother, only a determination to ensure a happy and peaceful death. She had seen enough of death to know that the moment had come. As soon as she woke from her doze in the chair, she had heard the unmistakable sound of altered breathing. Short periods of silence were followed by a few rapid breaths, and then another silence. The Reverend Mother took her watch from her pocket and checked the time. Nine o'clock. Dr Scher was due within the next half hour but she was sure enough of her diagnosis to go to the door and then to whisper to the lay sister a request that the chaplain be ready to give the last sacraments.

Nature was merciful in the last hours, she thought, looking down at the sleeping girl. The terrible, heart-rending struggle for breath had died away. Now there was nothing but tiny, shallow, almost inaudible whispers of an inhalation interspersed with long silences. Dr Scher arrived, barely listened to his stethoscope, and shook his head sadly. He took out his syringe, then looked at her, nodded and put it away again.

'Not long now,' he said with a warning note in his voice.

'I've sent for the chaplain,' said the Reverend Mother. She spoke in a low voice, but to her surprise, the eyelids of the dying girl snapped open. There was a look of fear in them and the breathing became louder, more raucous, just as though a struggle had awoken the senses of the body. The Reverend Mother bent over and took the thin, cold hand within her own. She knelt beside the bed so that her mouth was close to the girl's ear.

'Don't worry, Nellie,' she said. 'Your mother has gone before you, but she will be there for you.'

She remembered a book she had as a child where all the angels and saints and those who had gone to heaven were sitting around in a sea of deep, deep blue, more blue than any sky in Cork could possibly be. And each was perched upon a fluffy white cloud, holding a celestial harp. Meant for little children, of course, but the face on the pillow before her was that of the young child who had haunted her mother's footsteps and so she went on with the story, hoping that all she had learned and had taught was, in fact, true and that those who had gone before would be reunited with those they had loved. But whether it was true or not, now was the moment to speak comfort to the dying girl and remind her of her long-lost mother.

And so, she spoke on, drawing on scraps of information from Lucy and recalling her own memories of the magnificent garden made by the woman who had died so tragically, leaving two small sons and a daughter to mourn her. Dr Scher carefully injected something into the bone-thin arm and after a few minutes, the girl's breathing relaxed again. Her eyes opened wide, moved around the room, and then went back to the Reverend Mother.

'I want to see the policeman and the priest,' she whispered, her voice a mere thread of sound. 'I must, I must, please, please! Now!'

'Dr Scher will fetch them,' said the Reverend Mother reassuringly. She gave an appealing look at the doctor. He would make sure that Patrick came. Sister Catherine was willing, but very diffident and likely to be put off by an officious constable.

She could go herself to the phone, but the thin fingers clutched her hand so desperately that she vowed not to move while the child still needed her presence.

'I'll be back in two minutes,' said Dr Scher, and she heard him pound down the corridor and, faintly in the distance, his descent on the uncarpeted staircase. The girl's eyes had closed. There was an almost unbearable tension until the loud sighing breath came again. The Reverend Mother prayed for the grace of a happy death until Dr Scher returned.

'Sleeping,' he said, with a finger on the girl's pulse. He bent down, gently pulled an eyelid, placed his stethoscope on the neck and then stood back. 'A couple of hours,' he said softly. 'Go down to the kitchen. Sister Mary Agnes will have tea and toast ready for you on a little table outside the kitchen, she told me to tell you that you will not be disturbed. Keep your strength up. Bring up Patrick when he comes. She will die peacefully once she has told all.'

The Reverend Mother followed his instructions. It was very thoughtful of him to arrange that she did not have to enter the kitchen or engage in conversation. The table was placed under a tree, laid with a linen cloth, the toast was in a covered dish and the teapot warmly clad in a cosy. She sat upon the cushioned chair, poured the tea, and forced a finger of toast down before swallowing a refreshing cupful. Her mind was busy. She had no memory of Nellie's mother, Eleanor Musgrave, but she sensed her presence. What was it that Lucy had said about her? Married very young, more of a companion to her children than a traditional mother, loved to garden, amused by the boys, adoring and adored by the youngest child, her little girl.

Thoughtfully, she finished her toast, drank her tea, called in a message of thanks at the kitchen door. Sister Mary Agnes looked up, tears running down her face. 'Nellie?' she said, her voice cracking on a heartbroken sob; she asked no question, just turned away. The Reverend Mother shook her head, but she, also, said nothing. Was it the presence of this woman that had influenced Nellie's decision to join the Sisters of Charity?

Seeing the police car sweep in through the gate, the Reverend

Mother went to join the elderly chaplain outside the church door. His face, she noticed, was very grave, and there were stains of tears on the cheeks which he had just mopped with the handkerchief in his hand. She honoured him for that. A man she could trust, she thought, as he listened carefully to what she had to say and nodded his understanding. She was, she thought gratefully, supported by men who could be trusted. No need for any explanations to Dr Scher who had instantly done her bidding. Patrick, also, had come instantly, and alone, and this chaplain could be relied upon for compassion and understanding.

'Come with me,' she said to both men and took them with her up the uncarpeted backstairs and down the echoing bare boards of the corridor.

The room was dead silent when they came in. For a moment, the Reverend Mother feared that the girl was dead, but then she heard a sound as a sighing breath was inhaled. The eyes fluttered open and fixed upon the priest and then moved towards Patrick.

'I want to confess to you both, to tell you what I have done.' The voice was tiny, but the priest and the policeman moved in unison once the words were uttered, both standing, side by side, beside the bed. Dr Scher moved to the other side of the bed, his back to the window and the syringe still held within his hand. The Reverend Mother took up her position at the bottom of the bed and all the laity crossed themselves as the priest began to go through the last rites raising his voice slightly as he came to the last words: '*Indulgeat tibi Domine, quidquid per visum, audiotum, odoratum, gustum, et locutionem, tactum gressum deliquisti*', speaking the words and making the gestures with practised speed, touching the eyes, ears, nose, mouth and limbs with the holy oil. And then he waited.

It took a superhuman effort, but the Reverend Mother had witnessed enough deaths to know that the administration of extreme unction brings moments of strength and lucidity to the dying person. The girl's eyes opened, and she fixed them, not on the priest, but on the gleaming medal in the centre of Patrick's cap, which he held clasped to his chest.

'I confess to Almighty God and to you, Father, and to all

here that I am guilty of the mortal sin of murder. I planned it. I stole some sugar from the kitchen and a bag of fertilizer from the garden shed and put it in the hole just beside my father's seat early in the morning before anyone else was up. I took a box of matches from the church, and waited until after lunch when we were scrubbing the church. I looked out, saw he was there and when it was my turn to fetch the bucket of water from the well, I threw the match down onto the sugar and the fertilizer and ran away.' She stopped there and Dr Scher bent over her, but the thin whisper began again before he had to use his syringe.

'My father was an evil man. He killed my mother, he drove my brothers across the sea and would not allow me to leave the convent where I was unhappy, though I had confessed my sin. I killed him, just I. No one else had a hand in it, no one, but me.'

The frail whisper faded out. The eyes shut for a moment and then opened again. The Reverend Mother took a step forward, touched Patrick on the arm, opened the door and kept it open until Dr Scher, also, went through. And then she closed it behind them and came back to stand beside the bed.

'My child,' she said gently. 'You have told your little story to Inspector Cashman. Now you must tell the truth to God and to Father Hayes. None other will hear it.' She gave a quick glance at the chaplain and reassured by the calm, elderly face, she went through the door, and closed it silently behind her. The two men were standing by the corridor window. She looked expectantly at Patrick and after a long moment he spoke.

'It doesn't make sense,' he said, and the Reverend Mother admired the ring of conviction in his voice. 'It doesn't make sense, Reverend Mother,' he repeated with even more energy. 'How could that frail, thin girl climb down into that hole, carrying a sack of fertilizer and a heavy iron pipe and stuff the fertilizer into the pipe, wearing that long white dress and white veil? How did she know where to find the fertilizer and that rusty downpipe? It was in the gardener's shed. How did she carry it over there? And then she says that she triggered the explosion by flinging a match down. That could never have worked. The match would have gone out well before it ever hit the top of the downpipe. In any case, a match doesn't stay alight if you throw it down a hole. And sugar doesn't ignite so easily. She's made the whole thing up. But why?' Patrick looked from one elderly face to another and the Reverend Mother looked expectantly at Dr Scher.

He did not fail her. 'These drugs!' he said, shaking his head. 'Diamorphine has great painkilling properties but can have strange hallucinatory effects. Poor child. Who knows what prompted that nightmare?'

The Reverend Mother nodded approval. 'God alone knows,' she said piously.

'The only thing that puzzles me,' said Patrick with a frown creasing his brow, 'is how on earth did she know about the fertilizer and the sugar. The bomb expert thought it was diesel, but sugar would have done too, he told me that.'

'I think I can explain,' said the Reverend Mother quickly. 'When she was a child, her brothers experimented with a combination of fertilizer and sugar and almost blew themselves up. She was younger than they, but it would have stayed in her mind, I suppose. My cousin Lucy told me that story. She said that she would never forget the way one of the twins stood in her kitchen, pouring blood and with a piece of metal stuck into his arm.'

'Oh, I see,' said Patrick. He took his notebook and pencil from his pocket and began to write rapidly. 'Do you spell diamorphine with a "y" or with an "i", Dr Scher?' he enquired without lifting his eyes from the notebook.

'With an "i",' said Dr Scher steadily. 'These hallucinatory effects are quite a common side effect of the drug,' he added helpfully, and Patrick nodded while continuing to write rapidly. He had replaced his notebook when he spoke again.

'No proof, of course,' he said decisively, 'but it's fairly obvious now that it was the IRA after all. And the wrong man, of course! I'll have a private word with Willie Hamilton, tell him that he might find the climate of Northern Ireland a bit healthier. If the IRA are after him, they'll get their man eventually. Well, thank you, Dr Scher. I think we'll just forget this confession; don't you think?' He looked towards the closed door with an air of sorrow. 'God bless her and give her the grace of a happy end,' he said with a note of deep feeling in his voice as he shook his head sadly. He replaced the notebook, bent his head to the Reverend Mother and then slipped out.

'Nice fellow, young Patrick. Did you notice the tears in his eyes?' said Dr Scher. He said nothing for a moment. Both their eyes went towards the closed door, but nothing except the steady voice of the chaplain reciting the prayers for the dead could be heard.

'A lot to be said for religion in times like these, I have to admit,' said Dr Scher and then with a quick change of voice, he said, 'Well now, Reverend Mother, perhaps you would like to tell the truth, the whole truth and nothing but the truth to an old heathen.'

The Reverend Mother stroked her upper lip meditatively. 'God alone knows the truth, the whole truth,' she said reprovingly, 'but there is nothing in the scriptures to say that man should not use the brains, the capacity for logical analysis and then ability to listen, with which He has endowed mankind. Perhaps in this particular case, the ability to listen has been more important,' she added and then when he did not respond, her voice became more animated. 'My cousin, Lucy, Dr Scher, has a great gift for making you see the people whom she describes. Certainly, she made the Musgrave family come alive for me. The father, a man for whom money and his place in Cork society was of the utmost importance. And then, his wife, warm-hearted, devoted to her children, amused by the twins and their jokes, encouraging them to experiment and to have fun, keeping the quiet, shy, little girl with her as much as possible, teaching her to share the love of plants, of gardens and of their design. Only God knows how they would have grown up, of course, if she had lived, but they may have developed into affectionate, loving adults who found their way to a rewarding way of life when they reached the end of their childhood. But then, of course, tragedy struck. The mother was killed, killed because her husband drank too much at a party and crashed the car on an icy stretch of road, something for which, certainly the boys and possibly the little girl, also, blamed him. A tragedy and worst of all was the effect on the children. They were banished from their home, sent to boarding school, grew up rebellious and badly behaved, the boys neglected their schoolwork, were troublesome and probably only the father's money and status persuaded the Jesuits to keep them in Clongowes. There were hints that the girl may have committed what to him was an even more serious sin. The adoption of the name of a reformed prostitute, Mary Magdalen, was most revealing.' The Reverend Mother grimaced with a feeling of distaste.

'So, the girl was forced into a convent, and the boys packed off to Australia,' remarked Dr Scher.

'Where, I'm afraid, they did not do at all well,' said the Reverend Mother. 'They wrote to their father and he responded, apparently, not by bailing them out, or giving them more money to invest in their farming enterprise, but by sending the bare minimum to purchase two one-way tickets. However, true to his class and to his breeding, he sent enough money for a first-class fare for each, and that was enough for the purchase of two return third-class fares. And so the plan was woven.'

'I'm quite confused,' complained Dr Scher. 'Why two return tickets? Surely just one of the twins came back to Ireland – Peter – and he arrived well after the murder. Patrick checked the landing register and he definitely arrived on the RMS *Orient* from Sydney and went back on it when it made the return journey.'

'One of the pieces of information which my cousin Lucy gave me,' resumed the Reverend Mother, 'was that the twins, as well as loving to play tricks by their likeness to each other, were also great mimics and fond of dressing up as people from other countries. I feel that the young German, looking for agriculture work, who assisted the nuns' gardener to dig the pit was probably one of the twins. The relationship between the boys was very strong, but I suspect they were also very fond of their sister and her letter sent at Easter, pleading for help to escape the convent triggered the plan. I also suspect, by the way that the twin who remained behind, let's call him Peter, covered his brother Paul's absence in some way, gave him an alibi for a week. Paul arrived in Cobh a week or so earlier, made his way up to the city, would have found the whereabouts of his father, hung around, noted that his father sat on this particular seat everyday and his boyhood prank of making a bomb from fertilizer and some form of sugar might have suggested a method of murder which would probably be attributed to the IRA.

I would surmise that once he had persuaded the gardener into digging the hole, he suggested that it be covered with the tarpaulin and then came back at dawn, with a can of diesel, and using a key to the gardener's shed, which he had purloined, he was able to rig up the bomb and probably a rope soaked in diesel. He would have been hidden from sight under the tarpaulin, though as dawn comes early in June, he ran little risk of being seen. He may well have lurked in the hole during the morning, but more likely hid in the woodland and waited until his father was in position and the coast was clear. The one dangerous moment was the lighting of the fuse or, more likely, the length of rope soaked in diesel when, in fact, he was seen by his own sister, but, if it had been anyone else they would probably have taken him for the gardener.

'So he tricked the gardener into helping him to dig the hole, perhaps suggested to him to cover it with planks and a tarpaulin, comes back at dawn with the key to the shed, he murders his father, takes the ship back to Australia that very night and probably passes his twin brother, Peter or Paul, somewhere near Gibraltar! Well, well, the God of Abraham and Isaiah, put a lot of ingenuity into the human brain,' exclaimed Dr Scher.

'Indeed,' said the Reverend Mother, quietly.

'But what put you onto it?' He had raised his voice slightly and then looked guiltily at the door. The steady sound of Latin words still came to their ears. Dr Scher went across and noiselessly turned the handle and looked in and then closed it again and came back to the Reverend Mother. 'No change,' he said to her and lowered his bulk back onto the windowsill.

'The twins, of course,' continued the Reverend Mother in a low voice, 'were notorious for their mischief in the respectable confines of Montenotte and they were not popular with the householders on the whole. Luckily for them they were, according to my cousin, endowed with the sort of good looks, the blond hair, the very large pale blue eyes, that old ladies love. One such old lady, a sharp old lady, named Mrs Maureen Clay, who lived in Montenotte up to a couple of years ago, but who is now in a nursing home in Cobh, a nursing home built quite close to the sea, saw a familiar-looking young man at the harbour front – and she recognized those pale blue eyes. You may not have noticed, Dr Scher, but here in Ireland we have brown eyes and green eyes, but when the eyes are blue they are almost invariably a very dark blue, "put in with a smutty finger", so they say. Pale blue eyes are unusual and much admired. So there was a young man on the harbour front at Cobh, a young man with those familiar pale blue eyes, but with a very scruffy and untidy beard which he had grown as a disguise, probably, but she is a sharp old lady and it didn't fool her. She probably tried to talk to him, but he brushed past her. However, when, the following week, she saw those familiar blue eyes again, in the presence of Eileen, she greeted him as "young Musgrave" and congratulated him on getting rid of his beard and tidying himself up. According to Eileen, who told Patrick about this, she didn't like the way that Peter Musgrave was rude to a very old woman from the nursing home, something that made Eileen, who has been well brought up, regard him with dislike.'

'I see,' said Dr Scher. 'And Reverend Mother Aquinas put one and one together and made it one hundred and one! So, now, what do you do?'

'Nothing,' said the Reverend Mother firmly. 'Their sister probably saw her brother, one of her brothers – who knows whether it was Peter or Paul – with a match in his hand to light a fuse in order to detonate the bomb, to set fire to a rope soaked in diesel – remember she had been scrubbing the porch and came out to get water from the well just before the explosion, but she was an adoring young sister, who knew how much their mother loved the boys, and so she offered up her life for them, deliberately caught diphtheria, and who am I to try to nullify her sacrifice? In any case,' she finished briskly, 'it would be an impossible and heartrending task for Patrick to accumulate enough proof to make even a case to apply for extradition; a safe conviction for murder would be an impossibility. Lucy tells me that Rupert was quite unsure as to whether it was really Peter who came to his office and declared that it may well have been Paul. No,' she ended decisively, 'the IRA have many unacknowledged sins upon their conscience; let them bear the weight of one that is undeserved.'

She stopped, listened, then went to the door and opened it. The old priest was by the bedside holding up a small, carved crucifix. The girl was very still, as still as death almost, but then a long sigh came from her and her eyes fixed themselves on a patch of sunlight on the ceiling. The Reverend Mother came forward, fell upon her knees beside the bed and then there was one more sigh, this time louder and harsher and an unmistakable change in the blue eyes, still fixed on the ceiling, but now wide and without sight.

The Reverend Mother crossed herself, then rose to her feet and gently closed the girl's eyes, pressing down the lids and holding them in place as she prayed that the last image had been that of a very beloved mother and that little Nellie was safe in loving arms. Softly she quoted from Revelation: '"And God shall wipe away all tears from their eyes; and there shall be no more death, neither sorrow, nor crying, neither shall there be any more pain: for the former things are passed away."'